COME HERE TO ME

SABRINA BURNS

For Jenna, who insisted I find someone I could be my whole self with, and then insisted that I write.

ONE

Leaves crunched under my feet as I strode through campus, my overfilled bookbag straining at the seams and leaving me lopsided as it weighed down the whole right side of my body. I paused momentarily on the sidewalk to hoist it higher up my shoulder while I shifted my phone to my other ear, a grunt escaping me as my many textbooks made another attempt to take me down.

"Are you okay, Emma? Where are you right now?" my mom's voice echoed through the earpiece. As usual, I'd made my weekly call to her while on my way to do something else. I loved her dearly but preferred talking to her when there was a set amount of time bracketing our interactions. Beyond fifteen minutes, she would stop being Mom and start being

Professor Brice, quick with critiques on the latest draft of whatever paper of mine she had insisted I send her or opinions on the published contributions of one of my professors. While growing up with two lit professor parents had its benefits, there was a definite downside, especially when you also pursued a career in academia. Even on my best days, I just did not have the emotional armor to withstand her well-meaning meddling without dissolving into a puddle of goo she could easily manipulate.

"I'm fine, just walking to Viva to get some work done," I said, narrowly dodging a biker who'd decided to cut through the quad. The autumn breeze was strong enough to whip my hair into my face and obscure my vision, a hazard given the high energy buzz on campus with the quarter just starting. That same breeze carried a hint that mild days like today were numbered, and that soon the jacket I'd slung over my bag just in case would be a necessity. I caught a whiff of someone burning leaves not too far off campus, mixed with one last hurrah of a cookout, and my heart ached. *Remember this*, I told myself. *All of it. Those students lingering on the benches between classes, the rumble of the Metra passing, every single second you have left here.*

"Are you sure you'll be able to focus there? All

that noise," Mom said with a note of distaste. I could picture her shudder down to the theatrical turn of her head and eyes squeezing shut as if in pain. She did all her work cloistered in her office, surrounded by a world she had ordered down to the very last paperclip. Meanwhile, I'd found that I preferred noise—the chatter of fellow students, the bustle of activity, the sense that I was on my own but never *alone*—to do my best work.

Growing up, I had classmates who dreamed of becoming astronauts, doctors, firemen—but as early as five, I told my teachers that I wanted to be a litera-ture professor when I grew up. (Sometimes I wonder if hearing the word "literature" coming out of a kindergartener's mouth was charming or disturbing, but I only remember encouragement of my aspira-tions.) My childhood bedroom was filled with books —not children's books, absolutely not. What was I, *simple?* My bookshelves were double and triple-stacked with age-inappropriate reading sanctioned and supplied by my parents. While my friends read Judy Blume, I read *Ethan Frome* and *Madame Bovary*, which my parents discussed with me over dinner with a seriousness more akin to ceasefire negotiations than casual conversation. Granted, the main message I took away from *Ethan Frome* was that his wife was "mean," so I was by no means exceptionally mature or astute, but my parents were not interested in a child with average intellect. My vocabulary was deemed "precocious," my writing "advanced," and the obvious pride my parents took in my report cards ensured that my main goal in life was a stack of A's and teachers who would report that I was "a pleasure to have in class." To my good fortune, this came easily to me. There was no denying the hand I'd been dealt.

"Yes, I'll be able to focus. It's better than the apartment, anyway—George and Anika are fighting again," I said. I shared a railroad apartment on 53rd with two other UChicago postgraduate students, and while our cohabitation was mostly peaceful, today an argument that had started over whose turn it was to do the dishes had escalated into a heated debate about Foucault and neoliberalism, and the conflict left our apartment radioactive with tension. Therefore, I'd settled on Viva Coffee as a perfect alternative work environment. It was just far enough away from campus that the clientele wasn't exclusively UChicago students, and I had a good shot at snagging a table. The cozy atmosphere always reminded me that reading was a treat and not a punishment, even when my professors seemed determined to suck dry any drop of joy we might wrest out of our assignments. I was enough of a regular there that most of the baristas knew my usual order—soy latte and a chocolate croissant—and started pulling shots and frothing milk before I even made it to the counter. That warmed something in me every time, that sense of belonging. Here, everyone knew my name.

"Oh Jesus, what is it this time," Mom said, eager as ever for an intellectual dispute she could authoritatively settle. In turn, I was thrilled to provide her with one that took the heat of her critical gaze off me and my work. On the days that I didn't manage to redirect her attention from my academic pursuits, Mom's perpetual concern that I wasn't applying myself would be our only topic of conversation, so a successful distraction was always a win in my book. When I pulled it off, I could assuage the slightly ill sensation I got in my stomach whenever it had been too long since I'd spoken to my parents for at least another week.

The sky took a turn for the threatening as I relayed the details to Mom, doing my best to disguise my slight breathlessness as I powered my way toward Viva, hoping to beat the rain. I heard pans clanging in the background and knew she was making breakfast for herself and Dad, a weekend ritual they'd enjoyed my whole life. They would still spend the day holed up in their respective offices, grading papers and working on their own research while downing a frightening amount of coffee, but the morning was theirs. I often timed my calls to her to coincide with this routine, as it brought out the most relaxed version of my mother—though no one who'd met her would ever describe Geraldine Brice as relaxed.

While both my parents had their hearts set on their only child embracing their same dream of "the life of the mind" (read: school until you die), it was especially important to my mother. Since I had no real interests outside of pleasing them while I was growing up, I was happy to embrace that shared dream. When the college acceptance letters came to our house (and they were all acceptance letters— professor parents have the eagle eye when it comes to college applications), it was a foregone conclusion to commit to the University of Chicago, where my parents had met. Their pleasure and pride in me and my choice was so great that it was almost like feeling that way myself. We went out for a fancy seafood dinner the night I committed, and all of us spent the next two days sicker than dogs with food poisoning. It became part of our family lore, the beginning of the story we'd tell when one day I was a lit professor, just like them.

College hadn't been a completely seamless transition—classes were pass-fail rather than graded, praise focused more on the strength of your arguments rather than having the "right" answer, and I was no longer one of the bright stars, since bright was the expectation—but I had never felt more at home than at UChicago. The campus was just as old and beautiful as movies had led me to believe college was meant to look; it was practically a scholar's fairy tale kingdom, the picturesque dictionary definition of "campus." My main social skill was a preternatural ability to suss out what people wanted me to be and do and adapting quickly, but here I was just one in a sea of students who took their studies more seriously than they'd ever taken their social lives, so in a strange way, I felt like I finally fit in with minimal effort. At last, my endless shapeshifting to please others was at least somewhat less necessary. The demands of the curriculum wound their way around me like the ivy on the buildings, and I felt safe and cocooned, knowing exactly what was expected of me. I loved UChicago so much that I stayed to pursue my master's there rather than broadening my institutional horizons at a different university. It was the first decision I ever made that baffled and concerned my parents.

As I relayed the morning's fracas, it didn't take long for Mom to grab hold of one of Anika's arguments and start poking holes in it with glee, which allowed my mind to drift back to my inescapable preoccupation these days: the looming cliff of graduation, this final year of grad school. My cozy, safe cocoon was about to kick me out. My student loan debt had reached a balance so high that it had lost any meaning for me beyond the realization that it would be absolute insanity to continue with my PhD without alleviating at least *some* of my debt or finding a reasonably viable source of income first. This summer, I had reluctantly come to the conclusion I should seek out adjunct professorships after graduation—all within Chicago, so I could stay in Hyde Park—until I could justify applying for a PhD program back at UChicago.

My preemptive nostalgia about leaving UChicago and the community and traditions I'd knit together over the years was another topic I avoided with my parents, along with any concrete planning for my future or discussions of "next year," which meant I was in the absolute minority among my peers. My boyfriend, Adam, was starting 3L and already preparing for the bar and applications for internships with law firms and clerkships with judges, which meant that he had even less time to spend with me than usual. He had his top ten choices ranked and spent hours talking up New York and California to me. I always listened with a pang, wishing he expressed a fraction of that same excitement about me anymore, but maybe after two years together that was an unrealistic desire.

Meanwhile, all I wanted was an indefinite lease on the life I already had—studying literature and dissecting it with the smartest people I'd ever met. That and sunny summer days at the Promontory, loud brunches at Valois, and hours combing through 57th Street Books before warming up next to my favorite radiator at home. I could not imagine it was possible to love life more. Adam could spin me whatever tales he wanted about how much better things would be when we finished school, but I couldn't wrap my mind around a future that didn't revolve around the academic calendar—it wasn't just the only thing I'd experienced, but the only thing I'd ever had modeled for me, ever been taught to want.

Deep down, so deep I was afraid to acknowledge it, I worried my desire to stay was a kind of suspended adolescence, academia as an excuse to avoid entering the real world with all its mundanity and disorder. How would I structure my life outside syllabi and deadlines and my professors' approval? I couldn't relate to my classmates' complaints about the rigors of postgraduate studies, but I suspected it was because there was nothing and no one I wanted outside of what I was already doing. Adam understood the myopic focus I kept on my studies—he was in the same boat since law school had essentially swallowed him whole shortly after we met. We met at a party the week before he started 1L—and on uncharitable days, when he canceled our plans at the last minute or posed the idea of a quickie as stress release instead of romantic desire, I wondered whether our relationship had only stuck these past two years because he hadn't had the free time to go look for someone else to have semi-regular sex with. I shoved the intrusive thought down every time it surfaced, since I couldn't claim to be much better— my social calendar was woefully unbalanced with my work calendar, and I'd never considered seduction one of my stronger skill sets—but his perfunctory approach to our relationship still stung sometimes. I'd never been with someone who fit so easily into my life, like he was a puzzle piece designed just for me, but lately I hadn't been able to shake the nagging thought that there might be something *more* to romantic relationships than comfort and ease. I'd been studying literature long enough that I knew eternal passion was a fictional concept. What we had worked. I knew better than to ask for the impossible.

I half tuned out Mom's ongoing monologue to my latest fantasy, getting my adviser on board with me pursuing my PhD at the same university where I'd gotten my BA and MA. If I could get her to agree with my plan, I told myself, what was another hundred thousand dollars in debt? My student loans were already so insurmountable that I couldn't imagine ever being able to pay them off. They might as well have been Monopoly money. But even I knew that was swiss cheese logic, which is why this particular fantasy remained private. My parents were horrified that I was waiting to pursue my PhD—stopping at my MA was tantamount to running away to join the circus since I'd never get tenure with such dubious credentials. They were all for digging my pit of debt deeper, but I was enough of a realist to know that I was entering a job market radically different from what they'd experienced thirty years earlier, not to mention the accompanying exponentially higher cost of living. As much as I hated doing it, I pushed back on their expectations and tried to wrap my mind around a different version of the future than the one I'd held close for all those years.

I heard a cabinet door bang in the background and snapped my attention back to the present. "I've been meaning to ask you, how did Dad's consultation with the surgeon go?"

Mom sighed heavily. "You know your father. He insists that he knows better than the doctor and that he's perfectly fine without a hip replacement. A doctorate in literature is not an MD, as I keep reminding him, but will he listen? Meanwhile, climbing a flight of stairs leaves him bedridden for days, which means *I* have to do all the yard work."

By the time I finally reached Viva Coffee, I was able to end our call with a quick update on Adam (at least the latest I knew about what he was up to) without the topic turning to my thesis or the many differences of opinion my mother had with my adviser, Professor Houghton. This qualified as a major success as far as I was concerned and meant I felt lucky when I entered the café, scanning for the best available spot to park for the day. It appeared that the impending rain inspired most of the usual crowd to stay home, so I was able to snag a prime seat right next to the fireplace, which was already roaring away cheerfully. I unpacked my laptop and reference texts across the coffee table next to my latte with its foamed milk heart and felt a hum of pure satisfaction through my veins with the afternoon unfurling before me. The rain started as I took the first sip of my latte. It couldn't have been more perfect, another puzzle piece slotting elegantly into place.

Hours later, my paper on surrealism and André Breton abandoned for the time being, I watched the rain sluice down the windows of the coffee shop, even more grateful that this was the day I'd snagged the armchair by the fire. What had started as an ambient rainy day escalated into a lashing storm, effectively grounding me at Viva, which wasn't a tragedy since it was exactly where I wanted to be. My laptop sat blankly on the coffee table in front of me, offering at least the impression that I might get some work done today, though I knew it was only a pretense at this point. I'd slid off my boots hours ago and tucked my feet underneath me, as cozy and at home as I'd been in bed with my picture books as a toddler. This was the precise kind of day I was afraid of losing after leaving UChicago—one where none of my work was so pressing that it demanded I do anything other than to please myself. Hence, the preemptive nostalgia (and nagging sensation that what I loved most might not be academia itself) tinged what could otherwise have been a perfect afternoon.

That was when the bell above the door clanged, jarring through the space and drawing my eyes from the window. An almost impossibly tall man stood just inside the doorway, dripping on the inadequate floor mat, looking like some supernatural forest creature who had just crawled out of a bog. His dark hair was long, maybe three inches past his shoulders, and woefully bedraggled from the rain. At least he wore a jacket and boots, but I doubted they were waterproof, given the slightly blue tinge to his pale skin. He looked relieved at finding himself out of the deluge and bashful at the sudden attention since all heads had turned toward the door at his entrance. He glanced around the space, seeming dubious at the prospect of tramping water further into the shop, and for some reason I couldn't explain, I couldn't stomach the idea of him walking back out into the rainstorm.

"Over here!" I called and waved, trying to modulate my volume to reach him across the room and avoid offending the studious quiet of the coffee shop patrons. I stood and moved over to the couch opposite the fire, freeing up the armchair in the prime fire-place-warming position. My instantaneous and instinctive decision to stand and greet him short-circuited my verbal skills. I wouldn't call myself shy—I had plenty of friends, or at least people who wouldn't object to me using that term to describe them—but most of them were extroverts who liked to collect introverts like myself. I didn't have a habit of making the first move or pursuing friendships. If someone didn't pluck me out of the crowd and claim me, I was perfectly content alone with my books. My relationship with Adam was a good case in point, in fact. I wouldn't have singled him out of the crowd at the party where we met, but after he doggedly struck up conversation with me three separate times, I let him walk me home. I was so flattered that he saw something in me even when I felt slightly outside the raucous group that it had sealed an almost instanta-neous loyalty to him in me. My best friend Charlie—not Adam's biggest fan—was quick to point out that I probably got more sexual satisfaction and reliability out of my scheduled reread of *Jane Eyre* each year. I didn't admit to her and tried not to admit to myself that lately, she had a point.

The giant first appeared confused by my over-ture, like he was trying to place me, then just grateful, picking a tender path through the scattered tables and cozy couches over to the fire. The closer he got, the more my heart rate sped up as I reckoned with the outcome of my uncharacteristic impulsivity. My cheeks flushed imagining how strange he must find the gesture and the idea that he'd think I was making a pass at him. I tucked my hair behind my ears and tried to smile in an impersonal way, cutting my eyes over to the chair by the fireplace. I would just offer him my seat and get back to work. This was simple courtesy, nothing more. That justification didn't address the sensation that I'd just plunged into an icy pool and hadn't brought a change of clothes, but I was determined to ignore that.

When the stranger finally reached me, I was startled by how much he towered over me up close. I had been able to tell he was unusually tall from across the shop, but up close, he was maybe the tallest person I'd ever seen in real life off a basketball court. What was he, six foot five, six foot six? Was I going to need a step stool to talk to him? "Hi," I said, nervous and already half apologetic with nerves. "You looked like you needed to warm up." I gestured to the armchair I'd just vacated like I was Vanna White and this was *Wheel of Fortune.*

The giant smiled back at me as rainwater

dripped off his nose. He wiped it away with a self-conscious grin. "You'd be right, thank you," he said, soft and lilting in an accent I couldn't immediately put my finger on. He set down his bookbag close to the fire, also soaked and starting to puddle on the old hardwood floors, then turned back to me. "I'm Declan. I'd offer to shake your hand, but it might be kinder not to."

My eyes flicked down to his hands, his long fingers looking like they could span my entire waist. I offered him a weird little wave, the sense that touching him would be an enormous mistake flashing in my brain like a warning. "Emma," I said. We continued standing there, staring at each other, until I laughed at the awkwardness. "Anyway, sit! Get warm. Best seat in the house." I dropped down onto the couch, busying myself with my laptop, attempting to hide what I was afraid was a growing blush across my cheeks.

Declan lowered himself into the armchair with audible relish, and I couldn't resist peering over the top of my screen to watch him. Now that he was closer, I could make out the lankiness of his build, which was somewhat hidden within his oversized jacket and pants. He was less imposing now that we were both sitting—being relatively tall myself at five eight, I wasn't used to craning my neck to look up at many people. He shrugged his way out of his jacket and draped it over the back of the chair, but getting dry still looked like it would be a losing battle since his long hair was already dampening his shirt.

Before I knew what I was doing or where this new impetuous version of myself had come from, I reached into my backpack and pulled free a UChicago hoodie I'd packed for my walk home in case the temperature dropped. "Here," I said, tossing it over to him, still too cautious to close the distance between us. He caught it by reflex, looking at me like he didn't know where I'd come from either. "I doubt it'll fit you, but you can at least dry your hair with that." Jesus, I was jittery today. Maybe it was the caffeine.

"Are you sure?" he asked, peering at the clean sweatshirt. By now, I thought I had nailed down his accent as Irish, soft and country. "You'll need a dry layer yourself when you leave. No telling when this will let up. It's bucketing down," he said, gesturing back to the windows.

"They have coffee and chocolate croissants here. I could stay all day," I said, and he chuckled, nodding with gratitude. The fact I was the one who had gotten that low and musical laughter out of him had me absurdly pleased, considering we had just met. It felt like an achievement. I was usually the one who laughed at someone else's joke, not the one making the joke.

"Then thank you again," he said, using my hoodie like a towel to wring the rain out of his hair. The sight oddly mesmerized me. I wished I could wrap the strands of his damp hair around my body, feel it that close. In the few minutes since he'd sat by the fire, his hair had already begun to curl and frizz into an untamable array that made me wish I could paint. I could imagine it in a wild leonine mane in my mind's eye, something I'd want to run my fingers through.

All the reading for my Comparative Fairy Tales class must have been making me fanciful, I thought with an internal reprimand. I didn't have any business fantasizing about a stranger's hair. This must be pure envy—my own hair was long and dark, almost black, but stick straight, unwilling to hold a curl even with all the advances of hair science at my disposal. If this were a fairy tale, I would definitely be the mortal, and I was projecting qualities onto this man that were far from helpful. I clicked out of several browser tabs to remove distraction and attempted to ignore the fae-like prince sitting across from me, dripping. It was ridiculous and cliché to get so tripped up over an accent. I told myself that if I talked to him, I would discover he was an idiot, and the fanciful bubble expanding in my mind would burst. It was past time to get back to my work.

"That's very good," Declan said, and I glanced back at his face, startled and afraid that he'd caught me staring. After all, he was just a human and not the fantasy my brain was spinning. "*Endymion*," he said then, nudging my backpack with his foot, where the book was poking out of the zipper, and I felt like my heart had fallen out of my chest and landed on the table in front of me.

"Right," I said, at a loss for anything cleverer. "I should be focusing on my reading for class, but I keep coming back to it. I have a bit of a thing for the Romantics." My cheeks heated as I admitted it. Why was I babbling? Men didn't make me nervous, not ever, certainly not when I wasn't single.

"I can relate," he said. "My recreational reading gets me in trouble as well. When I was writing my thesis on contemporary political fiction, I kept procrastinating by reading Jacobean verse." In anyone else's mouth, it would have sounded like pretentious braggadocio, a pathetic attempt at stating his own brilliance, but coming from him, it seemed genuine. I stared back at him, unwillingly rapt.

He shook out my hoodie, his hair frizzing and puffing out like a halo away from his thin, bearded face. "Ah lord, this is terrible. You'll have to let me wash this and bring it back to you. I'd be embarrassed to give it back to you like this," he said, brushing an errant hair off the logo. His face was so endearingly chagrined that I would have rewound time to re-loan him my hoodie ten times over, relishing the faint bloom of embarrassment in his cheeks.

"Don't worry about it," I said, reaching for the hoodie and secretly hoping I might brush his hand. *How weird. Stop it.*

"I insist," Declan replied, pulling the hoodie out of my reach. Something in me thrilled with curiosity about him—the accent, the un-American choice of words, the strangeness of his size all mysteries I wanted to untangle. I felt as if I'd both encountered a mythical creature and a friend from another life that I just couldn't place.

"Give me your phone, then," I said. "I'll give you my number, and we can schedule this hoodie hand-off." Despite the twinge of guilt, I decided there was nothing weird about that. It was pure practicality. I would need my hoodie back. The fact that I wanted to see him again was beside the point.

He looked dismayed. "I would, but I haven't gotten an international phone plan worked out just yet."

"Oh? Where are you from?" I asked like an idiot as if I'd just noticed his accent wasn't classic Midwestern. Would he lie to me to spare my feelings if he didn't want to give me his number? He must think that I was hitting on him. I should drop a casual comment about Adam; that would set the record straight. I didn't want to give him the wrong idea.

"Wicklow. It's in Ireland," he said.

I nodded as if I had any idea where Wicklow was. "What brings you to Chicago?"

Declan held up the hoodie he still wouldn't give back to me, gesturing to the maroon letters spelling UCHICAGO emblazoned across the front.

"Nice. Me too. Um, obviously." Inside my head, I was screaming at myself. I had proven time and again to be at least a socially competent adult, but for some reason, faced with this man, my ability to form sentences reverted to the sophistication of a ten-year-old.

"'Let knowledge grow from more to more...'" he began, reciting the school motto with a bashful grin.

I held up a hand. "I have to stop you there. You're better off knowing now that the unofficial motto is more accurate."

"What's that?" he asked.

"'Where fun goes to die.'"

His mouth quirked, unwilling to be fooled. "Are you messing with me?"

I shook my head, and he read the truth of it in my eyes. A guffaw broke out of him, cascading notes of glee, and I grinned back like a Cheshire cat. My sentence formation appeared to be back online. Somewhere between the hoodie and his laughter, I decided I wanted to keep talking to this person more than I wanted to get back to my work. Wasn't meeting interesting new people part of what school was for?

As the afternoon and the rain wore on, Declan bought me a fresh latte and a chocolate croissant—*to thank you for your kindness*—and I learned more about his life in Ireland. It was similarly cold and wet where he came from so there was no excuse for his lack of umbrella today. He'd just earned his postgraduate degree in English literature at Trinity College in Dublin and was after his PhD next. The alignment of our studies felt like kismet, and I settled into our conversation like a comfortable bed at the end of a long day. Our discussion washed over me with a sense of relief I hadn't known I'd been missing. Adam tried to show interest in my coursework, but his own workload in law school left him with little time or brain space for anything else, and the subtle implication that my work was frivolous and his was meaningful made me less eager to share it with him as the years wore on. It was such a joy to discuss imagery and the nuances of different translations with someone who was just as excited about them that I could have purred.

"So why UChicago specifically?" I asked, my hands wrapped around my latte, enjoying the sight of Declan uncoiled and warm by the fire. When he'd entered the café, he'd been actively trying to hide his size, and the difference in physicality when he relaxed enough to take up space was striking. Instead of the uncertain man who'd walked into the café, here was a man whose movements became liquid and confident the more engaged he was. I felt as satisfied and responsible for the change as if he were a kitten I'd rescued from a monsoon.

"Mainly the quality and reputation of the literature program, but I needed a change of scenery as well," he replied, breaking eye contact with me for the first time.

Something in his evasion made me say, "Bad breakup?" I wanted to crawl inside his mind and look around. His face made me hungry. I fought down the disquiet that I felt such curiosity about a strange man, reminding myself that I wasn't cloistered. Talking to men wasn't illegal because I had a boyfriend.

He smiled wryly. "You mischievous thing. What makes you say that?" Which wasn't an answer, but it wasn't not an answer, either.

"'A change of scenery' feels like a euphemism." Two hours earlier, this would have felt like an inappropriate bid for intimacy I hadn't earned, but I was already confident Declan wouldn't take offense. He may have been a near stranger, but I already sensed it would be hard to rattle him.

"Ah, a close reading, I should have known," he said, tucking some of his escaped hair behind an ear. "Something like that." His eyes, mostly brown but flecked with gold and green, were far away like he was watching a film screening inside his mind. In the short time since we'd started talking, I'd already gotten used to the presence and candor of his expression, which felt rare, almost remarkable. Seeing him shut off felt jarring, discordant, a reminder that he *was* an actual stranger.

For reasons I didn't particularly want to examine, I didn't like the idea of Declan hurting. "Is it working? The change of scenery?"

He seemed to land back in the moment, settling back into his chair. His eyebrows were thick, and I could watch his thoughts play across his expressive forehead with every furrow and wrinkle. "It's certainly proven a distraction, but I'd be lying if I said it wasn't lonely as well. I don't know anyone here. The idea was to get as far away from her as possible to get some perspective, but I didn't quite take into account that it would be distance from everyone else I care for at the same time." He attempted to soften the sadness of it with a smile, but it didn't fool me. He was lonely and questioning his decisions, and I wanted that to change immediately. The prickling of possessiveness I felt when Declan used the pronoun "her" was another thing I didn't want to examine.

"Well, that's not true anymore," I said. At the questioning look in his eyes, I added, "You know me now." My heart rate picked up, unaccountably hanging on his reply.

"Yes," he said, the glow of the fire turning his chestnut hair gold where it touched. "Now I know you."

A flare gun of rightness went off inside my chest. I felt like we'd been granted a boon—that we somehow had needed each other without knowing it, and here we were against the odds. I was not fanciful by nature, and I'd never believed in the concept of fate, but there was a sense of a missing piece almost audibly clicking into place at that moment.

The afternoon passed in a haze of conversation and little work. The rain petered out, fortuitously enough, just as Viva Coffee started closing up for the night. I felt a pang as I packed up my belongings —I didn't see how we would find each other again if we didn't even have each other's numbers. It may be for the best, but it still stung like a loss that we would only have this one conversation, this one afternoon.

We both hovered on the sidewalk outside, the evening sky starting to darken already. "Well, it was very nice to meet you, Declan," I said, feeling an unaccountable thrum through my nerves at using his name for the first time. I liked the shape of it on my tongue. "Think you're dry enough for a handshake now?"

He grinned down at me from his lofty height and opened his arms for an embrace. "I'm more of a hugger if that's all right with you."

With a rush and a laugh, I stepped into his arms, going on tiptoe to wrap my arms around his shoulders. Much less intimate than around the waist, I rationalized. His shirt (still slightly damp) smelled smoky, almost peaty. The strangeness of chemicals struck me—how someone's smell can feel either so right or so wrong, regardless of all the rational reasons you may have to be drawn or repelled by a person. If I could bottle Declan's scent, I would have kept it in a vial to sniff like smelling salts whenever I was rattled. *Yes*, my body said. *This.*

He gave me a friendly squeeze across my upper back, which shouldn't have sent electricity through all my nerve endings, but it did. He stepped back as my heels returned to the ground. "My pleasure," he said. "Without you, I may have drowned. Where are you headed?"

I pointed north. "Up on 53rd."

Declan looked regretful. "I'm down on 57th. Wanted to stick close to campus in an unfamiliar city and all that."

"Makes sense," I chirped, like the idea of our time together ending didn't make me irrationally panicked. "I guess I'll... see you around."

"Wait a minute," he said, gently smacking his head like a thought had just occurred to him. Heedless of the knee of his pants dampening, he knelt on the wet sidewalk to pull a spiral notebook out of his bookbag, then scribbled on the corner of a page and tore it off for me. "That's my email—so we can coordinate the reverse hoodie heist. I may not have cell service, but my apartment *does* have internet."

I glanced down at the scrap of paper, his uchicago.edu address scrawled across it, and felt my sinking heart bob back into my chest from my stomach. "Glad to hear you're not a complete Luddite. Here." I pulled my phone out of my pocket and shot him a quick email—subject line: *Hi,* body text: *This account belongs to the loud hoodie owner.* Then I pressed send. "Now you have my address too."

Declan smiled, his eyes crinkling at the corners. "Slán leat, Emma."

I rolled my eyes even as the warmth spread from my chest to all my extremities. "Goodbye, nerd."

I only turned back once as we went our separate ways, catching just a glance of the bounce in Declan's step, still identifiable with his wild head of hair cresting over the flow of foot traffic as the distance between us increased.

I had a sneaking suspicion I had just met my new best friend. Though the slight ache in my chest with every step separating us said something different, that was what I told myself.

TWO

That night, I blessedly had the apartment to myself. George had announced he had a string of new quarter parties to attend, and Anika was in the throes of a new romance that meant she spent most of her nights at her new paramour's apartment. I pulled up Otis Redding Radio on Spotify and made myself a cup of green tea, my personal studying jet fuel. I'd texted Adam an invite to come over after leaving Viva, but his response had been a misspelled string of words implying a mountain of drudgery he couldn't avoid. I was determined not to let that hurt my feelings and instead view a night free of interruption as a perfect opportunity to work on the paper I should have finished that afternoon.

With all my study aids in place, I was startled to

hear a key in the lock and hoped that George or Anika had just forgotten something at home on their way out to their respective evenings. This early in the quarter, there were plenty of parties to choose from before midterm stress sent the majority of us into social hibernation. Even though I'd had years to acclimate to their bickering and the inevitable noise human cohabitation creates, any distraction would complicate the serious dent I needed to make in this damn paper.

Instead of Anika or George, it was Adam, letting himself in with the key I'd given him six months into our relationship. "Hi!" I said, rising from my spot on the couch, a slight sense of guilt right on the heels of my irritation at the interruption. After all, I'd invited him, and then been upset when he declined. Was I so unreasonable, could he do nothing right for me? He leaned in for a hello kiss, one hand on my hip, one holding an overnight bag. "I didn't expect to see you tonight! I thought you were slammed." It was a more frequent occurrence that we'd plan to meet but have something interfere, but it wasn't out of the norm for Adam to show up for an overnight unannounced. I tried to see the nonchalance of his comings and goings as a testament to our closeness— my home was his and all that—but sometimes it felt more like disregard. I did my best to shrug off the way it grated.

"Disappointed?" he teased, though the exhaustion in his voice was apparent. He flumped onto the couch next to me, taking off his glasses and rubbing the bridge of his nose with his thumb and index finger. He looked drained and in need of a week of sleep, and the guilt overwhelmed my irritation. I knew what his days were like. I should be grateful to spend any time with him, knowing how thin he was spread, without being put out by the lack of communication. I didn't want to miss him while he was right here with me.

"Not at all, just surprised," I said, sitting back down. He reached over to squeeze my knee.

"I don't know if you have grandiose Saturday night hopes, but I'm beat. Just wanted to see you tonight." I breathed an internal sigh of relief at the subtext that he neither expected me to go out or have sex with him. My much-needed night of studying could continue almost entirely undisturbed.

"I was just working on this paper for my pedagogy class. No big plans."

"Jesus, we're party animals." I mimed taking a shot, to which he offered a perfunctory ha. "Next year, I promise to be more exciting." I refrained from commenting that as a first-year associate in a law firm or clerking for a judge, he was unlikely to have any more time or energy at the end of the day—but excitement was never what I'd asked for or expected from him, anyway. More of this was fine, more of this was good enough for me.

"Don't worry about it," I said. "This is perfect."

He gave me a wan smile. "I love how low maintenance you are." Officially, he was joking, so why did that hurt? I flashed him the smile he was expecting, but it was all teeth and no feeling. "What were you up to today?"

"Nothing special, just studying at Viva Coffee." I turned my attention back to my laptop with a flicker of unease. I wondered if Adam would be able to tell I was leaving something out. There was no reason not to tell him about meeting Declan; he'd probably be thrilled I had someone else to talk to about Seamus Heaney's translation of *Beowulf* since he most certainly didn't want to hear it. But something inside me said *no, that's yours—it's not to share.* "How was your day?" I kept my eyes on the screen, schooling my expression to be as unconcerned as it should be after such an innocuous question.

When Adam didn't immediately respond—he often had an impassioned tirade to make about the amount and tediousness of the reading he had to do or how his IP professor unjustly hated him—I turned to face him. He had already fallen asleep, collapsing into the couch cushions as if he couldn't hold his body weight up one second longer. I felt a flicker of tenderness at his slackened face, the tension mercifully gone from it for once.

As gently as possible, I took off his shoes and covered him with a blanket, then settled back in with my laptop. But even in the silence, my fingers lay still on the keyboard, the words on the screen a blur. What rolled through my brain was *Endymion*. "A thing of beauty is a joy forever: / Its loveliness increases, it will never / Pass into nothingness..."

Declan and I had only brushed against Keats in our conversation today. I allowed myself a moment to wonder if we'd have a chance to dig deeper, then focused on my paper, Adam's soft snores just the white noise I needed to concentrate.

I WOKE the following morning eager to check my email. My body flushed with joy to see a reply to my message waiting from Declan. *Your hoodie has been laundered with the finest of hypoallergenic detergents available at Walgreens. Ungrateful thing, it still just whispered 'I miss Emma' to me.* I laughed out loud and shoved my phone in my pocket when Adam came shuffling into the kitchen, looking for coffee and asking what was so funny. I gabbled a lie about a text from Charlie and put the kettle on.

Later that same day, I was perusing the fluorescent-lit aisles of 57th Street Books for thesis source materials when a shadow appeared on the copy of *The Castle of Otranto* I held. I looked over my shoulder and jumped, clutching my heart with a yelp.

"Didn't mean to frighten you." Declan grinned. I couldn't believe how close he'd gotten to me before I noticed him. "I saw the back of you from across the shop and wasn't sure if it was you."

I wondered what was so distinctive about my back that he would recognize it after one meeting where we were almost exclusively face-to-face, but I wapped him lightly on the shoulder with the book to cover my embarrassment over how jumpy I was. "Well, in the future, you'll be able to recognize me from my screech of terror. Hi." Now that the startlement had drained from my veins, I expected my heart rate to slow. It didn't.

"More romantic poetry?" he asked, angling for a glance at the cover of my book.

I flipped it around to face him. "Not recreational this time, sadly. My thesis is on gender representation in the gothic novel. This one is usually cited as the first." My mother, whose own dissertation had revolved around gothic literature, had been thrilled with my choice. To be honest, she'd steered me toward the topic so resolutely I hadn't felt there had been any other viable option for me. She'd been advising grad students on their theses for decades, so it seemed churlish to reject her free guidance, even if nothing about the subject matter stirred genuine interest in me. Not all projects were passion projects. I knew that well already.

Declan nodded, his head just shy of the hanging lights in the basement shop.

Flustered by his muted reaction, I changed the subject. "What about you? Are you looking for something in particular?"

"Not exactly," he said, running a finger along the spines lined up closest to his eyeline. "I find bookstores peaceful. There's a shop right on the Liffey I used to go to most weekends, and when I realized I wouldn't be doing that for a long while, I got a bit homesick. Thought this was as good a place to go as any."

This time, I nodded without saying anything.

Something in my heart reached out as if to grab his hand and give it a squeeze. Since we didn't know each other well enough for that—and I dreaded finding out that our meeting at Viva Coffee was a fluke and not a friendship he'd want to continue outside the context of proximity to a warm fire on a wet day—I said, "Do you also drink coffee when you're homesick?" I thought back to our meeting the day before and how he'd nibbled at plenty of pastries but hadn't ordered a drink.

His mouth quirked. "Tea, actually."

"I should have guessed. Come with me," I said, gesturing that he follow me up out of the basement bookstore. "We'll go to Fairgrounds. You can have a cuppa there."

His laughter, big and warm, faintly echoed off the walls of the glassed-in stairwell. I was glad my back was to him so he couldn't see the ridiculous size of my answering smile.

Walking to Fairgrounds, Declan adjusted his gait to match mine. His pace was luxurious and unhurried, while I sped up with nervousness, both physically and with inane small talk. I was desperate to recapture the ease we'd had yesterday and flailed verbally to find it. The third time he stopped walking to pull peanuts from his bag to toss to the squirrels, I had to ask.

"Do you seriously carry around peanuts for the campus squirrels? Most people consider them pests," I said. A quorum of the cheeky rodents gathered around his feet, waiting for their due. "They look like they're going to climb you next. They probably think you're a tree."

He laughed, a faint blush suffusing his cheeks in a way all the more beguiling for being unexpected. "I do this at home too. I like knowing they're a little less hungry when we meet. It makes me feel needed. Food is one of my love languages," he added, a little sheepish.

Jesus, I thought. *The romance-starved women of UChicago are going to eat him up.* "Well, be careful," I said. "I don't know what the squirrels are like in Ireland, but these might eat you next. If you're that lonely, join a club or something."

Declan tossed a few final peanut shells into the grass, and the squirrels were off to hide their treasures. "I was hoping I'd run into you," he said, which didn't seem like an answer to my suggestion.

My heart skipped a beat. "Oh yeah?"

"The Horticultural Society didn't appeal to me,

so yes, I hoped I might meet the interesting woman with the weakness for recreational reading again." His eyes slid over to me, sparking with hope and nerves. He looked like a kid offering to split his dessert on the playground, worrying he might be turned down.

"Don't lie. You just want to raid my wardrobe." I did my best to sound nonchalant, far too pleased that a near stranger—particularly this one—had taken a liking to me right away for once. Usually, I was an acquired taste, adopted into friend groups as part of a couple or crowd and not singled out for myself. *She grows on you*, I could imagine my friends saying. While I was grateful that my appeal had some staying power, it stung that I never seemed to be the person who captivated others at first glance—that on the surface I was apparently so bland. Every so often, I wanted to be the one who grabbed the attention— and with Declan, it seemed I had done it.

"I have been looking for more outerwear that will end somewhere above my navel, true," he said, checking my reaction in his periphery. I couldn't contain my satisfied smile.

"You haven't met anybody in your classes?" I knew he'd both teach and attend classes as a PhD student. As the rare postgrad who could actually pull off the glasses and elbow patches look with an accent to boot, I had no doubt he was already a heartthrob among his undergraduates. He seemed the type for that kind of attention to sail right over his head, though, which was another layer of appeal I shouldn't have noticed.

"The quarter has barely started. Am I being timed?" he protested.

This was my opportunity to prove my platonic bona fides, then. Invite him into my circles, introduce him to my friends, take him to parties where he'd have the chance to mingle with more people who shared his interests. Yet if I was already envious of the attention he gave to squirrels, how could I introduce him to my roommate Anika, who was both cartoonishly beautiful (giant eyes, tiny waist) and intimidatingly intelligent (a molecular biophysicist, for fuck's sake)? Would he still find me *interesting*? Why would it feel like such a loss if he didn't?

I delayed the inevitable. "You're right. There's plenty of time to make non-squirrel acquaintances."

"Though I'd never abandon them. It wouldn't do to be a fair-weather friend."

"You'll make menaces of them all. *Worse* menaces than they already are. And they're famously assholes!" I said. But even at that moment, I knew I'd think of him whenever I saw a squirrel from that moment forward. Suddenly, I was fond of those combative rat bastards.

Declan looked puzzled. "These particular squirrels—wild animals, I'll remind you—are considered assholes for being hungry?"

I flapped a hand at him. "It's a thing. Remember the UChicago slogan I told you?"

"'Where fun goes to die'? You're really making me question my choice to leave Ireland. Which wasn't easy, either. The visa process was painful."

I tilted my head in acknowledgment of the challenges he'd faced to come here. "They really should put these things in the marketing materials. I hate to tell you there's another one."

"Another slogan? I'm afraid to ask."

"'Where the squirrels are cuter than the girls and more aggressive than the boys.'"

Declan groaned. "Now I know that one isn't true." It happened so quickly that I could have imagined it—did his eyes flick down my body for just a fraction of a second before he found my eyes again? I didn't have the kind of figure that inspired lusty glances—my build was more athletic than curvaceous—he wouldn't have looked at me like that just to flatter me, would he? *It doesn't matter, Emma, this is not sixth grade*, my brain screamed. *You are not this thirsty for validation.*

I was twisted in knots. I decided to ignore the look and the implied compliment, too horrified by the thought of being wrong. "You've crossed an ocean to attend a university populated by dweebs, Declan. Maybe you *should* focus your energy on the squirrels."

"Sounds like I'll fit right in," he says, unperturbed by the revelation that he had moved across the world to a peculiarly sexless environment. UChicago was pretty much the antithesis of a party school. I knew what he meant by fitting in. He definitely looked the part of an academic: wiry instead of muscle-bound, dressed as if he could fit into a classroom any time between now and the 1970s—but on him, it was appealing instead of off-putting. The intelligence and wit that sparked behind the glasses he took on and off, the intensity of his attention, the accent—he seemed so *alive* in every movement, and while it was obvious that he was shy, he wasn't socially hobbled, he just needed some time to warm up. If he hoped this transatlantic move would help him heal his broken heart with a lot of random hookups, I didn't think he'd have a problem achieving that, UChicago's reputation be damned.

I was grateful to reach Fairgrounds and the opportunity to change the subject. I knew I had no right to object, but I found I didn't like the idea of Declan hooking up with the lonely female population of UChicago (and it was legion). "Here we are," I said unnecessarily, opening the door for him like I was a valet.

He insisted I order first when we reached the counter, and while I opted for my usual soy latte, he got his "cuppa" of Earl Grey. We snagged a table, and once again, I was overcome with awkwardness. Did my offer to take him out for tea qualify as asking him out on a date? Had I crossed the line from friendly to flirtatious? I wrapped my hands around my latte and wished I'd ordered tea so I'd have something to blow on and keep myself busy.

"So I have a thought," Declan said, sitting across from me, looking nervous. "Please say no if it's an imposition."

My heart sped up. "What is it?"

"I just arrived a week ago and haven't seen much besides my apartment and the registrar's office. Would you mind showing me around Hyde Park a bit? Help me get the lay of the land?" He looked like he half wished he'd never asked before he even finished the question. But something about his face made me think the other half of him held his breath as he waited for my answer.

"Sure!" I sounded way too enthusiastic, but it was too late to moderate my excitement now. "I mean, I've lived here for six years. It's safe to say I know my way around," I added, attempting to temper my eagerness.

"I know how involved working on a thesis is, so if you're just saying yes to be kind—" he said, but I cut him off.

"I'm not. That sounds fun." And it did. Relief flooded my body at the realization that our collision at Viva Coffee didn't have to be a one-time thing. Instead, the idea that I might have a real friendship with someone who lived in the same city as me (unlike my beloved Charlie) bordered on sublime, but I wasn't going to tell him that. Showing him around didn't sound romantic. It wouldn't be wrong of me to do that. So yes. Yes, I could have this.

This doesn't have to be over echoed in my mind, comforting and thrilling all at once.

He flashed a smile at me, bigger and brighter than any I'd yet seen from him. If I had any misgivings, they were quickly drowned out by the pleasure of knowing I'd inspired that smile.

. . .

AFTER OUR CONVERSATION AT FAIRGROUNDS, we began sending each other brief, nonsensical emails a few times a day, but beyond that, I started seeing Declan almost every day, whether we'd arranged to meet up to explore Hyde Park together or not. It helped that he stood out anywhere on campus like a beacon, the autumn wind catching his hair as he stood a full head higher than the next tallest person in any crowd. If he saw me first, his standard greeting became "*There* she is," like he'd been searching for me everywhere. The recognition and relief of it made me smile every time. "Come here to me," he'd add, gesturing that I join him wherever he walked next. If I saw him first, I liked to circle back and bump into him from behind because he was so adorably polite, he would fall all over himself apologizing for being a stationary obstacle until he realized it was me. I was amazed that the same dorky practical joke worked on him every time. Something about his guileless attitude made me feel like I could play—I didn't have to be pulled together and serious all the time, the Emma Brice who shot to the top of the class with her unwavering work ethic. A part of me felt like I was experiencing childlike play for the first time in my life.

This silly prank played out the same way every time. Once Declan realized I had plowed into him on purpose, he would abort his acrobatic apology with a smile and a "you wagon," and we'd walk off in search of a snack (if he didn't already have an apple or packet of cookies for me in his bag) or a place to work together until one of us had class. What started as something impromptu and casual became a little tradition, a part of my days that felt essential. If we didn't manage to run into each other or I hadn't received an email from him by the time I headed back to my apartment for the evening, I walked a little slower and felt a little sadder. I had friends, and obviously, I had Adam, but I hadn't had a symbiotic friendship like this since my freshman year of under-grad, when Charlie and I walked around campus together like we were in an eternal three-legged race. When she transferred to UT-Austin the following year, I was bereft and moorless for months. Eventu-ally, I adjusted, but I never stopped missing the inti-macy that came with lightning-strike chemistry. Charlie was still my best friend, but the physical space between us and the competing demands of her MFA and my postgrad work meant our lives weren't as closely woven together as before. The appearance of Declan in my life out of the clear blue sky gave me a similar feeling of immediate sparks—kismet, fate, destiny. Whatever terminology you wanted to apply, it fit.

The first few weeks of any quarter usually provided the most opportunity for free time before everyone's workload swallowed their social lives, which was how I justified the sheer number of outings I planned for us over the next three weeks. Since he'd already been to Viva and 57th Street Books, I decided the next local institution Declan needed to experience was Valois, a cafeteria-style restaurant famous for being one of Obama's favorite spots. When Friday night rolled around and Adam canceled our dinner plans due to a fast-approaching deadline for a law journal submission, at least now I had an available alternative to stewing in my resentment over always coming second. After assuring Adam I didn't mind—low maintenance to the core—I shot off an email to Declan. *You up for breakfast tomorrow morning?* I knew he'd see the message; he left his email open in a browser on his laptop all day. Considering email was his main source of contact with his friends and family back home, I understood his impulse to be plugged in at all times.

His reply pinged my phone minutes later. *Name*

the time and place. I typed in the address and *9AM* and went to bed early, already anticipating the morning.

Valois was an easy walk from my apartment— both were on 53rd, so I expected to beat Declan to the restaurant. However, as I approached the exterior loudly proclaiming its slogan ("See Your Food"), he was already waiting for me on the sidewalk out front.

"*There* she is," he said, leaning down for a brief hug. I'd gotten used to them in the past few weeks— the smoky smell of his clothes, the way he had to round down to meet me and I *still* had to stand on tiptoe. *This is what safe feels like*, my nervous system said. *Take a pill, you neurotic*, I told myself.

"I'm on time," I protested, his hair tickling my nose.

"I'm merely expressing that I'm happy to see you." I felt a flutter in my stomach that I did my best to ignore, letting my heels return to the earth.

"Welcome to Valois," I said, gesturing to the building's facade with the showmanship of a circus ringleader.

"Lovely, I could do with a fry-up," he responded, but I shook my head.

"This is not that kind of place," I warned him.

"But there are rules I want you to remember."

"Rules? For breakfast?"

"If you don't want to get yelled at, yes, there are rules."

"Why would anyone be yelling?" he asked, looking bewildered and possibly like he was in for more than he'd bargained for.

I ignored that, giddy at the prospect of seeing his reaction to the bustle of cafeteria service. "The keys are this: You must be decisive. You must keep up. And you must be loud." I grabbed his elbow and steered him into the restaurant, instructing him to grab a tray as we got in line to order at the counter.

"Fortunately, there's always a little bit of a wait on the weekends, so you have time to decide what you want," I shouted over the cacophony of the dining room. "But god help you if you haven't decided by the time you get up there." Even with a line snaking to the door, we had fifteen minutes tops until we made it to the counter.

A wrinkle of concentration and barely concealed panic creased his brow, and it was so cute I couldn't decide if I wanted to wipe it away or find more ways to make him nervous. My mind started concocting other tasks I could set him with a stopwatch.

When we did make it up to the assembly line

counter, Declan wore a determined face. "I can tell you're repeating your order to yourself in your head," I said to him while we waited for our turn. Magnanimously, I'd already offered to go first to show him how it was done.

"Hush, you, or I'll forget the word for pancake."

I grinned and bellied up to the counter. "Three pancakes and hashbrowns!" I bellowed at the sweaty man behind the counter, who nodded brusquely and started dishing up off the grill and onto my tray.

"You?" he prodded Declan, irritated.

"Could I please have—"

"I can't hear you!" the cook shouted back at him.

Flushing, Declan raised his voice a few decibels. "Three pancakes and sausage links, please!"

The cook dished up his food without making eye contact, already on to the next customer. Declan looked over at me, shell-shocked. "I told you—you have to be loud," I said, flashing my UChicago ID for the discount and paying with cash before Declan could scramble up his wallet and hold up the line further while he made sense of American currency. He'd incited the cooks' ire enough for one day.

"But I was decisive," he protested as we made our way toward an open table. "That was incredibly stressful. Why did you bring me here?"

"I wanted to see if you were capable of speaking in a tone and volume other than one would use to read a bedtime story to a child," I said, grinning. Gamely, he smiled back, and I notched a point for myself in the unofficial tally of successfully acclimating Declan to Hyde Park and the United States at large.

Not every outing was as psychologically grueling for Declan as Valois. I also introduced him to the magical grilled cheese at Medici on 57th, took him to a guided tour of Frank Lloyd Wright's Robie House, and acquainted him with the jewel that was Hyde Park Produce (though in that instance he was disappointed that they didn't stock Walker's Crisps).

"Are you playing up your Irishness with me?" I asked once as we walked to the Regenstein Library (more commonly known as the Reg) for an afternoon of studying. I'd rarely, if ever, felt so comfortable with someone so fast, and I wondered if I was simply thrown off by the accent and his agreeableness. I was so used to being the agreeable one that maybe all this was disorientation; I was just knocked off my axis.

He tilted his head slightly, glancing down at me. "What do you mean?"

"I mean, the things you say. Like 'come here to me' or 'bang on.' Leaning into the slang. Are you playing it up?" Not to mention the insistence on calling chips crisps and fries chips.

Declan looked puzzled. "Does it not make sense? That's just the way I talk. We're both speaking English."

"No, it makes sense, I just—" I wasn't expressing myself well. "Is this how you're making new friends? Playing the exotic foreigner?"

"Emma, I hate to disillusion you, but I don't *have* any friends." I groaned and punched his arm. We were a month into the quarter, and he could have had plenty of new friends by now if not for the fact that he never seemed to approach anyone. He carried himself as if he'd learned long ago that being as tall as he was would intimidate people and he had to be as unassuming as possible. The juxtaposition of his size and his self-effacing manner didn't just catch my eye —women checked him out wherever we went. A few even hinted at going out, and he seemed to miss the innuendo every time.

He grinned at my irritation, having heard my speech about his social skills multiple times. "And I was never good at acting." I could attest to the truth of that. I'd discovered that while he was painfully polite, he was incapable of not telegraphing his feelings, whether they be discomfort, glee, or sadness.

He wanted to provide whatever was asked of him, but I could see when those actions fit uncomfortably for him written all over his face. You could call Declan many things, but you couldn't call him "smooth."

"Never mind," I said. "I forgot that being tall, handsome, and smart is such a handicap when meeting new people." I would have been embarrassed at calling him handsome if not for the fact that he was too excited to poke back at me to notice.

"Are you playing up your Americanness with me? Because I can assure you, it's unnecessary. Your portion sizes gave it away." I punched his arm again, harder this time, and we called a truce in order to settle in quietly at a table in the Reg.

"Be nice to me or I won't show you all the best neighborhood spots," I warned him in a whisper. "You can eat at Giordano's for all I care."

"There are more restaurants where the staff shouts at you?" he asked, feigning shock.

"You make me tired," I said, but it wasn't true. He made me feel appreciated, interesting, alive, confused, and guilty. Never tired.

After the first time we ran into each other on campus, and as our time together became woven inextricably into our routines, Declan started carrying my hoodie around with him in case we crossed paths. I gave him a litany of excuses why I couldn't take it back—no room in my bag, I was in a rush, it looked so much better on *him,* etcetera, etcetera (which was a blatant lie, the sleeves barely covered half his forearms)—that the failed handoff became part of a shared language we were building together. He would try to throw it to me, and I'd intentionally miss, then howl that he had to wash it again before returning it to me. Or I would claim I was transferring to Brown and didn't want it anymore, or whatever weird bit occurred to me each particular day. The truth was, I liked him having it, imagining it mingling with his own clothes in the apartment I'd never seen, that he had a little piece of me.

I didn't question how we always managed to find each other over the course of that fall, and though I never asked about his schedule outright, I knew that Tuesday and Thursday afternoons he would be free. We would walk the campus east to west, Declan slowing his pace to match mine while we complained about our classes and debated the merits of whatever recreational reading we were frittering away our time on. Our conversations weren't always weighty or intellectual—more often they were silly and repetitive—but they made me feel like I had a home in this person who was always happy to see me. I hadn't realized how much I'd been missing that.

My initial fears that our time together would blur the line between platonic friendship and something more seemed unfounded. It felt like the window for something romantic had closed without that line being crossed—which was a good thing, I reminded myself when I wished for him to step a little closer or for our hugs to last a little longer. It meant I wasn't doing anything wrong.

It meant I didn't have to stop.

ONE COLD AND blustery October morning, I checked our mailbox in the breezeway before setting off for my day. It was largely the usual—a gas bill, some restaurant flyers stuck through the openings—but a letter from our building's management company addressed to George, Anika, and me caught my eye. I slit the envelope open while my brain whirred with frantic activity—we each addressed our rent checks individually, and my October check had already cleared, so I knew we weren't late—but it was a generic letter from our landlord letting us know that she was selling the building. We would get to see out the end of our lease but couldn't renew. This was always a possibility as a renter, and I'd known that, but the idea that no matter what I chose to do next year, I wouldn't be coming home to the cozy apartment I'd loved for the past three years left me gutted like I'd lost a friend. I was preemptively grieving my favorite radiator for drying wet socks, the balcony where George, Anika, and I would share our coffee on sunny days, and the built-in shelves holding our mismatched collections of books. It was one more horrible reminder that I was running out of time—to make future plans *or* enjoy my present. I was fuming with the injustice of it all—being forced to change when all I wanted was for things to stay the same. I had an emotional cloud over my head to match the October sky for the rest of the day.

Like most Tuesdays, Declan and I ran into each other on the quad after my classes. Unlike most Tuesdays, I was so consumed with my spiraling thoughts of change that I didn't notice him. He had to chase me down the sidewalk since I'd missed his first several shouts of my name.

"Whoa there," he said when I finally clocked that he was trying to get my attention. "What's happened? Are you all right?" The concern creasing his forehead was the first thing all day to break through my self-pity and remind me that, rationally, this was not the end of the world but a commonplace occurrence. That as awful as I felt, I didn't want to worry Declan.

"Hi," I said, a tearful wobble sneaking into my voice. "I'm fine, just a bad day, that's all."

That didn't seem to convince him, especially with the unsteadiness of my tone. "You don't seem fine, Emma. What's wrong? Where are you headed?" He blocked my path with a wide stance, all gallantry and sweetness, and it wasn't helping my determination not to cry.

"I was going to Viva—" I said. Going home would mean I'd have to tell George and Anika about the letter, and even if they weren't as upset about it as I was, I didn't want to tell them our home was almost gone and make it any more real.

"No," Declan vetoed. "You need something stronger than coffee. Come here to me."

I stepped closer, and he linked his elbow with mine, steering us both resolutely toward Noyes Hall.

"Where are we going?" I asked, buffeted along in the wake of his long stride, almost trotting to keep up.

"To get you a pint," he answered, like the answer to my problem was simple as breathing.

You know, I didn't think a pint would make

anything worse. I followed him into Noyes Hall and down the stairs to the basement, where the Pub was housed, a private club where students paid a nominal membership fee to have access to a bar on campus.

Declan parked me at an empty table and walked up to the bar to order us a round, brooking no arguments from me. When he returned, pushing a frothy stout and a basket of waffle fries my way, he sank into the seat across from me and said, "Talk."

I covered my face with my hands. "I feel so stupid. I'm overreacting. Don't pay attention to me."

"That's impossible," he said. I dragged my hands away from my face.

"It's nothing, I just... I got a letter this morning that my apartment building is being sold. I'll have to move out in June. That's all. See? I'm overreacting." My eyes had started to tear with the admission, so I sipped my beer, which was creamy and malty, just the way I liked it.

"That's awful, darling. I'm so sorry. I know you love your apartment." He sounded genuinely sad at the loss, and he'd never called me darling before. He'd never even been to my apartment, but I talked about it like it was a living person, and his tone made it clear he understood just how deeply the prospect of leaving it cut.

"It doesn't matter. When I graduate, I probably would have had to move anyway. This is just forcing the inevitable," I said, waving a hand and looking away to dispel the lingering sense that the perfect place for my cheek right now was pressed against his chest.

He contemplated that. "So what's next for you, given this news?"

"Another beer, that's for sure," I said.

"Well, that's a given," Declan said dryly, "but I meant more along the lines of your life. Academically, professionally, what you're planning to do. Since you are graduating, as you said." He was watching me closely, though he'd asked the question casually.

I sighed. "Don't remind me." I found myself dodging this topic whenever it came up, but I'd walked him right up to it. Graduation still felt like a countdown to a future I didn't want. Inadvisably, this reluctance to face facts had also led to the bad habit of giving my thesis short shrift in favor of literally anything else—cleaning my apartment, calling my parents or Charlie, researching exhaustively for any paper outside my thesis, grading for the undergrad courses I was TAing. Spending *lots* of time with Declan.

He didn't respond, waiting me out. "I don't know. Everyone I know has a five-year plan set in stone, and I have no answer. I have this visceral reaction to every option I can come up with—*not that*. I've had all this time to think about it, and I just want to relive this year over and over again. I'm in suspended animation."

"Sounds very Groundhog Day. Might get old," he joked gently, trying to coax a laugh out of me.

"I didn't know you were such Bill Murray fans across the pond," I said, unable to laugh but happy to redirect the conversation. Saying it all out loud felt like pressing on a bruise, an ache that would linger long after we climbed out of the Pub.

"It's not *him* I'm a fan of. It's more of a Punxsutawney Phil thing."

He got me on that one. I grunted a laugh and took a long pull of my stout. Declan preferred dark beers, though he said he'd never order Guinness in the States. ("This far away from Dublin? Sacrilege.")

"Fine. In an ideal world, I'd pursue my PhD next—it would make sense—but I'm already so deep in debt, and after undergrad *and* postgrad at UChicago, there's no way they'll want me here. My adviser wants me to apply elsewhere to round out my educational and pedagogical perspective. Which I understand, but I can't imagine leaving." Even the Pub, with its concrete floor and well-worn pool tables, had the glow for me that only nostalgia can lend. "I've been holding on to this hope that even if I have to leave UChicago, I could stay in my apartment, you know? Find a job in the city, get to stick around." Now that I was hearing it, the idea sounded like getting fired from a job and still showing up for work every day. Were all my future plans this half-baked?

"It is lovely here," he allowed, sipping his porter.

"I can hear the 'but' in your voice, Declan," I said. I was past my initial surprise at how easy I found it to bicker or disagree with him by that point —normally the merest hint of confrontation or snappishness sent my blood pressure skyrocketing and I would immediately shift gears into my most accommodating self, no matter how I really felt, but Declan seemed to take whatever I had to say in stride. It was so freeing, and felt so *good*, that I found myself teeing up little debates on a regular basis just for the pleasure of expressing an opinion without the fear of judgment.

He held up his hands. "Not at all. I certainly

don't want to lose you. I have years ahead of me here."

I felt my cheeks warm. "Oh please. Not this 'you're my only friend' thing again."

He grinned. "Even if you weren't my only friend here—which is true, though I don't want to belabor the point—I would miss you." He looked a little embarrassed with his own earnestness but not sorry he'd said it. I suddenly felt close to tears—losing the apartment had softened me up, but it was more than that. The simplicity of his unforced affection was something I was hungry for—and the more I got of it, the more ravenous for it I became.

I blinked back the tears before I could start crying at the bar and really make things awkward. "It's your round. Get me a Guinness, you softy." If I started thinking about missing Declan on top of everything else that would change after graduation, I was done for.

He grimaced at me but made to stand. "This is cruel and unusual punishment."

"Just trying to make you feel at home," I trilled as he walked away from our table, my incipient tears averted with the joy of needling him.

I was taking deep breaths, trying to level out and come up with a new topic of conversation with enough pull to keep Declan's focus off my future plans, when the sensation of being watched grabbed my attention. I caught the eye of a third-year law school student named Ben across the room, holding a pool cue and clearly watching me. I'd met him at a few law parties with Adam, though Adam considered him a competitor more than a friend. Ben waved, looking like he was about to walk over.

Panicking, I pulled out my phone while I waved back, pretending to get a call. I noticed a woman struggling to hold her bookbag and beer while eyeing Declan's empty seat in the crowded bar. I leaped up, gesturing to the table while still miming a phone call in case Ben was watching. The woman—clearly a student if the eye bags and sense of desperately needing a drink were anything to go by—smiled at me gratefully and collapsed into my seat with her beer and overloaded bag. I cleared our glasses and scanned the bar for a corner where we could stand with our next round away from Ben's eye line.

I was surprised to find myself self-conscious about being seen out with Declan by someone who knew me through Adam. I hoped he hadn't been watching when I was near tears; that would *definitely* get back to Adam. I knew there was nothing to hide. Declan and I were just friends, and Adam was so busy with 3L that I knew he wouldn't begrudge me hanging out with someone, especially when he didn't have the time or emotional bandwidth to hang with me himself if our string of recently canceled plans were anything to go by. But my time with Declan had become like the flame off a match to me: something I wanted to cup my hand around to protect it from any battering winds. It felt safer as mine alone, and worth guarding.

What was harder to justify with every day that passed, even to myself, was not mentioning Adam to Declan. It would be so simple. All I had to do was drop in a casual comment, "I'm meeting up with my boyfriend, but I'll email you after." It should be no big deal, but I couldn't bring myself to do it. Weeks had passed, and the longer I put it off, the weirder it seemed that I'd never mentioned him. Every time I pictured it, all I could imagine was something crucial fracturing between me and Declan. The idea of introducing that whisper of a boundary felt like it would wreck the easy sense of kinship and belonging we'd found and add a layer of restraint to our interactions. We'd probably still hang out, but something would be missing. We'd see each other less and less frequently until our friendship faded away like so many do in school.

That was, if Declan even still wanted to spend time with me after finding out I had a boyfriend, which some dark, paranoid corner of my mind assumed he wouldn't. It had happened before that I'd thought I made a guy friend and one mention of a boyfriend rocketed him out of my life and into the ether. I didn't think Declan was the kind of guy who thought women were their partners' property, but his almost courtly manners didn't make it seem like a stretch that he might consider backing off the (misguidedly) chivalrous move.

Ben seemed to take the hint of my pretend call and sudden relocation and returned to his pool match. I hastily put my phone away as Declan returned with our next round after finding me in a corner near the bar. "Here is your inarguably inferior American Guinness. Did I interrupt a call? I can give you some privacy." He stood a few feet away from me, prepared to walk away and give me space, but I edged my way further into the corner to make room for him to join me.

We'd had the Guinness argument before. "It was just a robocall. How can a beer possibly be inferior based on the location where it is consumed?" I asked, taking the pint off his hands.

"I could go into detail about the cleanliness and

calibration of nitrogen tap lines, but I suspect you don't want an answer. You just want to be difficult," he said, smiling.

"My one true talent." At least with Declan. And it was addictive as hell.

He ducked his chin, giving me a doubtful look. "I hate when you do that, you know."

"Do what?"

"Downplay yourself. You act like you're a walking disaster and everyone else has it all together, when the truth is pretty much everyone feels how you do, they're just not honest about it. And speaking of, what happened to our table?" he asked, though it sounded like he already knew the answer.

I flapped my beer-free hand. "It's really crowded in here, I felt bad hogging a table."

Declan blinked at me. "Tell me, do you look for opportunities to inconvenience yourself for the benefit of others? You have every right to *sit*, Emma."

"It's not a big deal," I said, slurping the head off my beer and dying for a change of subject. However, Declan didn't seem inclined to let it go.

"This is just another way you try to make yourself smaller. You realize that not many people are accepted to UChicago in the first place, don't you? You are verifiably intelligent and impressive." He peered over the top of his stout at me, waiting for me to accede to his point.

I sighed, stowing the compliments away for later perusal. His vehement defense of my worthiness felt so good I couldn't trust it. "I didn't use to feel this way. Just... graduation has really been throwing me for a loop. I don't know how to be anything other than a student. I never even *planned* to be anything other than a student. And I'm twenty-five years old. Seems like I should have picked up some other skills by now, considering how unmarketable this one is. Maybe woodworking." I slugged back a mouthful of beer.

"I don't think many people know how to *be* anything, to be fair," Declan replied. "It's more the doing one can know."

Ignoring the slightly nonsensical philosophy a few beers could pry out of Declan, I leaned a hip against the wall and decided I'd had enough of being the center of attention. "What about you?"

"What do I know how to be?" he asked, intentionally missing the point and waggling his eyebrows at me.

"No, smart-ass. What's your big plan after you finish your PhD?"

"I have three more years to figure that out."

"Come on, telling me you have a plan won't make me feel worse than I already do. No one spends a decade in universities for no reason."

He conceded the point. "I'd like to teach university, I suppose. Continue writing."

"Is that what you've always wanted to do?" It was already hard for me to imagine Declan doing anything else—like he'd emerged into the world as a fully formed adult with glasses on his nose and a book under his arm, professorial elbow patches and all. I'd experienced the spectrum of teachers over my academic career—from nurturing parental figures to bitter, resentful profs out to ensure you're every bit as miserable as they are—but I knew Declan would be the most memorable and impactful kind of them all. He would be a teacher genuinely invested in the emotional health of his students without sacrificing an ounce of the challenge and rigor they would need to grow. I had no doubt his students already sought his respect and attention—and would remember him fondly for the rest of their lives. I knew I would.

He pondered that. "I think so. I'm a bit of a black sheep in my family—my brothers played football or I guess soccer, you call it?—and went into finance for the lifestyle, but chasing money never appealed to me. I loved school from the beginning, which everyone in my family found strange, but it suited me. And during postgrad, I learned I love teaching— watching people discover a new skill or a new passion. It feels like a gift to spend my days doing that."

Teaching would suit him "down to the ground," as he would say. I wished I felt the same way, but I found myself jealous of my students instead, wishing I was being graded instead of the other way around. I was envious of that natural fit for him, that sense of vocation. "Are you planning to do that here or... somewhere else? Since you came to the US for your PhD and all," I added.

"I'd like to go back to Ireland someday," he said softly, tracing a bead of condensation on his glass with his fingernail. I almost shuddered, fantasizing about just one finger touching me with that same attentiveness. "But it's a small island. I suppose I'll go where opportunity leads me."

It felt like a hand squeezed my heart, imagining Declan any further from me than the six inches between us at that moment. "Let's run away together and leave all this behind," I half joked.

"Finish your Guinness. That should help with your ennui, even if it is inferior this side of the Atlantic." He clinked his pint to mine. I tried to remember the last time anyone had gone out of their way to drag me out of a funk like this and came up blank.

"Right, I always have better ideas about my future a couple beers deep," I replied, the sarcasm thick enough to clog a drain.

"You are possibly the least Irish person I've ever met," he said. It could have sounded like an insult, but hearing any superlative applied to me from Declan's point of view felt like I'd carved out a place in his life, and I relished it. I said a silent, secular prayer to stop time.

IT WAS around that time that it became harder to ignore that my friendship with Declan had settled into a gray area that I couldn't define. Sometimes I would catch him looking at me in a way that caught my breath—but in the same moment, I'd doubt my own instincts as paranoid or wishful thinking. Those looks were inquiring, hopeful, cautious—but never blatantly flirtatious. We explicitly used the word friend to describe each other. Lately, I'd been tempted to call him my best friend, and that didn't scream romance. Even that term felt like risking too much intimacy, that we'd run screaming into passionate dependence on one another within a month, but it didn't feel inaccurate.

In characteristic problem-solving mode, I found myself compiling a list of evidence he wasn't interested in me—which simultaneously depressed me and reassured me that I wasn't doing anything wrong. When we were out in public, I watched to see if Declan checked out other women—but if he did, it was so subtle that I missed it. One day at Viva, Declan had flinched so hard when a woman flirtatiously touched his arm that he sloshed hot tea on his pants and looked like he'd peed himself for the next two hours.

"Please stop laughing," he whispered to me after evading the woman in question's advances, slouching low in his chair as I snorted into my hand. The busty redhead had fled to the opposite side of the café, making a meal of setting up a study station to telegraph her indifference. "It hurts."

"Do you need some ice for your groin?" I wheezed. Actual tears were leaking out of the sides of my eyes.

"No, my ego. Think the barista could help?"

"Only if she has a time machine," I answered. "Did she electrocute you? You almost splattered yourself on the ceiling."

Declan groaned, closing his eyes. "I didn't mean to make her feel bad. She just startled me."

"If arm touching is startling for you, I have some bad news," I continued gleefully. I was way too pleased by Declan's rejection of a pretty girl, and leaning into the shit-talking was the only way to disguise my less-than-supportive thoughts.

"She's a stranger! We exchanged all of three sentences, and she *touched* me! How was I supposed to react?" Declan looked like he wanted to drown himself in what was left of his tea.

"Declan, she didn't *grope* you. She touched your arm. You're not a shut-in. You have been in relationships before, or so you've led me to believe. You have to know how to flirt, at least a little."

"I never went around touching strangers' arms and hoping it would lead to a phone number, I can tell you that."

"Do you want to go out with her?" Suddenly, I didn't feel like laughing. "She's still over there. You could try again. Maybe leave your drink here this time." I owed him this, I thought. If he wanted to date, I should be supportive, no matter how much it made me nauseous.

"No," he said definitively. "Let's get out of here." He'd already started packing up his study materials and the undergrad papers he'd been grading.

"Fleeing the scene of the crime," I answered, my humor bubbling back with his denial.

He practically used me as a human shield as we exited Viva to avoid further eye contact with the redhead, who I couldn't help but notice looked pretty irritated as we left. I felt a flash of sympathy—getting rejected in a public place is no picnic, one of the many reasons I never made the first move. I ducked my head to avoid making eye contact with her, afraid she'd see something there I wasn't ready to admit to.

It was an unseasonably warm late October day, so we decided to take advantage of what would likely be one of our last opportunities to enjoy Promontory Point before the wind off the lake became nasty instead of refreshing. After our escape from Viva, we sat side by side on the rocks, looking out at the lake, placid and bright blue against the sky. The greater the distance from the coffee shop, the more Declan relaxed and seemed to enjoy my affectionate ribbing, though now he appeared ready to turn the tables.

"So what's your signature flirting move, then? Do you also grab passersby in the hopes it will charm them?" He glanced over at me, a little furtive. He was testing a boundary.

I ignored the warmth spreading to my cheeks. It was a question I wanted to ask him too—so I'd know whether I was wrong to think he was flirting with me every so often. Was he wondering the same thing? "Don't change the subject. We were talking about *your* moves."

"You're a sadist," he said, giving up on eye contact with me and skipping a rock into the lake.

"But seriously, Declan," I said, "setting what just happened aside, you're telling me you haven't met anyone who interests you since you got here? Even women who don't squeeze your bicep while you're holding a hot beverage?" I resisted the urge to hold my breath. As long as he didn't say *It's you, it's always been you*, I could keep seeing him without feeling guilty, right? Yet that was all I wanted him to say.

He winced at the memory. "I do recall telling you that I came to Chicago for distance after a breakup," he said, continuing to avoid eye contact with me. "Let me lick my wounds in peace if you're so concerned about my love life."

I hated the term "love life" as applied to Declan. I wasn't interested in sharing him.

And the thing was, he didn't strike me as wounded. The day we'd met, I felt a shadow over him, some ache that was still present but fading. But since then, I mainly saw the more cheerful side of Declan—teasing, quick to laugh at himself—or the quiet intensity he'd slip into when discussing something that fascinated him, especially around any piece of writing, like he wanted to pull it apart and see how all the individual pieces worked. He seemed a little lonely, a little unsure in this new country, but he didn't seem heartbroken. I knew it was pure ego to give myself any credit for his healing, but was it wrong to hope I'd played some part in it?

I busied myself with digging through my book-bag, just as eager to avoid his eyes as he was to avoid mine. "Do you want to talk about her?"

"Who, Maeve?" He looked at me like I was crazy. "Why?"

"It might help you process the breakup if you need to 'lick your wounds,'" I said, widening my eyes cartoonishly when I quoted him. I stopped myself from mentioning the ex-boyfriends I'd monologued about to Charlie, unprepared to field any follow-up questions. Strangely, my heart was in my throat.

"No," he stated definitively. "I do not want to talk about Maeve, and I don't need to 'process' anything. Stop pestering me, woman." His voice was mock stern, but I knew he wasn't actually upset with me, just eager to end my line of questioning.

I backed off, obscurely relieved. "Whatever you say," I said. "I'm sure Red will recover from her disappointment in time." *Just because he's not interested in anyone else does not mean he's interested in you,* I told myself. *Don't be so self-involved.*

I changed the subject, but my mind strayed back to Viva, the way he'd unconsciously shifted closer to me to escape the redhead's advances. How my fingers had itched to reach out and pull him in.

THREE

With all the time I'd been spending with my new friend, I was several weeks into the autumn quarter before my neglect of my best friend knocked me over the head.

I was hunkered down at Hallowed Grounds (where I'd have access to coffee on practically an intravenous drip), attempting to make sense of the disparate threads of my thesis based on Houghton's most recent feedback, when my phone began to buzz in my bag. I silenced the ringer and was ready to write it off as a spam call when the first insistent buzz ended and another immediately followed it. I didn't need to look at the caller ID to know who it was. I pulled my phone from the depths of my bag and answered the call, whispering, "Hello, Charlie," into the receiver.

"So you are alive, just screening my calls," she responded, the clatter of cups and the distant rumbling of a coffee pot in the background.

"Sorry, sorry, sorry," I said, standing and making my way to the door. Hallowed Grounds was a student-run coffee shop located inside Reynolds Club, and while it didn't have a dead-silent vibe, I still didn't feel comfortable carrying on a full-volume phone conversation there, which always made me feel exposed and rude. "I know I've missed your last few calls," I said as I circled the staircase. "I've been meaning to call you back, but things have been crazy over here."

"*Three* calls. I will not be ignored, Dan," Charlie said, her voice still scratchy with sleep, though I'd been awake for hours. "And besides, are your thumbs broken? You are aware of the concept of texting, are you not?"

"I have been unforgivably remiss, I know. It will never happen again. Please don't boil my rabbit in retribution."

"Mmm," she hummed. "I suppose I'll give you a pass this time. If I didn't, I'd have no rational touch-stone in my life." Charlie was pursuing her MFA in acting in North Carolina, and our opposite schedules exacerbated our difficulty finding time to connect. Her rehearsals and shows ran late, and I was usually in bed with chamomile tea by nine o'clock. Once she was in tech and I was approaching midterms, our relationship would descend into sporadic texts full of the skull emoji and GIFs of Elmo with a backdrop of raging fire to express our current mental states.

"What sensible perspective can I offer today?" I asked, sitting on the top step and settling in for a long chat. It was a Saturday, and Charlie wouldn't have call until at least noon.

"Nothing in particular," she said. "I was just beginning to think I'd imagined you for all these years. Crisis averted."

"Okay, okay," I said. "You've made your point. Mea culpa, mea maxima culpa."

"Cut the Latin, we all know you're smart. So what's your deal? Has Adam been keeping you up all night whispering the secrets of con law to you, all sexy-like?" I could just picture the piercing gaze she'd pin me with if she asked me this question in person and squirmed. I hadn't seen Adam in two weeks. Our relationship was in one of those stretches when it consisted of sporadically answered texts. That used to make me itch with the constant sense that something was out of place. This time around, I'd barely noticed.

"You know that's not his style. He's more of a torts guy," I said, evasive to the max.

"I'm just assuming he's the culprit behind your recent disappearance. Everything okay there?" Charlie was a fount of jokes, but the thread of genuine affection and concern was always there in her voice. Even when she wasn't a fan of one of my boyfriends, rocky patches in my relationships got her full attention and mama bear energy.

"Everything's fine," I said, my voice pitched slightly higher. "He's really busy with 3L. I think it's been two weeks since I last saw him." Hearing myself say it out loud felt jarring; it was just another reminder of the rut we were in. *We need to talk*, I resolved to myself.

"Jesus, what is the actual point of having a boyfriend if you're not getting it on the regular?" Charlie's concern was replaced by indignation, which I was much more comfortable with.

I scoffed. "There's more to a relationship than 'getting it on the regular,' you perv."

"I wouldn't know," Charlie cooed. She was more of an intense showmance or three-night-stand kind of girl than a serial monogamist like me, and happy to be that way. That kind of emotional whiplash sounded like a hangover every day for the rest of my life, but Charlie thrived on the intensity and ephemeral nature of brief connections. I asked her once if she missed the support and continuity of long-term relationships, but she just blinked and said, "Why would I need that from a man? I have you."

We'd always been a bit of an odd couple, even back when we were inseparable freshman year, but the differences between us seemed to grow bigger with every passing year. Charlie at eighteen was an eccentric dresser, the kind of theater kid who aggressively owned the things that made her weird and dared you to laugh, while I embraced my normalcy, from how I dressed to how easily I contorted myself to fit into any friend group. Now, Charlie was intimidatingly gorgeous—a real leading lady—and carried herself with the confidence of someone who knew she was very, very good at what she did and looked very, very good doing it. Whereas I... seemed to be aging in reverse. I felt more like an insecure middle schooler with each day that marched me closer to graduation.

"So is there someone new in the picture?" I asked, eager to redirect the conversation away from

Adam. They'd met several times when Charlie was between shows and could manage a weekend visit to Chicago, but they'd never hit it off. Their effortful attempts to find common ground stressed me out, so I told Adam that I relished the girl time when she was in town. With visible relief, he assured me that he was disappointed but understood. Charlie was less diplomatic with her pleasure about the change. I told myself that Charlie never liked my boyfriends—which was true to an extent—but her particular friction with Adam scraped against my nerves in such a way that their interactions wore me out. If it turned out Adam and I did move in together next year, I worried Charlie might give up on visiting me altogether.

"The fight coordinator on *Comedy of Errors* is gorgeous, but thus far has remained impervious to my charms," she said, sounding supremely unconcerned and slurping her coffee.

"Give it time," I said. "I have absolute faith in your ability to wear him down." Charlie purred on the end of the line, and I laughed.

"Well, if not a vomit-inducing picture of domestic bliss, what is your life like these days? What's so exciting that you've been leaving me to my own questionable devices? I hate that we have to have these info dump update calls instead of actually *seeing* each other." I would second that plaintive statement.

"A lot of studying," I said, half truthfully. "And..." I hesitated for the length of a breath, debating the wisdom of informing Charlie of another competitor for my time and attention. "I made a new friend."

"I knew it! I've been replaced!" she crowed. "Betrayed! Ghosted! You faithless wretch!"

"Calm down," I replied. "No one could live up to the level of histrionics you bring to my life. There *is* no replacing you."

"Harsh, but fair. So what does this new chick have to offer? Besides sheer physical proximity." Charlie's voice sounded like sharpening knives. I suspect she knew I secretly loved her possessiveness and made sure to play it up with me. I'd never been so utterly claimed by anyone, and it had an anchoring effect I craved.

"Not a chick," I said. "His name is Declan. He's an English PhD candidate I met at Viva about a month ago. He just moved here from Ireland, and I've been showing him around Hyde Park."

"Ah, so what you share is a love of smelly books and being tortured by academic sadists about the originality of your insights. I'm fine with ceding that portion of my territory," she said, sounding somewhat mollified. "You took him to Valois, right?"

"Yes, obviously, and... I don't know," I say, a tiny thrill in my gut at finally sharing what made my time with Declan feel so vital. If anyone might understand it, it would be Charlie. Indescribable emotion was the air she breathed. The more complex or fraught, the better. It was what all the great roles were made of. "I don't know what it is about him. I just felt like I could be completely myself with him right away."

"Wow," Charlie said. "High compliment."

"I mean, it's just nice to talk to someone interested in the same things I am. I don't have to worry about impressing him or boring him. He just gets it," I continued. "Adam tries to understand my work, but I'm sure he feels like I do when he talks about civil procedure."

"Bored and obscurely abused?" she quipped.

"Right," I said, laughing at the pinpoint accuracy of her reply. "It's refreshing not to have to explain myself or justify my choice to get such an 'impractical' degree."

"I can't relate. I decided to go tens of thousands

of dollars into debt for a degree in acting," she deadpanned.

I laughed. "Exactly. And it's not just work. We can talk about anything. It's a no-pressure, easy, great new friendship. You'd like him." And suddenly, with absolute certainty, I knew it was true. I imagined the two of them meeting—how Charlie would be charmed by Declan's earnestness and coax him out of his shell, and how Declan would admire Charlie's bravery and wit and want to discuss dramatic literature with her.

"I'd be inclined to say 'good for you' if not for the suspicion this Declan person is the reason you haven't been calling me back."

"No, that's just because I'm asleep long before your witching hour."

"Well, that too." I heard the clunk of Charlie putting her coffee mug down. "I am glad, though," she said in all seriousness. "I know you don't always find it easy to make new friends, which is baffling since you are beautiful, intelligent, and weirdly funny, so I get why this is a big deal for you. I'm happy for you."

I swallowed a big old lump of feelings. "Thanks, Charlie." As possessively as she guarded her place in my life and time with me, I knew she worried about my hermit-like tendencies. Our biggest fight had been a year earlier when she called Adam a "relationship of convenience" and urged me to get back into the dating pool instead of settling. More and more of late, I suspected I had reacted so badly because, on some level, I knew she had a point.

"So I'll give this Declan person the provisional Charlie stamp of approval. Though I do, of course, reserve the right to revoke it when I meet him if he doesn't pass the written and practical exams."

I smiled. She may have been engaging in her usual hyperbole, but she wasn't far off in spirit. "Of course, we can't deviate from the regular operating procedure for the Charlie stamp of approval. No one is exempt from the exam. But I owe *you* a visit next. What are the dates of *Comedy of Errors* again?" I often scheduled my visits to North Carolina to align with whatever show Charlie was currently in, at least when they didn't clash with midterms or finals, but she made a vehement noise of rejection at the question.

"This one's a shit show," she said. "I'd rather no one who I actually respect see it and think less of me. Other than the gorgeous fight coordinator, mostly because it's already too late, but also because he might take pity on me and throw me a fuck to comfort me after we close."

"Ah yes, the classic comfort fuck." I had no experience with those, and we both knew it. "The show cannot be that bad, Charlie. And I'm sure you're great in it."

"Emma, the guest director is a coke fiend who thinks it's a great idea to direct a Shakespearean comedy in the style of Bertolt Brecht. It *is* that bad."

"Well, now I'm curious." I giggled. I didn't get back to my thesis for another hour, but I didn't regret a moment of the work time lost.

I HAD neither of the necessary resources—time or money—to travel for the brief Thanksgiving break, so I decided to use the extra few days to hunker down for my end-of-quarter studying sprint early. The hell of it was that even locked in my room, noise-canceling headphones in place, and my desk arranged with all my reference materials just so, I still managed to find a plethora of excuses to avoid my thesis. I went on an undergrad paper-grading spree, got ahead on reading for all my classes, and then spent hours staring at the cursor blinking in my thesis document. I made a brief

FaceTime appearance with my parents on Thanksgiving Day itself and begged off a law school friendsgiving Adam had invited me to, citing my workload. Adam accepted my excuse with ill grace, grumbling enough that I had a bad feeling his patience with my pretexts to avoid him was running out. After hanging up on his call, my head felt so heavy that I rested it on my desk while I took calming breaths. *I should call back and accept*, I thought. *I'm not being fair.* And then the image of an apartment full of law students shouting over each other while I drank my way through a bottle of wine out of sheer boredom would bubble to the surface, and I'd start my round of calming breaths all over again.

While my mind spun about whether I should call Adam back, my email pinged with a notification. Grateful for any reason to get off the justification merry-go-round, I peeled my forehead off my desk, my face immediately warming when I saw the new email was from Declan.

I'd say Happy Thanksgiving, but as an Irishman, I am genetically incapable of appreciating holidays that celebrate colonization. That said, I hope you're having a lovely little time off.

I could almost feel my elevated blood pressure

stabilizing as I read. *I'm no colonial apologist,* I typed back, *just trying to get a jump on work.*

His reply dinged my inbox almost immediately. *Woman, do you ever stop working? Another thing to fault your American heritage for—that Puritan work ethic.*

The gentle teasing brought an involuntary smile to my face. *Well, what else would you suggest I do with all this unscheduled time?* I sent the reply and found myself unaccountably holding my breath.

I've just the idea. Meet outside the Reg in fifteen minutes?

I hesitated for just a moment. *You're on.*

Fifteen minutes later, I was breathless in front of the Reg, having finally caved and pulled out my winter coat to ward off the late November chill. I saw Declan coming from what felt like a mile away, his wild hair escaping from a knit cap in a mushroom cloud of curls. A part of me I didn't want to examine was thrilled to see him rushing to meet me, loping with his long strides into a near jog before sweeping me into a hello hug.

"I thought we were long past time for *me* to plan an excursion for us," he said after I pressed him on where we were going. "Let me enjoy keeping you in suspense for once."

Declan ushered me onto a bus, wishing the driver a Happy Thanksgiving, and then spent the ride deflecting my guesses about our destination.

"I do have a life outside of you, you know," he chided me. He meant nothing by it, not really—just that I didn't know everything about how he spent his time—but the statement knocked the wind out of me, how viscerally I felt the sting of wanting to know it all.

It turned out that Declan's surprise outing was a run-down bowling alley in Chinatown.

"I would say I'm surprised that this is open on Thanksgiving, but I'm surprised this is open at *all*," I whispered to Declan as we laced up our rental shoes, taking in the almost empty alley in all its grimy glory.

"I know, it's a gem, isn't it?" Declan beamed, childlike in his joy—whether because of a heretofore unknown-to-me passion for bowling or because of surprising me for once, I didn't know. Either way, his glee was contagious. I smiled so hard my face started to hurt.

It turned out Declan was a pretty good, if inconsistent, bowler—he would rack up three strikes in a row only to throw a gutter ball, though my heckling may have had something to do with that. I couldn't remember the last time I'd been bowling—possibly a grade-school birthday party—and Declan was eager to coach me on my approach and swing as well as help me find the right size bowling ball, but he didn't hold back either. After two merciless routs, I crumpled to the ground in a dramatic heap, crying uncle. Declan joined me on the shiny parquet floor with a shit-eating grin, aglow with his victory.

"How did you get so good at this?" I asked, massaging my shoulder.

He shrugged. "I used to play a fair bit in high school with my mates. I found this place a while back and came here for a few games when I was getting nowhere with my work."

We spent so much time together, and I'd gotten so familiar with his schedule that I imagined these games would only happen on the rare evenings I was with Adam. Remembering him and his friendsgiving invite for the first time in hours, I flushed and reflexively checked my phone. No messages from him—just a text from my classmate Helen begging me to meet with her and share my notes from the latest pedagogy lecture. I sighed and typed out an offer to study together tomorrow.

"Sorry," I said, sliding my phone back into my pocket, disconcerted to realize that Declan hadn't taken his eyes off me during the interruption from our conversation.

"Is everything all right?"

"Everything's fine," I said.

"I don't mean to pry, but you seem stressed, Emma," Declan said. "What's got you so worried?" He reached out and rubbed the space between my eyebrows with a thumb, a gentle but insistent gesture.

"It's not a big deal, just this girl who never takes notes in our pedagogy class and then panics and wants to study together every other week. It's annoying, but it's easier to just meet with her and calm her down."

Declan blinked at me owlishly. "Easier than what?"

I leveled a quelling look at him. "We're not in class, Professor."

"I'm serious, Emma. Meeting with her every other week when you have the workload that you do is easier than what?"

I squirmed, hating the honest answer. "Easier than... dealing with her being upset with me."

"Is this a good friend of yours?"

"God no, I barely know her." I shivered at the

idea of spending any more time with Helen than absolutely necessary.

"Then why," Declan continued gently, "does it matter if she's upset with you?"

"I just... hate the way it feels," I said. It was an anemic reason, but no less truthful for that. Even the thought of disappointing someone else made my skin crawl with shame and self-loathing. The effort it took to please others felt like a small price to pay to avoid the choking weight of disgust and guilt.

Declan looked like there were so many things he wanted to say to me that he didn't know where to start. "Oh, Emma," he said.

I flapped a hand at him. "Please stop. I've been having such a good time. I don't want to ruin it talking about this stuff." Or the fact that Helen's text was just a fraction of what had put the worry on my face that Declan was so fixated on.

The set of Declan's jaw told me he wanted to argue, but he just said, "Okay."

"One more game?" I asked.

"I thought you'd had enough," he said.

"Come on, you have to give me a chance to salvage my dignity," I insisted. "I don't think he'll care if we play another game," I said, gesturing to the lone employee staring into the distance behind the shoe rental counter.

"I don't think he'll care if we start shooting up in the middle of the lane," Declan countered and offered me a hand off the ground.

THE MORE I wished for time to slow after Thanksgiving, the faster it screamed by. The autumn quarter's impending end had the entire campus in panic mode. Anxiety attacks were endemic on campus, and it was clear in the short tempers and disheveled appearances on display that everyone in Hyde Park was burning the midnight oil to wrap up term papers and study for finals. I was in self-imposed lockdown trying to beat my thesis into submission, my adviser's increasingly dire warnings about its flimsy state ringing in my ears. I rarely left my apartment, considering the time spent commuting to the library or any secondary studying location as a frivolous waste of time. Adam was in a similar state of academic frenzy, essentially going radio silent after I turned down his invitation to friendsgiving. My only contact with Charlie consisted of her bleak text updates about the run of *Comedy of Errors* that left me groaning and laughing simultaneously whenever I could tear my eyes from my laptop for ten seconds. Declan and I sent each other brief, mournful emails about how screwed we were throughout the course of each day, but there was no time for casual campus walks or Hyde Park adventures. Weekends came and went unacknowledged, which I spent locked in my bedroom, resenting the interruption of bathroom breaks.

Woe is me, etcetera, etcetera was one such email from Declan, along with a screenshot of his word count, which hadn't changed appreciably since his email three hours earlier.

I'm basically chained to my desk, which I'm pretty sure is a violation of the Geneva Convention, I replied, along with a photo evidencing my hastily foraged meals strewn across my desk—dry cereal, a banana peel, and the crust left behind from my grilled cheese sandwiches (which I'd burned running back and forth from my desk to the stove).

Why does no one in this godforsaken city know how to make curry chips? he bemoaned. *I can't be expected to concentrate in these conditions.*

I stood for the first time in hours (my joints protesting as if I'd aged decades since sitting down), walked over to the living room window to snap a picture of the Christmas lights and garlands going up on my street, and attached it to my reply. *These are distracting me by reminding me joy exists, someone needs to take them down.*

Ah, that's lovely, he sent back a few minutes later. *Now, they're distracting me too.*

We would get progressively loopier as we marched into the early morning hours at our respective desks each night. Our emails grew more frequent, our work grinding to a slow crawl, the pace of a death march. *I think my veins are about 90% caffeine at this point. I tried to melt a candy cane into my last cup to be, you know, FESTIVE, but the main result was just a sticky coffee mug. I can't believe I'm saying this, but I'm actually looking forward to going home for Christmas,* I sent.

I have been searching for the source for this one citation everywhere and can't find it, so now I'm afraid I imagined it, Declan replied. A line break later: *I can't believe this has never come up before—where is home for you? It's hard for me to imagine you outside Chicago (or at this point, unchained from your desk).*

Home is Framingham, Massachusetts—it's outside Boston. My parents both taught at universities in the city (Mom at Boston College, Dad at Brandeis). Usually, I loved Christmas break, everyone loose and unfrazzled for once. Mom and Dad would be done with a flurry of grading papers and exams, and I could attempt to wipe my brain clean until the start of the next quarter, but over the past year, it had begun to feel there was no sanctuary from my mother's increasingly strident admonitions regarding my future. A month earlier, I would have been dreading ten days of forced proximity with that kind of pressure. Now, I was so exhausted that any change of pace was welcome. It couldn't be worse than crossing my eyes trying to make sense of my own writing any longer. *A full night's sleep is so close I can practically taste it, Declan.* I chewed on a pen, staring at my screen. *What about you? Are you heading home for Christmas?* Waiting for his answer, I stared at my email browser, neglecting to click back into Word.

I like to imagine you fully rested and full of Christmas cookies. Cheers. And then a few lines down, *I wasn't planning to, but my mother threw a wobbly, so I booked a flight. Two weeks to get my fill of curry chips and decent tea.*

The idea of an ocean between us felt unnatural. I felt an irrational fear that if Declan left Chicago now, he might never come back and tried to push it away. It wasn't like he was boarding a steamer for a six-month voyage. I was not the dramatic one. That was Charlie. I was the realist.

At this point, I gave up on the pretext that I would get any more work done that night. *Wow*, I replied. *Enjoy your family time.* Declan regularly weaved his brothers into our conversations, and his affection for them was evident, even as different as they all were. After some hesitation, I added a question: *Do you think you'll see Maeve?* I pressed send and felt a superstitious urge to hold my breath. I had a sudden image of Declan having a romantic reunion with a stereotypically redheaded and green-eyed Irish beauty, followed by them opening Christmas gifts together, and felt sick to my stomach.

Declan's response pinged in my inbox two minutes later. *It's always "Maeve this, Maeve that" with you. Nosy.* I managed a shallow breath at his playful tone. *I don't imagine I'll be seeing Maeve. She just got engaged to the man she left me for, so I'm not inclined to go out of my way to be friendly.*

I gasped out loud, my eyebrows shooting into my hairline. Declan so rarely doled out details about his breakup that this was the first I'd heard Maeve had left him for someone else. I wanted to crack open his brain and learn everything—how long they'd been together, how he felt about her, what happened between them—though it didn't matter, right? It was over. Why did it feel so important? I was dying to know and terrified to push too hard. How brutal that she was already engaged less than a year after their breakup. I felt it in my chest like she had left me, along with a simmering rage that I'd never seen any evidence of in Declan. *There's no accounting for poor taste. At least she's someone else's problem now.* If he was too mature for petty vindictiveness, I wasn't.

I could picture his face if I'd said that to him in person—disbelieving, uncomfortable, sad. I hated it. And just as in person, he didn't respond to my defense of him (or shot at Maeve) in email either. *Get some sleep, Emma. Talk tomorrow. xx*

I'd gotten acclimated to his habit of ending messages with those casual x's and knew better than to read into them, but these, in particular, made my heart ache. I finally went to bed as the sky began to lighten with the dawn, but sleep was elusive. Instead, I thought of Maeve's new engagement and hoped that Declan was as blasé about it as he made it sound. I knew I wasn't.

· · ·

OUR DEAD SPRINT to the end of the term didn't kill us. In the end, papers were turned in, finals for undergrads were proctored, and scores of exhausted students across disciplines crowded into dorms and apartments to celebrate their temporary respite from academic torture. Adam had been drunk with his law school friends for days, and I'd slept for fifteen hours straight after turning in my last final.

With the hell of this quarter behind us and that of the next quarter still to come, Declan and I made plans to have a celebratory drink and reunite after our weeks of social isolation. We decided to connect off campus to avoid the oppressive party-hard atmosphere bedeviling our usual haunts. Before I set off to meet up with Declan, I made an appearance at my friend Kathryn's end-of-quarter party with Adam, who I also hadn't seen in weeks. I spent the evening watching the clock and nursing my beer until it was warm and unappealing, waiting until I felt I had performed my girlfriendly duty and could leave without guilt. Were these parties getting more tedious, or was I the one who'd changed?

"Come on, stay," Adam pleaded in that tipsy in-between period between buzzed and smashed, where he was affectionate and clumsy. I was putting on my coat and saying my goodbyes, the party already promising to rage long into the night. "We've barely seen each other all quarter. I miss you," he cajoled, stepping closer to nuzzle my neck and stumbling in the process. It was clear he envisioned ending the night in my bed, but I doubted he'd be in any shape to do anything about it if he did.

"I know," I said, pulling back slightly, turned off by his drunken wobble. I wrapped my scarf around my neck and waved to Kathryn across the room. "I just made these plans before I knew Kathryn was having a party. I can't back out now." Declan's flight was in the morning, and tonight was my last chance to see him for weeks. I had no patience for the same old party chatter when I could be talking to Declan instead.

Adam looked like he wanted to stomp his foot to get his way, to see if transitioning into full-on petulant child mode would get him what he wanted. It wasn't unheard of when he'd had one too many. The old adage "familiarity breeds contempt" flashed unwillingly in my mind. I cut it off at the pass.

"You know I'd rather be here with you, but I have to go. If I can get away early enough, maybe I'll come back." I did my best to make it sound like this was an obligation drink I resented, knowing from experience that would soothe Adam's ruffled feathers. I smiled at him, placing a placatory hand on his elbow, which doubled as support as he swayed like a tree in the breeze.

"Fine," he said, a little pouty but mostly pacified. "Who is this friend, anyway, dragging you away from me on a Friday night? I should have dibs." His teasing tone hid genuine curiosity beneath it.

My face blanched—over the past three months, our conflicting schedules had provided sufficient cover to explain my absences without ever having to mention Declan. Adam had never asked directly before. The sick feeling I got in my stomach each time I avoided saying Declan's name was enough for me to know it was wrong, but I'd convinced myself that as long as I wasn't telling Adam deliberate lies, I was toeing the line.

"Just a friend from the English department," I said, wondering if that qualified as a lie. "He's new this year, so he doesn't have many friends."

"So it's a HE, is it?" Adam asked, his voice too loud even in the cacophony of the crowd.

"Yes, Adam, it's a he. I have male friends. This isn't middle school." Irritation crept into my tone. Adam had plenty of female friends and I didn't make a fuss about it. Adam mostly didn't make an issue about my male friends, either, but he tended to smugly imply they were either gay or in love with me but unable to compete with him. I didn't want to hear either about Declan.

"Hey, you're the one abandoning me to go spend your evening with some other guy. And you're mad at me?" His playful drunk demeanor could easily tip over into Adam becoming a handful. It would take me hours to extricate myself from if I let this escalate.

I took a deep breath. "Of course I'm not mad at you. I just have to go." All our conversations lately had a similar circular pattern of annoyance, followed by smoothing the other's ruffled feathers, and ending with mutual dissatisfaction. It struck me for the thousandth time that I didn't know what I was doing with Adam anymore. Our relationship had been enough for me for so long—fun enough, comfortable enough, convenient enough—that it seemed it would sustain itself indefinitely. Nothing about Adam had changed in the past three months, but I felt completely different. How long was inertia and guilt for changing my mind about what I wanted supposed to carry me forward? It was obvious Adam wasn't satisfied with the way things were going either. What was the charade for? Ending things gracefully would benefit us both, but for some reason, I couldn't bring myself to do it. I grew more disgusted with my failure to act with each day that passed. My cowardly wish was that he would either lose patience with me or do something so unforgivable it would force my hand.

"Stay," Adam said. "At least until you're not mad anymore. Have another drink." He tugged at my hand, trying to draw me away from the door.

"I don't want another drink," I said, tempted to stomp my foot. Right on the precipice of saying something I couldn't take back, exhaustion kept me talking before my brain had a chance to override my feelings. "Adam, what are we doing?"

He locked eyes with me, startlement shocking him a little closer to sobriety. "What do you mean?"

"We barely see each other anymore. And when we do, we fight," I said, hiding my shaking hands in my coat pockets. I hadn't meant to do this now. I was all about playing out possible outcomes and gaming a strategy when faced with something difficult, but I'd just careened into this conversation without a road map. Maybe it was better this way, but still, my brain scrambled for a way to regain control. I'd never broken up with anyone. Was it even possible to do this without disappointing and hurting him? I spent my life trying to avoid those outcomes, to exhausting effect. Was my only way out convincing Adam that ending our relationship benefited him? "What are we doing together? Lately, I've been thinking that I'm just not the right person for you anymore." Saying it out loud was simultaneously terrifying, sending my heart beating against my rib cage like a bird trapped behind a window, and a tremendous relief, a shackle removed from my ankle.

"Whoa, whoa, whoa," he said, stepping closer to me and opening the door to Kathryn's apartment. "Let's step into the hallway and talk." I followed him out, the sudden hush of the landing and the hum of the party trapped behind the door making the situation all the more stressful. "This is getting blown way out of proportion. I'm sorry I gave you shit for going to see your friend. I know your friends are important to you. I didn't mean to imply you're a bad girlfriend or—'not the right person' for me or whatever." His eyes were blazing with focus despite his somewhat dilated pupils. He'd widened his stance, too, as if he were bracing for a fight. "But don't have a tantrum about it. Let's talk like adults."

"Adam—" I protested, already feeling outmatched if this was going to come down to which of us was more stubborn. "We aren't the way we were two years ago. Our lives are taking us in different directions. I don't want to hold you back."

"You're not. You couldn't," he said. The supreme

confidence that had intrigued me at first was now just one more thing that exhausted me. "We might be going through a rough patch, but that's part of being in a relationship." It had never been part of one of mine before, but maybe that was because I'd never placed much importance on my romantic relationships. "Don't make that mean more than it does. I know that neither of us has much time right now, but next year will be better. I promise I'm thinking of you. I know you've been pissed at me, but you're overreacting."

"What? I'm not—" I didn't even know which part I was going to deny—that I wasn't pissed or I wasn't overreacting—but Adam cut me off before it got out of my mouth.

"Emma, you hide it well, but we've been together for two years. I know you well enough by now to pick up on when you're pissed. Otherwise you wouldn't be trying to duck out right now. You want me to chase you."

I would have spluttered if I'd been able to force any words past my lips. I had no idea how he'd drawn such an offensive conclusion when I'd spent the entirety of our relationship playing agreeable and low maintenance. I stood stunned, taking in his expression of absolute certainty. He'd be harder to move than a boulder. "Adam, I am not playing a game with you. I'm leaving because I have plans to meet my friend, and I don't want to be late. But I'm tired of fighting with you about every little thing." I knew I wasn't framing it well. If I didn't make our split out to be his idea, he'd only dig his heels in further. "If such a small thing leads to a fight like this, something's really wrong here."

"Go meet your friend," he said in what I privately considered his "reasonable" voice. He was a born litigator—he used it to manipulate and shape situations when you were furious with him to make you think he was doing *you* a favor. You'd leave knowing you were bamboozled but unable to pinpoint exactly where it happened. "I know you've needed support the past few months while I've been busy, and I don't begrudge you that. Go blow off some steam. It's been a stressful quarter. Let's not displace our anger onto each other. We can talk more about this later." For someone else, it would be exactly the right thing to say.

I bit my tongue to stop myself from telling him not to infantilize me. If I stayed any longer to fight it out with Adam, I would be late to meet Declan.

What the hell. I didn't want to be here.

"We'll talk later," I said, shouldering my purse. "I have to go."

"We'll talk later," he echoed in a soothing tone as if I was a high-strung child. "Text me when you get home safe?"

"Fine," I said and sped down the stairs. I didn't look back, but I could see Adam's face in my mind all the same, safe in the assurance that we'd smooth things over.

AFTER MY STANDOFF with Adam outside Kathryn's party, I raced to my apartment to grab Declan's Christmas present and then off to Cove Lounge, a hole-in-the-wall on 55th where Kurt Vonnegut was rumored to have written (at least parts) of *Player Piano*. *I love a pub with history.* Declan had replied, *I'm in*, when I suggested it. I was happy to slip back into my Hyde Park tour guide role.

I was stewing over my near breakup on the walk to the bar, my spiking adrenaline warming me in the freezing temperatures, my mind crowded with the hundreds of ways things could play out from here. I felt like my brain was overheating. I picked up the pace even further, in a rush to see Declan, knowing that would help return my equilibrium.

I was in such a hurry to get to him that I risked wiping out on the icy sidewalks on 55th, the tote bag holding Declan's Christmas gift banging against my shoulder with each step. He had complained so volubly about the "strange" flavors of American "crisps" one day at the library that I'd gone home and tracked down a seller on Amazon who shipped multipacks of Walker's from the UK as a surprise for him. It took six weeks for them to arrive, and they had probably been ground to fragments in transit, but I'd been proud of the idea since I wasn't a naturally inventive gift giver. Now that I knew he was returning to Wicklow over the break, I felt silly and insecure about the impulse—was it too much? We hadn't discussed exchanging gifts, but in the end, I decided to give them to Declan anyway. Prawn Cocktail didn't sound like a flavor I wanted to sample myself.

As I stomped the snow off my boots at the door, I saw that Declan had beaten me to the bar. Just like I'd hoped, the sight of him quieted the voices in my head shouting that I needed to formulate some master plan to disentangle myself from Adam. It didn't seem so urgent now that Declan was smiling and waving in my eyeline. Even the rapid beat of my heart felt better, the tiny but crucial shift from anxiety to excitement.

He had snagged a corner of the picnic table closest to Barack Obama on the wall's mural and stood to get my attention as I made my way to him— as if I wouldn't be able to spot him towering over the sparse crowd. His happiness to see me and obliviousness to the way he drew my eye were adorable, like he'd been just as impatient as I'd been for my arrival.

As I unwound my scarf, I leaned in for a much-needed hug when I reached him. We had become casually affectionate with touch—hugging hello and goodbye and smacking each other's hands away from our studying snacks. Declan curved his long spine over me and kissed my cheek, a first. My heart stuttered at the brush of his lips against my skin, though it was brief and chaste. Was this simply a European greeting and I was reading too much into it? I was glad I could blame the cold for the red in my cheeks. "It's freezing out there," I said, settling onto the bench across from him.

He unceremoniously removed his knit cap and pulled it down over my ears. Suddenly, I wasn't cold in the least. "What's up, you? You look upset." A tiny furrow appeared between his eyebrows as he scanned my expression.

"I'm not!" I chirped, plastering a broad smile across my face.

"Well, maybe not upset, but preoccupied. Is everything all right?"

I opened my mouth to do it—finally tell him about Adam, tell him I'd tried to break up with my boyfriend tonight but he wasn't having it. We told each other everything else—nothing would change between us, would it? I sealed my lips and shook my head, gripped by the fear that telling him would blow up our little corner of the world. "It's no big deal. I'll tell you later," I said, chickening out and dropping my tote onto the bench beside me.

Declan looked like he wanted to press the issue but would respect my wishes. Part of me wished he'd force the point and take the decision out of my hands. "What's in the bag then, woman of mystery?" he asked, indicating my tote.

I pulled out his gift with a flourish, which I'd wrapped in free local dailies, eager to move on from the delicate subject of my preoccupied state. "Just something to remember me by."

Something warm sparked in his eyes, crinkling at the corners as he smiled. "Oh, I don't think I'll have any trouble with that."

"Even so, I'm not carrying this back home. You'll have to be a gentleman and take it."

Declan pulled the wrapped box closer to him, grinning. I had a mental image of him as a child on Christmas morning, humming with excitement. "I'd say it feels like Christmas, but I suppose it is." I hummed a few bars of "Santa Claus is Comin' to Town" as he unwrapped his gift—careful and intentional but excruciatingly slow, like he was going to save the paper.

"Oh come on," I said, "rip it! Is there anything you ever do that's messy?"

He raised an eyebrow at me, a challenge in his eyes that suddenly left my mouth dry. Unwelcome images of other things he might do slowly and carefully crowded my mind and I was afraid they were written all over my face. I found myself holding my breath as he ripped a tiny corner. "Happy?" he asked, the slightest huskiness in his tone making me aware of every nerve ending in my body.

I rolled my eyes to disguise my discomfort. "Deliriously."

He chuckled, and to my relief, the moment's tension was broken. He continued his painstaking unwrapping process, and I attempted to get my heart rate under control.

When Declan had neatly piled the newsprint wrapping to his right, he opened the box to discover his crisps with a gasp. "Em! My favorites!"

"I went for the Meaty variety pack for you. I thought they'd help you feel more at home, but now you're *going* home, so..." I shrugged, both pleased and embarrassed by his reaction, afraid he was putting it on to make me happy.

He was already opening a snack-sized bag of Roast Chicken-flavored crisps. "Ah, but these shall remain my home stash, perfect for ill-advised noshing when working late." Hearing him declare his Chicago apartment home rather than Wicklow made me feel ever so slightly better about his upcoming flight. He popped a crisp into his mouth and crunched it with glee. "Thank you, Emma. This is a truly wonderful gift." I loved the softness of his h's— they weren't silent, but so unobtrusive in comparison with his t's that "thank you" had become one of my favorite phrases to hear him say.

Before I could say "you're welcome," Declan reached into his omnipresent bookbag and withdrew a neatly wrapped gift, clearly a book. "Not nearly as exciting as your gift, I'm afraid," he said.

"Declan," I said, gingerly touching the actual red-and-green-plaid wrapping paper, "you didn't have to do that." All the same, I was absurdly pleased and surprised.

"I know, that's half the fun. Go on, see what's inside. You can tell me you have it already, and I'll be heartbroken."

I ripped the wrapping paper, not just to get a rise out of him but because I couldn't wait to reveal the first gift Declan had ever given me. Behind the plaid wrapping, I found a beautiful illustrated version of *The Lady of Shalott* by Tennyson. "Declan," I breathed. "This is too much." I traced my fingertips over the embossed words on the cover, delicate and stunning. It was the most beautiful book I'd ever owned and the loveliest gift.

"So you don't have a copy already?" He sounded painfully hopeful, and my heart squeezed.

"No, I've never even read it. I've always meant to, but..." I gestured back in the direction of campus. "Other books got in the way."

"I thought that all the gothic novels you've been reading might give you nightmares if you don't give yourself a palate cleanser. Thought you could use some medieval lyricism for a change." He had the evangelical glow of a reader gifting a book to another reader. I knew it well and felt his pleasure as keenly as my own.

"Isn't she isolated in a tower? Until her tragic death?" I asked.

"I thought you said you've never read it."

"I haven't, but it is a pretty famous plot. I'd be a pretty terrible English lit master's candidate if I had *no* idea what it was about." Declan bobbled his head side to side, conceding my point. "I'm just saying that thematically, it's not far from a gothic novel—curses, towers, tragedy, and all that. Plenty of nightmare fuel."

"You've got me there, but I thought you'd appreciate her sense of autonomy, unlike your gothic heroines. Tragic ending it may be, but she chooses it."

That was the crux of the thing, wasn't it? Choice.

"You are a delightfully specific gift giver," I said. "And a little more emo than I'd given you credit for. This is gorgeous, thank you."

"I'm glad you like it," he said. "Now you'll have something to remember *me* by."

"There's not a chance I could forget," I said. Before I could get even more sentimental, I stood to go order for us at the bar. "This is a pitcher kind of place. What do you say to MGD?"

He made a face. "Whatever you say, Em," he said, resigned to another evening of shitty beer but fond all the same.

As the evening wore on and I carefully refilled our pints far away from my beautiful new book, the beer settled my jangled nerves about Adam and peeled back my inhibitions just enough to press Declan more on what he'd let slip in his emails about his relationship with Maeve and how it ended.

"I need more context. How long were you with her, anyway?" I asked.

Declan sighed and sipped his beer. "So many questions. You have the essentials already. What good will the context do you?"

"The first time we met, you told me you moved across the ocean because of a breakup and then completely shut me out of the rest of the story! And since then, you've barely mentioned her. It's a classic storytelling technique to build suspense. If you don't fulfill the promise of the premise, you're a tease," I joked, nudging him with my foot under the table.

"I wouldn't define avoiding a personally painful story as a tease, Emma," he said with some asperity.

I was leaning in so far that I practically lay across

the table. After staying sober at Kathryn's party, I'd dove headlong into the pitcher I was sharing with Declan, and it was starting to show. I so rarely got drunk that I was just now learning how stubborn and heedless it could make me. "Friends are supposed to know these things about each other. Why tell me anything at all if deep down you don't actually want to talk about it?" I said, tipsily proud of my logic. "I'm so wise and perceptive."

"I think that's the drink talking," he replied, looking both wearied and inexplicably charmed by the reveal of my obnoxious drunk self.

"Come on. It feels weird that you won't tell me about it—we talk about everything else. I want to know things about you." More and more, I was sick with envy over any piece of his life that I didn't share. I was one drink too deep to realize that by pressing this line of conversation, I was inviting Declan to probe my romantic history in the same way. I had to know this part of him—imagining being loved by Declan took my breath away. How could anyone walk away from that?

He blinked at me, owlish and remote, until he seemed to decide I wouldn't let the issue drop. "All right. I was with Maeve for four years, and we lived together for two. The last year or so we were together, she got to be close friends with a guy at her work—really close. He'd come over for dinner at ours, he started running with our group of friends and fit right in, even dated our friend Aislinn for a while. I never worried if she was out late after work with him. Six months ago, she told me she was in love with him and leaving me. I'd just been accepted to UChicago and University College Dublin for my PhD, so I chose the one where I wouldn't risk running into her and Brian down the pub. And now that's something you know about me." He took a long pull of his beer while I reeled with the information. There was a grim set to his mouth, and the way he avoided my eyes as if he was afraid this story somehow reflected poorly on him broke my heart. I reached a tentative hand across the table to grab his. He allowed it, though his returning grip was loose, and he focused on the table instead of making eye contact with me.

"I'm so sorry," I said, both for what happened in the first place and obscurely for making him relive it. I gave his hand a little squeeze, his grip tightening just a little. "He was your friend too?"

"More hers than mine, but yeah, I considered him a mate." He drained his glass and pushed it away. "I haven't spoken to him since. When it all came out, she gave me this impassioned monologue about how they never meant for it to happen and that I wasn't to blame him. I could tell that the hardest part of our split for her was that someone might not think well of him. I was an inconvenient detail in their origin story after four years together, nothing more. I have no doubt that when strangers ask her how they met, I'm nowhere in it."

His voice was calm, resigned, like he'd spent a lot of time wrapping his mind around the brutal details and a lot of practice stripping his voice of any hint of pain. I wanted to find Maeve and push her down a flight of stairs.

"That is outrageously shitty. I'm so sorry." It wasn't enough, but I didn't know what else to say.

Declan shrugged, disentangling his hand from my grasp. I tried not to take it as a rejection. "That's why I didn't want to tell you. It's over, there's no need to go feeling sorry for me. I should have seen it coming."

"How could you have?" My forehead wrinkled in confusion.

"I've gone over and over it." He still sounded bewildered. "There must have been signs, but I didn't see them. I couldn't have been paying any real attention. She seemed the same as ever to me, happier, even. I thought it meant we were doing well, that we had a future together. I thought I knew her down to the ground. But when she told me how she felt about him—" His breath caught, and I knew he was back in that awful moment. Rage toward this woman I'd never met was building in me, a flame burning a path up from my heart. "I'd never seen her like that. It was like I'd only ever seen her in black and white, and now she was in color. I realized I must never have known her at all."

I had nothing to say to that, nothing that could ease any of the devastation of that realization. All my indignation, any words of comfort, were useless.

The dam in Declan seemed to have broken. He continued quietly. "What I wish I knew was how early it started."

"You mean when she started cheating?" I asked.

"I don't think she ever did." My face must have betrayed my disbelief. "At least physically, I don't think she did. But when it crossed over from being a friendship to being something more, when she knew it was over between us. I just wish she'd been honest with me as soon as she knew instead of dragging it out the way she did. I'd respect her more. I loved her and trusted her, and I wish... I wish she hadn't made me doubt myself for doing so."

"Right," I said lamely. "Maybe it was just as big of a shock to her as it was to you." The parallels between Declan's story and my relationship with Adam made me sick to my stomach, not to mention that I hectored Declan into telling me about it.

He shrugged, not denying the possibility but clearly unconvinced by the suggestion. "You know when there's a first and second place," he said. "But if I couldn't see that she was one foot out of our relationship for a year, maybe I don't have any business being in a relationship at all."

I felt like I had heartburn. "Declan, it wasn't your fault."

"That's kind of you to say, but how could you know that?" He finally met my gaze, and I immediately wanted to look away.

Because I know you, I thought but didn't say. I sipped my beer and struggled for the right words. Adam's face when I left him to come here and meet Declan scratched at the back of my mind. All my excuses for why Declan didn't know Adam existed felt shoddy in light of his experience with Maeve. I wanted to believe the two situations weren't the same, but I couldn't point to one pertinent distinction.

"I'm so sorry that happened to you," I said, aware

of how lame and inadequate it was and how many times I'd repeated it already. "But Maeve's choices say more about her than they do about you. Don't let them color your choices moving forward. She doesn't deserve that kind of power over you."

Declan smiled wryly and nudged my foot under the table. "Thanks, Em. But can we change the subject?"

I obliged, an ice cube of disquiet lodged in my chest. He'd have every right to ask me about my love life now. I'd teed him up perfectly. "Sure," I said, doing my best not to squirm on my bench.

"Did you know you get the most ridiculous blush when you're drunk? You're scarlet," he teased. I took my first full breath in what felt like ages and chucked a wadded-up napkin at him while he cackled gleefully.

We stood shivering outside underneath the art deco sign over the entrance a few hours later, saying our goodbyes for the holiday since Declan would fly out in the morning. He'd offered to walk me home, citing the darkness and my langered state, but I lied, saying that I didn't want to walk that far and called a Lyft instead. Declan's revelations had sobered me up pretty damn effectively, but I let him think the beer was the culprit behind my red cheeks.

"Happy Christmas, Emma," he said as I leaned into his warm and comforting hug. His long brown coat smelled vaguely spicy, and the wool scratched gently against my cheek. I closed my eyes, wishing I didn't have to let go.

"Happy Christmas to you," I said. "I'm looking forward to my holiday with the *Lady of Shalott.*"

He grinned down at me. "I'm looking forward to returning to my apartment and all my prawn cocktail crisps."

I made a face that said *better you than me.* "Have fun in Wicklow," I said, only half meaning it. As my ride pulled up to the curb, Declan opened the door and ushered me into the back seat, his hand lingering on the small of my back just a fraction of a second too long. I'd begged and begged to know the story about Maeve, and now that I did, I wondered if I'd just put the first chink in the armor of our plausible deniability. He closed the door behind me and stepped back, raising a hand in farewell.

As the car pulled away from the curb, I watched him begin his trek southward. The vision of him with the Amazon box full of imported crisps balanced against his hip, a long arm draped over the edge, tugged at my heart. He always looked a little vulnerable in a way that I found impossibly endearing—not just tall but a little too thin, a little awkward and hunched, bashful and funny and unaware of his appeal. The idea of three weeks away from him made me feel achy and afraid. It looked like the wind could blow him away.

The tops of my ears itched and I realized I was still wearing his hat.

FOUR

A few days and an empty inbox later, Adam and I loaded our bags into the trunk of an Uber and headed to O'Hare for our flights home. After our near blowout outside Kathryn's party, he was being especially conciliatory and easygoing, leaving me to feel that I had no leg to stand on in returning to the subject of our breakup—or maybe that was just my fatigue talking. Even though we'd booked our flights weeks earlier, Adam had once again offered to come to Framingham for part of the holiday to spend more time with my parents than the occasional campus meal afforded us when they visited Chicago, but I insisted it was more important he go back to Seattle and spend time with his new baby niece. ("You're so understanding," he said, relief in his voice. "But only if that's really what you want." I assured him it was.)

We'd planned our respective flights to Logan and Seattle-Tacoma to at least allow for an airport drink and meal in the same terminal before parting ways for the holiday. "Nothing more romantic than an airport bar," Adam said, scanning the menu for anything drinkable that cost less than seventeen dollars.

"I do love to spoil you," I quipped, but it was a robotic impulse. I didn't have the energy for another fight with him, let alone while trapped in airport hell. I was counting down the minutes until we could say our goodbyes and I could stop performing normalcy with Adam for a few weeks. I ordered a glass of red to help settle my flying anxiety, and Adam ordered a gin and tonic. We clinked our glasses together and descended into silence while we waited for our meals to arrive.

"Listen, I was thinking," Adam said as we dug into our food. "Instead of buying each other gifts this year, how about planning a trip together? Just a weekend, it obviously can't be too long with our schedules."

I blanched, thinking of the noise-canceling head-phones I had for him wrapped in my bag. I'd bought them before our fight and held on to them, feeling weird about gift giving while a breakup loomed. "Uh, that sounds great, but it might be hard to swing," I said, picking at my salad. The last thing I wanted was to become more entwined in our relationship and give the signal that we were taking the next step together. I'd been hoping a few weeks on opposite ends of the country might help Adam better envision a life without me.

"No, I get it, but I think it would be good for us," he said through a mouthful of his burger. "This year has been so crazy. I know you're frustrated with how little we've seen each other. I get it. I really do." He reached across the table and squeezed my hand.

He'd come to this conclusion just a few months too late. The near miss of it made my whole body feel heavy. "It has been crazy, but I understand, Adam. You don't need to stress out about me. We can talk about this later," I said, my stomach squirming uncomfortably while I left my hand limp in his.

"I know you understand, and you're amazing for that. But I don't want you to think you're not important to me just because 3L is so all-consuming." I nodded, distantly curious that this "good grade" from my boyfriend wasn't giving me the hit of pleasure it usually did. It felt frivolous and cheap in the absence of any real emotional investment. "Didn't you say Charlie didn't want you to come see her latest show? That should free up a weekend."

"That was back in November," I said. "I'll still go to her next show."

"Unless she doesn't want you to go to that one either," he countered like it was the KO move.

I swallowed my urge to tell him that wasn't likely, and that even if it was, I couldn't survive another three months of my life without seeing Charlie when I was perfectly content with the fact that Adam and I had only had sex four times since September.

"We don't need to make any plans now," I said, pulling Adam's gift from my bag and sliding it across the table to end the conversation. "Here. Merry Christmas."

"Shit, Emma," he said. "I didn't suggest a weekend away just because I don't have a gift for you yet. Now I feel bad."

"Don't," I said, and I meant it. He wanted his gift to be time together, while mine would help him shut me out more effectively.

I would have ten days back in Massachusetts without the distractions of work and Declan, and I resolved to spend them figuring out my exit plan.

Clearly, my spontaneous volley at Kathryn's party hadn't worked. There would be no romantic getaways in our future, but even as desperate as I was, I didn't have the heart to dump someone right before Christmas. If I was ever going to get out of this, I needed to figure out how I could divorce myself from my need to be blameless and easy. *Grow a spine, Brice,* I told myself.

CHRISTMAS IN MASSACHUSETTS started off like a postcard; snowy and festive, cheerful and relaxing, all things considered. Still, I found myself restless, wondering what Declan was up to in Wicklow, whether he would go see Maeve after all or whether he wanted to even if he hadn't been planning on it. I had this sick feeling in my stomach that he would never come back to Chicago if he did. What I would be returning to felt dull and draining if he wasn't there.

I tried to resist the urge to check my email and see if Declan was thinking of me too. If he was, he wasn't writing to tell me about it. He had become a part of my days so effortlessly that his absence robbed my time of shape and meaning. Even the denuded branches of the trees outside my window reminded me of his hair, untamable and always reaching for more space.

When I wasn't perseverating over the lack of communication from Declan, I jotted literal bullet points to convince Adam it was time to give up the ghost of our relationship while still softening the blow. He responded to logic, to evidence—maybe that was why my emotional outburst hadn't moved him. I would approach this breakup like we were in court and I had to convince a judge and jury.

I was ensconced on the couch with a mug of tea one morning after the holiday had passed, flipping through the pages of my illustrated *Lady of Shalott*. Mom walked into the room carrying a sheaf of papers that let me know she'd decided she was done with idleness during her own break between semesters.

"Back to work?" I asked. It seemed an innocuous enough question, but I should have known better.

"There's never enough time, is there?" she said, separating the papers into distinct piles across the coffee table. "I'm surprised you're not back at it yet."

I felt my jaw tighten. "I'm taking some time to decompress." I doubted a therapy-friendly buzzword would move her—Mom had never met an emotional problem that she couldn't solve with a professional accomplishment—but it was the best I could come up with at short notice.

"Well, sweetie, I hate to break it to you, but there's not a great deal of decompression time in academia." She chuckled when she said it, the condescension dripping off her. If I didn't know better, I'd say there was a note of grim pleasure in her voice at getting the opportunity to dress me down. We'd managed to avoid the topic of school my entire visit thus far, but apparently, the gloves were coming off now.

"I've noticed," I said dryly, though I felt instant regret. Any pushback was a sure way to get my mother to dig her heels into the topic. "I'll get back to it soon," I added in a more placatory tone.

"I wasn't going to say anything, Em, but you've been spending a lot of time on that book," she said, undiverted. Mentally, I settled in for the duration. She wasn't wrong that I'd been carrying it around and reading it over the past few days—but sometimes it just gave me something to hold, something to remind myself that Declan wasn't someone I'd imagined, while I tried to figure out how to solve my Adam-shaped problem. "That's definitely not thesis-related." She would know, as she had functionally chosen mine.

"It's just some recreational reading, Mom," I said. "It's not an application for a vocational school."

"I just don't see how you have the time for that if you're taking your master's work seriously," she said while marking up one of the stacks of paper with a red pen. I felt immediate kinship and pity for her students. It seemed that all it took for her to cross out whole paragraphs was a cursory glance and half a breath, and I was keenly aware of the hours of research, sweat, and blood that went into each sentence and citation.

"I am taking it seriously," I said. "I have everything under control." Neither of which was exactly true, but my mom had never been a person I could bring my struggles to. She would panic worse than I was, then turn around and assert that whatever situation I was in had been entirely avoidable if I'd just worked harder. I had learned the hard way that turning to her for help left me more stressed and lost than before.

The truth was I'd been slogging through my thesis for months, pretty much since the moment I'd started it. I told myself it was an emotional block because I didn't want to leave school, but I wasn't sure that was the whole truth. And all that was far too messy—and too far from the obedient daughter I'd always been—to share with Geraldine.

She raised a dubious eyebrow, and I suppressed a huff of frustration. I had the fleeting, nasty thought that she'd gotten everything she'd ever asked for in a daughter: compliant, high-achieving, even following in her academic footsteps, and somehow, she still found things to criticize.

"I don't want you to lose your sense of self in this relationship, is all," she said, throwing me for a loop.

"What are you talking about?" I asked, genuinely confused by the turn of conversation.

"Yes, Adam will be a lawyer, and I'm sure he'll be successful and well compensated. But you don't want to be someone's trophy wife, even if it's a comfortable life," she said, pronouncing "comfortable" like it was a dirty word. "I thought you wanted more for yourself than to ride on the coattails of someone else's achievements."

"The thought never crossed my mind," I answered truthfully. The gears in my mind spun, baffled by this new conclusion Mom had drawn. "Adam and I aren't even that serious," I said, which was true—at least as far as I was concerned. "What makes you think that's what's happening?"

"You've been so unfocused this year," she continued, my blood boiling at the justness of the criticism but still feeling she had no right to make it. "Choosing not to pursue your PhD, needing my help to select your thesis topic—"

"You wanted to help me pick it! I couldn't keep you away from it!" My voice was nearing a squeal. I needed to tamp it down if I wanted to prevent this from totally spinning out of control.

"Only because you showed every indication of picking an uninspired, totally retread topic! Graduate school is not the place to explore what you *like*, Emma. It's your opportunity to stake out a unique position and identity in the academic world, one that will make you *publishable* and *hirable*. It is to prepare you for a career, one that will last decades. It is not a time to be reading for *pleasure*."

I blinked at her, at a loss for what to say. I knew she was right about the business of postgraduate education, but hearing her lack of respect for my instincts still stung, especially since I'd spent over twenty years shaping my decisions to make her proud first and foremost.

"I know that's harsh," she said, making an effort to lower her voice. "But you need to know."

I swallowed, rebutting the one piece of her argument that I could. "I would have pursued my PhD except I don't have the money right now." It wasn't an accusation. My parents had saved all they could for my education, but seven years at a private university had more than gobbled it up.

"That's another thing, Emma. You only wanted to apply to UChicago—again. I'll never forgive myself for letting you stay there for your MA."

"*Letting* me?" I sputtered. "I'm the one who'll be paying for it, and I'm the one doing the work. Why would you be the person to pick where I choose to continue my education?" My one rebellion had been staying where I felt most at home and had first discovered any real sense of belonging. Why was that such a crime?

"It's too familiar; it's not challenging you enough. It's making you complacent." She swiped her pen across another entire paragraph.

I found myself dangerously near tears, unable to voice that I found UChicago plenty challenging, too much so lately. "I'm sorry you feel that way," I said, attempting to keep my voice level.

"Oh, Emma, don't be dramatic," she sighed. With effort, I gathered my book and tea and managed not to stomp my way upstairs. I couldn't think of a word that described me less accurately than *dramatic*. And I had a very big vocabulary.

I heard the decisive snap of her red pen hitting the table as I closed my door.

IT WAS THE MOST BLATANT, depressing fight with my mother I'd ever had. A chill settled over the house in Framingham, frosting unavoidable conversations and run-ins in the kitchen. I couldn't wait to get back to campus. If I'd had the money, I would have changed my flight back to Chicago to the next available out of Logan, but I had to tough it out in Framingham for three days after my argument with Mom. Our clash left me shaken. We'd fought so rarely over the years that I didn't know how to handle the unresolved tension, which made me feel physically achy and nauseated with anxiety. We'd come close to mother-daughter blowouts over the years, but I'd been so successful in de-escalating conflict before it really grew legs that this was uncharted territory. Mealtimes were mostly silent affairs, Dad baffled and darty-eyed, well acquainted with the sharpness of Mom's tongue but unaccustomed to me pushing back in any meaningful way. I knew he wanted me to do whatever it took to smooth things over and get us back to the status quo, but for once, I couldn't bring myself to do it. So instead, we settled into the silence. It was lonely but strangely restful to lay down all the effort that went into pleasing them.

Dad drove me to the airport alone. Mom claimed she was too behind on work to come along. We hugged stiffly in the foyer, a performance that fooled no one, and I got into Dad's Honda with relief. He attempted small talk with me on the ride, carefully avoiding the subject of my thesis and future plans, which gave me the impression that he'd heard or suspected more of our fight than he'd let on over the previous days of the Cold War in our house. I could imagine him hiding in his office, staying as far out of the fray as possible without physically climbing out the window. I couldn't bring myself to put any energy in my responses, drained by the week and a half I'd spent in the pressure cooker of my parents' house, the birthplace of all those people-pleasing habits I was beginning to suspect I'd have to work hard to break. With each successive visit since moving out, I'd been coming to terms with the fact that a pressure cooker was what it was and had always been, and this visit threw that truth into harsher relief than ever. I was starting to wonder if my life might be different today if I'd rebelled earlier and more definitively. What if I'd insisted on a different career, a different major, or even not to attend college in the first place? Would I feel less sick with fear all the time, less crippled by playing out all the potential outcomes before each minor decision? Would I be happier?

As we crawled through traffic to the drop-off location for Spirit departures, Dad's tolerance for the silence finally cracked. "Are you okay, sugar?" he asked.

"I'm fine, Dad." I didn't know how to answer otherwise. We certainly didn't have the time for a more comprehensive response.

"Your mom can be a bit of a bulldog, but she just wants what's best for you," he said, his eyes darting over to the passenger seat whenever he could tear them from the traffic inching forward.

"I'm not sure anyone, myself included, knows what's best for me," I said, unbuckling my seat belt. "I'll walk from here. Thanks for the ride, Dad."

Over his protests, I opened my door, forcing him to stop. I grabbed my carry-on from the footwell and turned back before closing the door. "I love you. I just need everyone to get off my back for a minute and let me figure some things out for myself, okay?"

"Okay," he said miserably. "I love you too, Em."

I closed the car door and walked into Logan,

looking forward to my glass of red and three hours free of questions and concerns, well-meaning or not, on the plane. Even a return to academic lockdown would be preferable to the continued standoff in Framingham.

Back in Hyde Park, my apartment looked even more homey than I remembered it: the brickwork in the fireplace the peak of craftsmanship and my IKEA catalog bedroom a thing of beauty. As much as I wanted to ignore all my mother's critiques as baseless and unfair, I knew I was way behind on my thesis, and my next meeting with Professor Houghton loomed large on the calendar in the first week of the new quarter. As I unpacked, I silently committed to parking myself at the Reg with my laptop and shutting out the world until the quarter started. It wasn't enough time to get my thesis to where I wanted it, but at a minimum, it would give me a rock-solid excuse to ignore Mom's phone calls.

Even so, my first day at the Reg put my resolution to the test. With every hour in the library, my heart sank further and further until I was convinced it was buried in the floor beneath my chair, Edgar Allen Poe-style. Even I couldn't make sense of what I'd written thus far. My thesis Word doc included every jotted-down note I'd tossed off for Houghton in our checkpoints last quarter, but even so, they seemed so disconnected I couldn't see how to cobble them together to support my central argument without the most tenuous of links. The few cogent paragraphs I had were, sickeningly, all ideas my mother had more or less fed me in our weekly phone dates throughout the fall quarter. I wanted to delete them out of spite, but if I did, I'd have almost nothing tangible to present to Houghton the following week, and we were well past the point when notes and ideas were sufficient. She wanted a draft. My building despair was like an immobilizing poison; the pipe dream of whipping my thesis into shape grew more hopeless with each breath I took.

From my bottomless pit of dread, I retained the awareness to notice someone approaching my work-station in my peripheral vision. As the figure approached, I realized with almost cataclysmic relief that it was Declan.

"*There* she is," he said, a dimpled grin appearing behind his scruffy beard. His hair was pulled back today, something I'd come to realize he did when he was studying and struggling to concentrate.

The solace I felt at seeing him flooded my body from the crown of my head to the soles of my feet. At that moment, I realized I'd started to believe my superstition that he'd never come back from Ireland. I opened my arms for a hug, practically limp in my chair. Declan chuckled and crouched down, enfolding me in his long arms. He tried to let go after a few seconds, but I just held on tighter, whimpering my rejection of his attempt to pull away.

"All right then," he said in my ear, his voice balanced between amusement and concern. "So not the best holiday?"

"Just squeeze the life out of my body," I murmured, my ear pressed to his chest so I could hear his heartbeat. He obliged, adding pressure and rubbing gentle circles into my back. I sighed, boneless and grateful that I no longer had to hold myself up. "Just keep doing that."

Declan gave his silent assent by sliding into the chair next to mine without letting go of me. To my alarm, I realized I was about to cry. I tried to disguise it, but my hiccupy breathing and the tears running into Declan's shirt gave me away. "Darling, you're breaking my heart," he said, the amusement long gone from his tone.

"Sorry, sorry," I said, pulling away and wiping my nose with my sleeve. "I don't know what's wrong with me." Declan kept his hand on my back, ducking down to stay near my eyeline, his brow furrowed with worry as he studied my snotty face. "I didn't hear from you all break," I whispered, painfully aware of how pathetic I sounded.

"Nor I you," he answered equably. "I thought I scared you away with all my whingeing." There was something guarded in his expression that I couldn't put my finger on, but I was too overwhelmed to pin it down.

"I missed you," I said, tears spilling down my face and dripping off my chin. Great. I'd never cried in front of Declan, let alone the whole library, but I guess I couldn't say that anymore.

"Emma, I missed you too," he said as if baffled that I could question it. He reached out and stroked my hair as if to soothe a frightened animal. Wildly enough, it worked a little. "It's all right, just talk to me. What's happened?"

I took in the crowded library, uncomfortably aware that we were already making too much noise, though people were trying to pretend they hadn't noticed my outburst. "We can't talk here."

"Then let's go to my place," he said, packing up my things without waiting for my assent. I opened my mouth to argue with him. I had a deep suspicion that if I was ever truly alone with Declan, I wouldn't be able to maintain the pretense that he was only my friend, but I felt totally devoid of the energy I would need to push back when all I wanted to do was curl up in Declan's lap while he told me everything would be okay. I nodded, gulping back my self-conscious tears, and followed him out of the library.

It was a short walk to Declan's apartment on 57th, his hand on my elbow to keep me steady on icy patches of the sidewalk. He seemed to know better than to ask me to explain my meltdown on the way, and we made faster time than usual with Declan in the lead, me following along in the wake of his long strides and the way his body took the brunt of the January wind.

We reached his courtyard building and climbed the stairs to a third-floor apartment. "I splurged on a one-bedroom," he explained as he let me in to a living room cramped with a loveseat, desk, and IKEA bookshelves. "I can't sleep if I'm next to a desk. All I'll think about is work."

"You may be on to something there," I said, taking in the notebooks and texts overwhelming his desk. It looked like a literary archive had exploded there.

"Here," he said, divesting me of my bag and helping me out of my coat. "Sit down. Make yourself comfortable. I'll make us some tea."

I did as he instructed, folding my hands in my lap and taking in the cozy chaos around me. The apartment couldn't have been more than 600 square feet, and I'd been in so many similar spaces that I knew how anonymous they could feel, but this apartment felt just like Declan. Books were stacked everywhere in haphazard piles, but I knew there was some innate logic and organizing principle to it all that I would never understand yet made perfect sense to him. The furniture was cheap and chosen for functionality (likely from Facebook marketplace and the neighborhood's alleys) rather than style, but the combined effect was still warm and welcoming. The sound of cabinets opening and closing, the kettle being put on, and Declan clinking around with mugs filled me with a sense of calm I'd been missing for weeks. I settled back into the couch cushions and tried to take deeper breaths, loath to start sobbing again when he returned.

A few minutes passed before Declan returned bearing steaming mugs of tea. "I didn't know how you take it," he said, "but as you're American, I figured you'd want it as black as your soul."

I forced a smile. "You'd be right. Thank you." I took the mug he proffered and wrapped my frozen fingers around it. "I feel bad. You don't have to treat me like some delicate flower," I said, primed to explain away my outburst in the library.

Declan folded his long frame into the seat next to me, setting his mug down on a rickety side table to cool. "I'm not treating you like a delicate flower, Emma. I'm treating you like someone I care about who is clearly upset."

The tears threatened again at his simple kindness. I went to take a sip of my tea to forestall having to answer that devastatingly sweet statement when he warned, "Careful, it's hot." I shot him a glare. "I'm sorry, you're not delicate," he said, and I lowered the mug, allowing the tea to steep longer.

"I'm sorry for freaking out on you," I said.

"I don't think you need to apologize for feeling human emotions."

"You are very contrary today," I said.

"I do disagree with you from time to time, yes," he replied, unperturbed. He leaned forward, resting his elbows on his knees. "Can you tell me now what's bothering you?"

"I just... Christmas was awful. My mom and I had the biggest fight we've ever had, and when I saw you, I just..." If not for the mug in my hands, I would have turned both palms up to the ceiling to indicate my helplessness to react any differently than I had. I couldn't tell him that the fight with my mom was compounded by my attempt to break up with Adam and how he'd boxed me out of it. "I realized how much I'd missed you. Jesus, I sound pitiful." I slurped away at the scalding tea, burned tongue be damned.

"What did you fight about?" Declan asked, ignoring my self-deprecation, his brown eyes bright and unblinking. Their unrelenting focus made me so nervous I stared into my tea instead.

"My thesis. My lack of originality and work ethic. What a shambles my future is in. What a disappointing daughter I am," I said, ticking them off one by one. "I mean, she's hinted at all of that before or nudged me in one direction or another, but just hearing all of it lobbed at me one after another—it was brutal." Declan hummed in assent, sympathetic and soothing. "I've spent my whole life trying to make my parents proud of me. I never rebelled. I made things so easy for them—or I thought I did. And she's still unhappy with me? I don't know what else I can give her." Without waiting for him to respond, I barreled on. "But the worst part is, she has a point. I mean, I haven't let her read my thesis—I'm not that insane—but I went to the Reg to work on it today, really get it in a better place before meeting with Houghton next week, and it's a fucking mess. Unsalvageable. It's like my mom could see into my head. She didn't *need* to read my thesis to know how badly it was going. Which makes me think my whole *life* has been a lie, she's been guiding my steps every inch of the way and nothing I've accomplished is even my own. So now I'm finally unraveling under the pressure, and she can see me for who I really am."

Declan looked like he was resisting the urge to rebut every part of my speech with great difficulty. "And who is that?"

"A pathetic people pleaser who isn't actually all that smart, just good at faking it because she had the right training," I said. It sounded so goddamn true coming out of my mouth that I realized I'd been feeling that way for a long time.

"Emma, you're spiraling," he said firmly. "Everyone feels that way."

"Sure doesn't seem like it, not in grad school, not at UChicago." I opened my mouth to say something about Adam and his pathological self-assurance but shut it again. Another knot I needed to untangle.

"I know you're not ready to believe me, but that kind of proves my point—that everyone here is just good at faking it. Everyone here is a golden child who is terrified of being told they've ever made a single mistake or not had original insight. I promise you."

"Do you feel that way?" I asked.

Declan screwed up his mouth, squinting at the ceiling. "I suppose I don't anymore. But I used to."

"What changed?" At the moment, I'd give anything not to feel the way I was feeling.

"Honestly? My personal life fell apart, and none of the rest of it seemed that important," he said. "Hence fucking off to America." He flashed a wry dimple at me.

"You make it sound so appealing," I said. He laughed softly. I stilled, watching the tension in his jaw. "I'm such a shit. I haven't asked you about your Christmas."

"Nice deflection, people pleaser," he said, nudging my knee with his own.

"I'm serious. I just had a mental breakdown on you in a public place before I even said hello. How was your time at home?" I looked at him properly for the first time since the Reg, scanning for any difference of expression that might give him away.

"Ehm," he hedged, shifting on the couch like it was suddenly uncomfortable. "It was eventful."

That sounded ominous. "Eventful? Now who's deflecting?"

Declan ran a hand through his hair. "Let's say I missed you too. I just felt like my brain was too full to email you. I didn't know where to start."

I scooted over on the couch until we were hip to hip, grabbing his wrist to force him to drape his arm over my shoulders. "You make me talk; I make you talk. That's how this works."

He smiled at me ruefully, tightening his arm around my shoulders to pull me closer. "Oh, is it?" My nerves all thrilled at the opportunity to have sustained bodily contact with him—to actually *feel* him breathe in and out, all while his fingers felt like they were burning through the fabric of my sweater. "Have it your way. I did end up seeing Maeve when I was in Wicklow."

The air left my lungs as quickly as if they were balloons that had been popped. "Oh? Was that her choice or yours?" I attempted to keep my face neutral, but I suspected my eyebrows were somewhere in my hairline.

"Hers."

I waited to see if he would add anything more, but the silence held. "And? You're making me nervous."

His hand squeezed my shoulder reassuringly. "It's nothing too terrible, I don't mean to be dramatic.

It was just hard seeing her. We were together such a long time. And when I saw her, she was so happy. Not to see me," he added at the look on my face. "She was terribly nervous to see me, but she seemed so different. And I realized she hadn't been happy with me for a long time. Maybe never," he said, his eyes trained on the floor.

"I can't imagine that's true," I said, almost in a whisper.

"That's what's so hard about it, I couldn't have imagined it either. I truly thought we were in it together, and she was never fully with me. I had pieces of her and never knew the difference." The grief in his voice gutted me. Declan gave so much of himself to others—his attention, his time, his affection—that the thought of him pouring all that love into someone who couldn't see it for the gift that it was enraged me.

"If she wasn't fully committed to you, it's because of her, not because of anything about you," I said, the pitch of my voice rising with my anger. If Maeve had been in the room, I think I might have hit her.

"Shouldn't I have known all the same? If I loved her so much?" His tone turned contemplative. "Did I assume that just because I was content, that meant she must be as well? It's really been wrecking my head, making me question myself. My relationships. Whether I have a read on any of them or just seeing what I want to see." He continued to avoid my eyes.

"Declan, you are the most thoughtful, caring person I know. If you didn't notice what was going on with Maeve, it's because she didn't want you to notice." An invisible hand clutched my throat, thinking back to how I stopped myself from mentioning Adam to him minutes earlier and how many times before that. With a sick feeling in my gut, I wondered if I was acting just like Maeve. And if I was so irate with her, I should be just as disgusted with myself. The tears were back, and this time I couldn't stop them from spilling over.

"Emma, darling," Declan said, apologetic and misunderstanding the reason for my renewed tears, "I don't mean to upset you. I'm really all right. You've enough going on without my navel gazing as well." He used his sleeve to wipe my cheek with such tenderness that I felt even worse.

I turned my head into his chest, traitorously seeking out my own comfort as I kept my secrets. I wrapped my arms around my ribcage to stop from touching him the way I wanted to. "You know, when we left for the break, I was afraid you wouldn't come back," I murmured into his sternum.

"Why would you think that?" he asked, his hand sliding from my shoulder to my waist. It could have been thoughtless, unintentional, but the shift felt seismic to me. My body came alive at his touch, which was always affectionate, respectful, and explicitly platonic, even when grazing the line of something more. I was afraid to move in case he took his hand away.

"I don't know," I said, struggling to make my voice as casual as possible as I swallowed my tears. "Just a bad feeling, I guess."

"You've not got rid of me yet," he said gruffly, and the air between us felt thick. His thumb slowly began to stroke my waist in light, feathery touches. I realized Declan was barely breathing, and the space between my thighs heated, quickly turning liquid in addition to the tingling of my skin where he touched me. This could be the moment, I realized. All I had to do was turn my face to his.

Ecstasy rocketed through my veins. We could do this. We could make this real. But just as quickly, guilt doused my joy. My big secret, Adam.

Don't do this to him, I thought. *Not like this. He'll never forgive you.*

I leaped from the couch like I'd been scalded. "Do you mind if I use your bathroom?" I asked, my nerve endings screaming at me to get back in his arms, back where I belonged.

"Of course," he said without commenting on my abrupt outburst, though his brow furrowed as he tried to read my expression. I ducked my head and made a beeline for the bathroom, where I sat on the edge of the bathtub, taking deep breaths until my heartbeat slowed from a sprint to a jog.

When I came back out, Declan was the same with me as ever—our conversation back on track, a fresh kettle on the stove. He was a gentleman, and I was a piece of shit.

FIVE

I avoided Declan for the rest of the week leading up to the new quarter, forcing myself to spend hour upon painful hour with my thesis, attempting to beat it into a shape that could perhaps one day resemble cogent literary analysis. I stayed in my apartment, refused to open my email, and declared to one and all that I was on a self-imposed work lockdown. For once, I was grateful that Declan refused to set up an international phone plan and wasn't immediately accessible to me if I had a moment of weakness.

However, that lack of accessibility didn't apply to Adam. The last night before the winter quarter began, he showed up at my apartment unannounced, straight from the airport. I met him at the door, already in my pajamas, my fourth mug of tea cooling next to my laptop on the living room coffee table.

"Adam, hi," I said, my stomach churning guiltily. The memory of Declan's hand on my waist and the way we'd both held our breath, suspended together for a moment in time, had been playing on a nonstop loop in my mind. "You're back."

Adam leaned in for a kiss in the doorway, the January cold still clinging to his skin. It felt churlish to duck. "Couldn't stay away. And you've been playing hard to get all break," he said, walking in with his suitcase and kicking snow off his boots. It seemed that the charm offensive was still in full force.

"I just have a lot of work to catch up on," I said. "It's nothing personal." But in addition to fantasizing about what could have been with Declan, I'd been steeling myself to finally end things with Adam once he got back to Chicago, his objections be damned. Since our fight outside Kathryn's apartment, I'd examined it from all angles. Whether anything romantic ever happened with Declan, I couldn't feign interest in this relationship any longer. Not when I knew how I could feel about someone without even being touched. My mind kept snagging on how to do it—when Adam had done nothing that qualified as wrong, when what he offered for years was the exact balance that kept my life the way I liked it. Moreover, he never shied from a fight and loved to win. I hated conflict and avoided it at all costs. Even if I laid out every iota of evidence that we were no longer right for each other, Adam was wired to respond to criticism by working harder, to be the best. That doggedness would make him a great lawyer. But it wouldn't make him Declan.

Adam had already rolled his suitcase into my bedroom and began unpacking while I stood in the doorway. Irritation prickled at my scalp. This wasn't unprecedented behavior—in fact, it had been the routine for much of our relationship—but the casual assumption that I would always welcome him without being asked rankled more each time I saw him. My thoughts slid back to Wednesday night, how completely Declan had shifted back into platonic friend mode at the first indication that I was uncomfortable with his touch (even though he didn't know *why*). Adam could assert that he knew me as much as he wanted, but he'd never proven it like Declan had.

"Adam, I know we need to talk, and I haven't

been returning your calls, but I just have so much work to do—" I started, attempting to soften the irritation in my voice. "Can we rain check? I have a meeting with Houghton on Thursday, and I need to be ready for it—"

"I know, you mentioned that," he said, unperturbed by my less-than-warm welcome. I had ignored his calls, but we'd texted throughout the break. He'd sent me pictures of his baby niece, and I had studiously avoided mentioning the fight with my mother. "You can work with me here, can't you? It's been weeks since we've seen each other. I miss my girl."

The subtle wheedling in his tone exhausted me. It wasn't the ideal timing I'd hoped for, but I couldn't do this anymore. "Adam, you're not listening to me. I need to focus on my work right now, and clearly, I'm not being fair to you. I've been thinking... maybe we should break up." My heart started pounding at rabbit speed, shocked at my own daring. I'd never broken up with anyone before. I'd always waited to be dumped or withdrawn to the point my ex-boyfriends had lost patience with me. It may have been cowardly, but it meant that at least I didn't have to be the bad guy. I knew something was wrong with my logic, but saying what I'd just said felt like asking for something I didn't have a right to. But I was trying to be braver than the voices in my head wanted me to be.

Adam looked up from where he'd sat on my bed, startled. "Emma," he said, "you're overreacting. It's just a meeting with your adviser. You'll be fine." It was clear from his tone that he expected that dismissive response to end the conversation.

I hissed in a breath through my teeth. "It's important to me, and I need to focus on it."

He held up his hands in a placating gesture. "I know it's important to you. We've always understood that about each other, haven't we?" I nodded, unable to deny it. "I'm not going to get in your way. But this isn't what you're really mad about. You don't have to play this game. You're more mature than this."

I blinked, at a loss for what he meant. "What are you talking about?"

"Emma, I know you've been ready to take that next step and move in together, and I know you want to stay in Chicago. I'm working on it. I told you that before Christmas."

I blanched. Over the summer, when Adam started organizing his post-law school plan of attack, we'd discussed the possibility of moving in together. Still, with both our futures up in the air, it had been far from a foregone conclusion. It was the next step and would make sense if we ended up in the same city, but we'd made no concrete plans. While I hadn't expressed enthusiasm for New York or any other cities where Adam was exploring internships, I hadn't demanded he stay in Chicago either. "Adam, I never said that you had to—"

"Emma, you never *say* what you want," he said, frustration edging into his tone for the first time. "Fortunately, I have a lot of experience guessing what you want."

It stung, but he wasn't wrong. I brought my hand to my forehead, attempting to rub away the tension between my eyebrows. "Adam, do you honestly feel like this is working? When was the last time we were actually happy together, not just treading water?" Treading water had felt like a successful relationship to me for so long; expecting anything more was the stuff of fantasy.

"We're plenty happy, Emma. Or we could be. You're not making an effort." He was mulish, digging his heels in to fight his corner. Any focus I may have had for work that night was shot. All I wanted was to crawl into my bed alone, but Adam wouldn't rest until he'd gained his point. What made the whole situation feel even more impossible was that I could imagine him having this same fight with almost anyone. He had an image in his mind of what his life was supposed to look like, and I happened to fit the girlfriend puzzle piece just well enough that he didn't want to start over with someone else. Not when it would throw off his timeline.

"How much of an effort do you think I should be making, Adam? How hard is it supposed to be to make a relationship work?" I was slumped against the doorframe to my bedroom, drained. I suddenly had a vision of our relationship as one long attempt to fit the wrong key into a lock.

Adam stood from my bed and walked toward me, holding me by the shoulders and forcing me to make eye contact with him. "Listen, we're both tired. Let's not make any rash decisions. You said we need to talk, so let's talk. Tomorrow." At the look on my face, Adam said, "This can work."

"Let's just go to bed," I said, surrendering. I had created an unwinnable situation for myself, one where I could make no one, least of all myself, happy. I decided to lie in the stupid bed I'd made.

Adam accepted the détente as a win and climbed into bed after me. I lay awake for hours, my mind juggling the new quarter's classes and teaching load, my meeting with Houghton, and my fight with Mom, but above all, how in hell was I going to extract myself from a relationship with a man who refused to let me go? Even when I was almost certain that what he was clinging to had nothing to do with me.

I BEGAN the new quarter feeling heavy and helpless, as if my body was filled with wet sand. I dragged myself to my new classes and taught my undergraduate sections, but the flurry of panic in my mind over my thesis and my relationship status had ground any concrete action to an absolute halt. I sent my thesis to Houghton in its current malformed state, bracing myself for whatever impact it would make on landing, and spent the rest of my time fighting with Adam. "It's just a rough patch because we're both stressed, Emma," he said. "I won't let you walk away from this for no reason." As much as it rankled me to be told I didn't have a say in my own relationship, I didn't know how to respond to someone who refused to be dumped *and* manage my workload at the same time, so I focused on preparing for my meeting with Houghton on Thursday and kicked the breakup can further down the proverbial road.

Even if the draft I'd sent Houghton hadn't been

a cobbled-together mess, I knew the meeting with her would be terrible based on my mental state alone. Houghton demanded you come prepared to battle with her over every thought, every citation, and every clause—and I barely had the energy to hold my spine upright. I told myself that it was only thirty minutes and I'd come out with some tangible direction to improve my thesis, so it would be brutal but necessary in the long run. I downed an inadvisable amount of coffee in preparation, hoping it would help to shake me out of my overwhelmed torpor.

"Frankly, Emma, I'm surprised," Houghton said with evident disappointment as she paged through the manuscript in front of her. Whole sections were circled and crossed out in red pen, furious margins full of question marks and exclamation points jumping out at me like the cast of a haunted house. *It looks like it's bleeding*, I thought. "You are much further behind than I thought based on our checkpoints last quarter. I have to say I'm alarmed. Your work is typically so rigorous. This is... muddy at best," she finished, like "muddy" was a particularly ugly euphemism.

"I know it's a little scattered," I said, trying to rev myself up to back my work. "I can make the connections stronger, provide more citations to support the underlying—"

"That would be the least you could do," she interrupted, holding up a staying hand. "But the arguments themselves feel recycled. There's no originality here, no fresh point of view. We expect a lot more of master's candidates at UChicago, and you are well aware of that."

I felt like she'd sucker punched me. Imagining what my mother might say if she were privy to this meeting sent me into near blackout mode. "You're right that I haven't been giving my thesis the amount of attention it deserves. I'm sorry about that, I really am, but I think it can be salvaged." It had to be. Otherwise, I didn't know what I was going to do.

"Emma." She sighed, peering over the top rim of her glasses, a note of compassion threading through her blunt words. "You'd be better off starting over entirely."

I didn't blink. I could barely breathe. I had no contingency plan for academic failure. If she had slapped me across the face, I couldn't have been more surprised and horrified.

"This may be a blessing in disguise," she continued, brightening her voice like she was speaking to a particularly dim kindergartener. "This topic really doesn't seem to hold your interest, I thought so from the very beginning. Why not take the weekend to think about what does interest you and schedule another meeting with me? I wouldn't advise taking any longer than that, but the weekend should give you some time to marinate."

"Start over?" I said, barking a laugh, wanting to believe she was joking. This was January. I was graduating in June. She might as well ask me to conceive and birth a fully gestated human baby in that amount of time.

"Emma, let me be quite clear. You are in very real danger of failing your thesis. If that happens, you may be entitled to resubmit, but I would think very hard about taking that risk. You've had an excellent grounding in English literature here, studied a great variety of texts over the years. Take some time to step back and think about what really speaks to you, what won't feel like a chore to spend your time exploring. What are you truly passionate about?" Houghton was tough as nails, but in moments like these, I remembered she was a mother—not a cuddly one by any means, but she genuinely wanted all her students to succeed. If she was recommending such a drastic change, it was because I was in much deeper shit than I'd realized.

I swallowed a dry heave. I think I nodded vague agreement, but the rest of our meeting passed in a haze of panic and disbelief, so I couldn't be sure. When she ushered me out of her office to meet her next advisee, I felt like I floated down the hall, completely detached from the sensation of walking.

I have no memory of how I made it back to my apartment, but suddenly I stood in my kitchen, staring at the teapot, when an emotional sinkhole of epic proportions opened beneath me. How was I going to break the news to my mother, who'd been right all along? Did I just waste the past seven years of my life? Was I ever any good at the only thing that had ever mattered to me?

I knew if I called Charlie, she would curse Houghton to Saturn and back, confidently stating she didn't know a good thesis from the hand up her ass, but considering Houghton had in fact read more theses than anyone living, the thought of Charlie's unquestioning conviction in my abilities just made my stomach hurt. Even if Adam and I had been in a good place, he was not the person to go to. He would shift into problem-solving mode and probably offer to edit my thesis himself, which I recognized as a well-meaning gesture of love but made me grind my teeth whenever he made a similar suggestion. Not to mention, if I went to him for help now, he would take it as tacit agreement that I'd given up on the idea of breaking up, and I was having a hard enough time making progress on that front.

For the thousandth time, I cursed Declan's lack of a phone. He'd told me he "found the quiet refreshing," which I had responded was both charming and obnoxious, and he could never get away with it if he were American. I pulled my phone out of my pocket like it weighed eight hundred pounds and opened my email to compose a new message, my first to Declan since our moment on the precipice the week before.

I should have offered some pleasantries, an apology for basically disappearing on him, but my cognition was barely functioning. In the end, all I typed was *Met with my adviser today. She basically asked if I've considered Burger King as a future career path.* I pressed send and tottered into the living room to collapse on our lumpy couch, wishing I could take the top off my brain and pour all the thoughts out of it. Possibly even flush them down the toilet.

Only two minutes passed before my phone buzzed next to my hip. Declan had replied. All his email said was: *I'm coming over. Address?* I hesitated for just a beat before typing it out. I looked around the living room with new eyes, wondering how Declan would react to the basket of yarn and abandoned knitting projects, the built-ins stocked with philosophy textbooks crammed in next to Harlequin romances. Instead of preparing for company, I slid back into a paralyzed, dissociated haze and waited for him.

When the intercom finally buzzed to announce his arrival, it startled me so much that I jumped, shouting "coming" to absolutely no one. I held down the buzzer for longer than was strictly necessary and opened the door, waiting for Declan to lope up the stairs with his long, easy gait. I didn't know what to expect—whether we were somehow back to normal or whether some awkwardness would linger from the last time I'd seen him—but once again, when everything felt wrong, he was the only person I wanted to see.

When Declan gained the second-floor landing and finally stood in my doorframe, his energy huge and peaceful and otherworldly, I felt like I had captured some mythical creature and brought it home. That was usually where it all went wrong in the fairy tales. Or the heroine's dearest wish was granted.

He held up a brown paper bag wordlessly. I thought of the peanuts he carried for the campus squirrels. "To drown my sorrows?" I asked.

"Or your adviser."

I chuffed something resembling a laugh and stepped aside. "Come in."

It only took two of his long strides before he stood in the living room, taking in all the homey detritus I'd decided I was too exhausted to neaten. "This is lovely," he said, and as simple as the compliment was, I held it close to my heart, like the rocks I'd collected as a little kid. *What's so special about this one?* my mom would ask. My answers were variations on a theme. *It's so smooth. It's so gray. It's so little.*

It's from Declan was what I'd say about this one.

"Just one more thing to kiss goodbye to, along with my academic career." I sighed, then regretted my word choice. "Fuck. Don't listen to me. I'm being overdramatic. It's a theme."

Declan looked over at me, his compassion too much to bear. "It's all those gothic novels, I knew it. Don't tell me you've also got a ghost troubling you."

I rolled my eyes. Gothic novels were the last thing I wanted to talk about. As was apparently evident to everyone around me. "I'll grab some glasses. Want the tour? It'll take all of thirty seconds."

He followed me down the skinny railroad hallway as I gestured to Anika's room on the left, hurrying past my door and the bathroom in a fit of self-consciousness, and George's next to the kitchen. Tour over, I stood on tiptoes to reach the top shelf of our dishware cabinet, where we kept the mismatched collection of tumblers we considered our "nice" cocktail glasses. Declan unsheathed a bottle of whiskey from the brown paper bag he carried, presenting the label to me like he was a server at a Michelin-starred restaurant.

"A classic," I said, nodding at the Jameson bottle. "I approve. Ice, I assume?"

We decided on one cube each and clinked our glasses together. "'For sinking your sorrows and raising your joys,'" he toasted as we clinked our glasses together.

I grimaced as the liquor scorched its way down my throat and brought tears to my eyes. "Jesus," I croaked, "I am really not used to this." I was an occasional beer drinker, or wine on special occasions, but the burning sensation had its own appeal in my misery. It provided a nice little sensory distraction for my less tangible pains.

"Let your ice melt a little, it will mellow," Declan said. "Come here to me and sit. Tell me what happened." He tilted his head back toward the living room. I had never considered our kitchen small until I saw him standing in it, but it did feel distinctly cramped at the moment.

He let me lead the way. Rather than flopping onto the couch again, I sat on the floor next to the coffee table, with the vague logic that sitting low to the ground would at least be fitting while I was feeling so low. Without questioning it, Declan joined me, crossing his legs and giving me his full attention, only inches between us on the hardwood floor.

"It's like I told you last week. Houghton's not wrong, my mother's not wrong," I said. "I'm what's wrong. That's the problem. My thesis is a mess. I'm so embarrassed that Houghton read it like that, that she thinks that's the best I can do. I know I could make it stronger if I really put the time in, but there doesn't even feel like a point in doing it when the problem is my lack of interest. I didn't pick my topic. I knew it would make my mom happy, and it looked good on paper. Which is how I've made every major decision in my life," I added darkly, taking another slug of the whiskey. It still burned, but I minded less and less. "Houghton told me I was in danger of failing, that I was better off starting over," I said, gazing down into my glass to avoid Declan's eyes, afraid to see disappointment or censure there. "Declan," I said, taking a shaky breath, "I don't know that I ever wanted to be an academic. My parents wanted it for me, and I didn't know what else to be." I had been afraid to say it for so long that speaking it aloud had felt dangerous. Now that I could sit with the words, the truer they felt.

He reached over to massage my neck, squeezing gently. The contact sent narcotizing comfort through my veins, the slightly rough quality of his hands a sensory shot to my bloodstream. "What is it you do want?" His voice was soft and low, free of judgment. I let out a breath I hadn't known I was holding—that our connection, as friends or anything else, was predicated on our similar academic pursuits, that without living up to the version of myself I'd performed for years, the future path that aligned with his, he would be out the door.

"Aren't you going to assure me I'm just overreacting to a harsh critique? Or tell me to write up a study schedule or something?" I asked. It was what my parents would have suggested. Adam too.

"I think if you've been working for months on a thesis that doesn't interest you, you've had plenty of people assume they know what's best for you. I want to know what you think." His voice was eminently reasonable and measured, encouraging me to take my time to answer. It felt like he was speaking a different language than everyone else around me.

At that moment, I realized I knew no better word to describe how I felt about Declan than *love*. That if love wasn't trust and respect and being willing to hear the hard truths, I didn't want it anyway.

A rush of feelings I'd been suppressing followed that realization. Knowing that I loved Declan for his gentleness, his shy chuckles, the way he would hunch forward to listen more closely to anyone who asked for his attention. I loved his cheekbones and how I wanted to fatten up his slightly underfed frame. I loved his contradictions—his fastidious organization and flyaway hair. But at that moment, what I loved most was the way I felt seen, known, and accepted exactly as I was: when I was furthest from the easygoing, perfect achiever I tried to be in order to belong.

The massive influx of emotion bubbled out of me in helpless laughter. "Oh Declan, the last thing I want to do anymore is *think*." His hand slid from my neck down to my upper back, rubbing in comforting circles as I doubled over with hiccupping hysteria, my head between my knees. My delirium didn't seem to throw him, considering he'd had a front seat to my mental health unraveling over the past few months. We stayed like that until my laughter faded and my breathing slowed, soothed by Declan's calming presence.

"Emma," he said, breaking the silence with sudden hesitance in his voice. He sounded like he half regretted what he'd started even in those two syllables. My heart stopped, and I straightened up to look at him. Declan withdrew his long-fingered hand from my back, and I felt the loss of his soothing touch like a shock. He rubbed his hand over his jaw, my eyes drawn to the flecks of red in his close-cropped beard. "Emma, after last week... I've been wanting to say... you must know." He trailed off in frustration with the inadequacy of words, hoping I would finish the thought for him so he wouldn't have to risk saying it aloud.

My breath caught. This was the moment we'd been hurtling toward since we'd met, the moment that I'd simultaneously hurled obstacles in front of and yearned to reach. We were about to blow up our willful blindness to what was happening between us at last, and I couldn't do anything to stop it. "Know what," I whispered, unable to pose it as a question.

"How I feel about you," he murmured, his brown eyes burning into mine. "I've never felt as close to anyone as I feel to you. You know me to my bones. Sometimes I'm sure you feel the same, and other times you pull away, and I can't tell anymore. I don't want to make you uncomfortable or assume you want the same things I want, but there's something between us, isn't there?" His voice had reached a pitch of earnest intensity I'd never heard before. "I haven't wanted to risk our friendship, was afraid to lose you, but I can't go on saying nothing. I want you any way I can have you, but the not knowing is killing me." I opened my mouth to respond, but the silence stretched between us, so fragile we could break it with a breath. A riot of joy and guilt and panic immobilized me to the spot.

"I'm sorry. I must have misunderstood. I shouldn't have put you in this position. I'll go," Declan said when he realized I couldn't speak, sounding so defeated I felt something crack in my chest. He planted his hand on the floor to press himself to standing, the heaviness in the movement unbearable.

"Wait," I said, reaching out to grab his wrist. He stilled. "There's something you should know." Panic welled in my throat, creating an almost physical barrier that stopped me from saying more. Our Christmas drinks at Cove Lounge pressed to the front of my mind; Declan saying he'd respect Maeve more if she'd told him how she felt about Brian as soon as she'd known. I may never have all of Declan, which was shattering enough as a possibility, but if I lost his respect—which he offered without reservation to everyone he met unless he learned they didn't deserve it—I didn't know if I could ever recover.

Declan's eyes flashed to mine with fear and worry—like he'd known something was wrong all along and had been waiting for the other shoe to drop. Knowing I'd caused that expression to cross his face, that if I'd been braver I could have spared him that, was wrenching. "I was with someone," I made myself say. I ducked my head and stared at his hand on the floor, afraid to watch him judge me, terrified to watch him recontextualize every interaction we'd ever had. "Until recently," I lied. I felt it land in my sternum with an ominous thud. *Wrong choice*, something inside me said.

I gathered the courage to look Declan in the face. "I'm sorry I didn't tell you. I didn't mean to send you mixed signals." That, at least, was true.

"Emma, darling, I never asked. You don't owe me anything." When I didn't appear convinced, he continued. "You haven't done anything wrong," he said, barely a sliver of hope in his voice, and still, he was comforting me.

I shook my head. "But I did. I wanted you."

I saw the pulse jumping at Declan's throat. "Do you still?"

I slid across the hardwood floor until our knees touched. I reached out tentatively, running my hand up his jaw to feel the scrape of his stubble against my palm. "I don't think I can stop." My voice was barely a whisper.

I felt his exhale of relief tickle at my wrist as he turned his face to lean into my palm. Taking the encouragement, afraid he'd see me trembling, I knelt above him and brought my other hand to his face, tipping it up toward my own. For once, I could see him from above, his strong cheekbones and soft, hopeful eyes. I leaned in slowly, taking in the flare of his pupils, each fleck of gold and green in his eyes, until our lips brushed. Declan's hands met at the base of my neck, tipping his chin up as he finally captured my lower lip between his, a sweet and lingering taste. Finally, finally, finally, I could really touch Declan. I didn't have to pretend that I hadn't been dying to for months.

Unable to stop myself, I climbed onto his lap, my

knees framing his hips. He hummed against my mouth, nudging his tongue against my lips for entrance until I melted against him, my center flush with his groin. I knotted my hands in his hair, the first time I'd gotten to really touch it, and opened for him.

Our bodies molded together, my breasts pressed to his sternum, one of Declan's hands behind my neck and the other cradling my shoulder blade to keep me close—as if I was even capable of pulling away from him. Our mouths tilted, negotiated, trying new angles and playing with pressure as if to say "this? Is this what you like?" in a thousand ways, as if we were the first people to discover kissing. It felt reverent, a revelation of how all the tiniest touches could become something holy with the right person. How tenderly he touched was foreign to me—not that everyone I'd ever kissed was rough or careless, but that I could feel how uniquely present he was. It made me aware of every nerve ending in my body, sparking and begging for his attention next. I found myself tilting my hips for more friction, grinding down into him. I could feel him harden beneath me. This could be so easy. We could just let it happen.

Declan pulled back gently, just far enough to break our kiss. "So that's how it is," he murmured, quiet awe and easy teasing in his tone. Drunk on him, I leaned back in, nipping at his upper lip, rocking against him. I didn't want to ever stop touching him. How I'd managed to hold back for so long was a mystery to me now that I knew kissing him felt as necessary as breathing.

He placed a hand on my hip, shifting me back until I lost connection with him. I could have whined. "Let's slow down," he said. "There's no rush." He pumped the brakes even as I felt his erection pulsing against me through our clothes, the consummate gentleman. I didn't want gentle right now.

But there is a rush, I thought. *The longer we wait, the harder it will be for me to convince myself I was just swept up in the moment. The longer we wait, the more it's a decision to cheat.* My lips were bee stung, my skin buzzing. I hadn't been this turned on in years. I'd forgotten I *could* feel this turned on. I'd spent years wondering if my libido was abnormally low, if something was wrong with me that I didn't seem to need sex the way other people did. I needed it now.

Still catching my breath, I forced myself to nod, elation and shame warring inside my chest. I felt dizzy, outside of my own body. What was happening between us was real. Declan and I were undeniable. There were no more excuses not to end it with Adam however he tried to refuse it. I could not do whatever this was halfway.

"You're right," I said, trying to pull away but drugged by the smell of his neck. I leaned in to breathe the skin behind the shell of his ear. "I have to go," I groaned, miserable and ecstatic. If I wanted to be in this with Declan in the way I wanted and he deserved, I had something to take care of before we went any further.

He playfully echoed my moan, placing a gentle kiss on the tip of my nose. "You're torturing me, woman," he murmured. "All right, you don't have to leave. I can keep my hands to myself." In fact, he sat on his hands with a cheeky grin at me. "But it won't be easy."

I forced myself to stay still and not reach for him. "I'm serious. I don't want to go, but I have to."

Declan looked puzzled at that but clambered up, shyly attempting to hide his erection (without success), and helped me stand with him. "I'll get out of here, then," he said. "If you've something better to do." His gaze was all that betrayed how off balance he was from all my abrupt mood swings since he'd arrived. I didn't deserve him.

"Not better," I promised. "Just necessary."

He kissed me goodbye at the door to my apartment, comfortable and confident we'd have thousands more. I closed my eyes and willed the moment to last. I watched him walking away from the living room window until he was out of sight, then raced down the stairwell, texting Adam. *Where are you?*

SURPRISINGLY, Adam responded right away. Even more surprisingly, he was home. *Come over,* he texted. *I have something important to tell you.*

My heart raced on the walk over to Adam's apartment. Could he possibly be thinking what I was thinking? Had I finally worn him down with my cold shoulder and unavailability? Was it possible that my life could be so easy and perfect at this moment that he agreed with me that our relationship had run its course?

I used my key to let myself into the building, imagining prying it off my key ring and knowing how light I would feel leaving it behind. As I breathlessly climbed the stairs to his fourth-floor apartment, I heard shouting and laughter. Did he have people over? Adam usually went out if he wanted to socialize, claiming he needed to get away from his desk. My heart rate picked up.

I knocked on his apartment door, but no one heard me over the whoops and music inside. I tried the handle, and it was unlocked, so I let myself in. Once I entered, I realized all the noise was coming from the kitchen. I could hear Adam's loud and jubilant voice rising above the others. As I entered the room, he turned around and held up an open bottle of champagne. "Emma!" he shouted. "I did it!"

Bewildered, I glanced around the room, which was populated with the other 3Ls who almost exclusively made up Adam's social circle by this point: Anish, Steve, and Hannah. "You did what?" I replied, smiling uncertainly, feeling like I needed to match the room's energy.

"This fucker got the internship at Kirkland and Ellis," said Anish, elbowing Adam with equal measures of affection and envy.

"Wow!" I said as Adam grabbed me in a one-armed hug and swung me around. "Congratulations, that's amazing!" It was jarring to feel his hands on me, not just because I had just come from Declan's, but because we had done so little touching in the past few months. I wanted to pull away, but having witnessed the work he'd put into reaching this moment over the past two years, I didn't want to do anything that might dampen his exultation at the moment.

Adam beamed and laid a smacking kiss on me. "Catch up, we're celebrating," he cried, grabbing a coffee mug from a cupboard and sloshing champagne into it (as well as onto the kitchen table). I took it to have something to do with my hands, working hard to keep my expression cheerful as my heart plummeted and my brain shifted into overdrive. What colossally awful timing. How big of an asshole would I be to ruin his moment of triumph by breaking up with him right now? But how could I possibly wait any longer?

The impromptu party carried on, and I sipped my champagne, the bubbles stinging my nose. Adam slung an arm around my shoulders and whispered in my ear, "I'm glad it came together like this. See, I told you—I know how important it is for you to stay in Chicago."

I felt like the worst person alive. "You have to do what's right for you, Adam," I said, looking down at my mug. "I've always said that. Don't make a decision like this for me. Especially right now," I said, attempting to allude to our near-constant fighting over whether our relationship should even continue without tipping off his friends.

"I am, I am! You know Kirkland and Ellis was my first choice. And if the internship goes well, odds are they'll make me an offer. We can find an apartment together, maybe I can swing Lincoln Park. No more roommates. I'll have more time for you. Things will be better."

The realization that Adam had been planning and working to stay in Chicago, even in part because he thought it would strengthen our relationship, made me feel even worse. He was celebrating us getting exactly what we'd wanted just a few months earlier, exactly what I'd wanted. "Mmm," I said noncommittally. "You should be really proud. You've worked so hard." And he had. It was part of why I'd been surprised when he texted me that he was home. He spent so much time at the D'Angelo Law Library that even before we returned from break and straight back into an argument, we rarely found an evening together. Most of the time we spent together, we were unconscious, sleeping over at one another's apartments once or twice a week, crashing out after one of our infrequent quickies or a side-by-side study session.

"Kathryn's throwing a party tonight at her place.

Do you want to come with me?" he asked. As fate would have it, we had met at one of Kathryn's kicking-off-the-school-year parties over two years earlier, right before Adam had started law school. "Really celebrate, you know?" His eyes were slightly unfocused, from drink or delirious happiness, who could say.

"Sure." I swallowed. "Let's go." I wanted to scream.

SIX

All I had to do was get through this one last night. I would do this one last small thing for Adam, and then I could end it gracefully and kindly. I repeated it like a mantra in my mind as I smiled blandly and watched Adam crow his good news to each new friend and acquaintance crammed into Kathryn's living room. This was the final compromise I would make. He got louder each time he said "Kirkland and Ellis," the bass line in the music drowning out conversations and the room feeling smaller and smaller as more bodies filtered in. I knew we'd be among the last to leave. When Adam did go out, he did his best to suck the social marrow out of the evening, not knowing when his next opportunity would arise.

I would do it in the morning, I decided. Let Adam have his night to celebrate, and tomorrow, no matter what rebuttal he might have up his sleeve, I would tell him I was out. That I was happy for him and grateful for our time together, but that it was over. He could stay in Chicago or explore his other options, but I was removing myself as a factor in his decision. I had my own decisions to make separate from him. Thinking about the finality of it—walking away from the back-and-forth and all the times I'd doubted myself over the past months—buoyed me, helping me to smile more easily at our friends' jokes even as my mind was elsewhere. After tonight, I wouldn't have to pretend anymore. Never again.

With my mood improving at the prospect, I turned toward the doorway, and there was Declan, looking absurdly tall in the crowded apartment and destroying the fragile equilibrium I'd found with my resolution. Heat flared in my cheeks at the memory of our kiss, along with joy and relief—*there he is!*— followed quickly by horror at the thought of him seeing me there with Adam. All my excuses for delaying our breakup fell tinnily on my ears, imagining saying them to Declan, especially after this afternoon and the lie I'd told him that it was already over. The ugly truth of it was I hadn't been brave enough even to admit my feelings to myself, and I'd prioritized keeping the peace over doing the right thing. I suddenly felt nauseous and claustrophobic, and too drunk on just two beers. It now seemed inevitable that he would end up at this party, that it was one more thing I was too stupid to have seen coming.

There was nowhere to hide—in order to leave the room, I'd have to walk right past Declan—but I tried anyway, like the coward I was. I crouched low next to a bookcase and pretended to peruse the bottom shelf, half hiding behind the curtain of my own hair while also scanning for when the coast was clear enough to make a run for the door. I thought I just might get away with it until my friend Daphne, an old floormate from freshman years in the dorms, squealed my name.

"Emma! There you are!" She tottered over to the bookcase, grabbing my hand and pulling me up for a sloppy one-armed hug. "It's so great to see you actually *out*! I can't remember the last time I saw you at a party!"

It was true that my social life had skewed more dinners with friends than house parties since freshman year (and since Charlie transferred), but as far as I was concerned, this night was not showing me the error of my ways. "Yeah, it's been a while," I said, trying to disentangle myself and turn us away from the doorway, but Daphne just clung harder.

"Where's Adam tonight? You old married couple, I know you two never go anywhere without each other," she said, finally releasing me and scanning the room. Before I could even respond, she spotted him. "Adam! ADAM! Get over here!"

He materialized behind me, immediately plastered to my back, wrapping an arm around my waist. I felt more trapped than ever. "Hey, Daphne," he said over my shoulder, at ease in his own skin and with his hands on me. I felt like I was having an out-of-body experience.

"Ugh, you guys," she said, making a pretend-disgusted face. "You're too sweet. Just look at you!" I tried to laugh, but it got stuck in my throat at the look of satisfaction on Adam's face. "You're so lucky you found each other—you wouldn't believe the dates I've been on lately. I'm this close to deleting Tinder." Daphne had the uncanny ability to zero in on whoever she'd cornered with absolute focus while still scanning the room for her next conversational victim. Her eyes lit up as they flit across the room, and I hoped that meant I'd be able to escape soon. "God, everybody's here tonight! Have you two met

Declan?" Daphne continued, gesturing toward the doorway. My limbs turned to lead. I should have seen this coming from miles away, should have known that eventually I'd have to pay the price for splitting hairs and hoping my problems would solve themselves.

"Who?" Adam shouted back.

"Declan! He just transferred from Trinity this year. I think he's doing English lit or a language or something—maybe you have a class with him, Emma! He lives in my building, and when I saw him at Hallowed Grounds, I invited him here tonight— he's that giant towering over there. His accent's gorgeous," she said to me, sotto voce, girl to girl. "DECLAN!"

His head turned at the sound of Daphne screaming his name, and my legs felt weak. Declan seemed to walk over in slow motion, politely making his way through the crush of people, my heart sinking with each step. I wished I could stop time at the moment he greeted Daphne before he realized who she was gesturing toward. I managed to slither out of Adam's grip, muttering that I was too hot, but I knew it was too late.

"...you should definitely meet her. I think she's in your program!" I heard Daphne say, as if I was underwater. "Emma, this is Declan. You've got to get him all caught up!"

He turned to face us, and I watched the emotions pass through his eyes like a flip book—surprise, delight, then confusion at my lack of warmth when hours before I'd had my tongue in his mouth. Adam made a bid to sling his arm around my hip again, which I deflected, but Declan caught it, alarm flaring in his eyes, the puzzle pieces starting to fall into place.

"Hello, Emma," he said, his eyes ablaze with the demand that I explain myself, his hands buried deep in his pockets. He hadn't even had time to grab a drink yet. No handshake was forthcoming—Declan didn't perform. His face was shuttered, so uncharacteristically unexpressive it was like I'd never seen him before.

"Hi, Declan," I muttered, trying to communicate with my eyes that this wasn't what it looked like, that I'd explain everything if I could just get him alone—even though this was exactly what it looked like. My mouth was too dry to say anything else when everything felt like a lie. I couldn't pretend I'd never met him. I couldn't turn to Adam and call Declan my friend. If the truth between the three of us came out right now, I only trusted one of these men to forgive me. I had to hope Declan would understand once I came clean.

Though we'd lost Adam's interest when Daphne said "English lit," Adam gave Declan a fraternal tip with his beer bottle. "Hey, man. Nice to meet you."

"Oh sorry, this is Adam, Emma's boyfriend," Daphne added helpfully, one more unnecessary nail in the coffin.

Declan nodded, his eloquent eyes blank. "Pleasure," he said. "If you don't mind, I see someone I need to catch up with. Nice to meet you." He detached himself from Daphne, who was flashing pouty eyes at him.

"God, have you ever seen someone that tall in real life?" she asked.

EVERY SECOND of the party had my skin crawling, being in the same space as Declan and not having the opportunity to explain myself. The living room was hot with bodies crowding together, the only movement possible if you were willing to stick your elbows out to barrel through the throng. I kept trying to catch Declan's eye across the room to signal that we find somewhere to talk—the balcony, the bathroom, anywhere—but he deliberately ignored my glances. I couldn't tell why he would stay at the party if he planned to freeze me out; I tried telling myself through my rising panic that he was waiting for the right moment to get me alone, get the story, but I knew that was wishful thinking.

Even though he refused to look in my direction, I knew he was taking in every time Adam slung his arm around my waist, possessively pulling me closer while he loudly shouted down someone's latest argument. I kept making excuses to create distance between us—I couldn't hear someone over the music, I was too hot—which Adam would accept but then forget about and reach for me again two minutes later. His laugh grated on me, a prickle of shame with each performative guffaw as he signaled to the room that no one could belong more than he did, and that I belonged to him. I had never realized before how casually Adam claimed my time and attention, how carelessly he touched me. Now that I'd kissed Declan and felt how responsive he was to my every breath and movement, how alive he was to the moment, I knew that touching was meant to be a conversation, not a monologue.

Even in the January chill, the heat of the room was stifling. I finally shook off my impulse to freeze in the face of danger and decided to find some privacy, hoping that Declan might come find me. I figured I would try the balcony first—in a January deep freeze, few people would be seeking out fresh air, and we might be able to steal a few minutes alone. "Hey, where are you going?" Adam shouted over the room's chatter, though he hadn't said a word to me for twenty minutes.

"Bathroom," I mouthed, the first thought to pop into my brain, which was in the opposite direction of the balcony. I'd have to do a lap. At that, the brief flare of interest in his eyes dimmed. He nodded and turned back to his audience, gesturing expansively with his beer bottle. He had his eye on joining the intellectual property practice at Kirkland & Ellis and was already strategizing out loud which partners he'd need to impress to get there.

The bathroom line snaked down the hallway, and the balcony turned out to be the site of an ill-advised beer pong tournament (complete with errant balls rocketing down to the street and sidewalk below), so I sought refuge from the noise in the kitchen, elbowing my way through the narrow hall-way. I found myself standing in the pantry staring at Kathryn's store of dry goods (how did she possibly have time to bake in addition to her double major in political science and economics?) and blinking back tears. My mind was nothing but static: no brilliant speech that would undo this evening popped into my head. My faith that Declan would seek me out grew feebler as the seconds stretched into minutes. I had to accept that he didn't owe me an opportunity to explain, and he wasn't coming.

With that gut-wrenching realization, all I wanted was to go home and crawl into bed, but getting out the door felt like it would be running a gauntlet of well-meaning friends. On top of that, I'd get an earful from Adam, even if I managed to escape, for leaving without saying goodbye.

I heard steps approaching and rubbed furiously at my eyes. Crying at a party was a sure way to invite the kind of attention I didn't need right now. "Oh," came a soft voice from behind me.

Inevitably, it was Declan, two steps into the kitchen and looking like he couldn't decide whether a fall from the third story window would be more painful than talking to me.

"Hi," I squeaked, realizing I was clutching a box of brownie mix in my hand. In all the time I'd spent that evening trying to catch his eye and wishing for this moment, I hadn't come up with a single thing to say.

Declan stared at me frozen with the brownie mix

like he'd never seen me before. "I didn't mean to disturb you. I'll leave you alone," he said, turning to leave. There went my optimistic theory that he'd stuck around to give me an opportunity to explain—maybe he'd stayed just to torture me. Before tonight, every conversation with him felt like curling up next to a roaring fire, comforting and warm and mesmerizing. Hearing him so cold and disconnected made me feel I'd lost something irreplaceable.

"I'm so sorry, Declan." The words rushed out of my mouth in an attempt to grab him and hold him.

"For what?" he said without turning around. And then, more softly, "It was just a kiss."

Everything in me rejected that. There was no *just* about our kiss. There was no *just* about us, no matter how long I'd tried to tell myself there was. "I fucked up. I never meant for you to find out about Adam like this. I know I said we were over, and we are, he just won't—"

That got Declan to turn around, a flash of righteous anger in his eyes. I'd never seen his temper before. "You don't look over from where I'm standing. Not to mention you've had four months to mention to me that you have a boyfriend. Not *had* a boyfriend. I have no interest in being the means by which you hurt someone else."

The words stung and deservedly so. The shadow of Maeve and Brian stood between us, and I'd known since our night at Cove Lounge that if he ever found out about Adam, he'd never see me any other way. I'd be just like her. "I know I should have told you. I just didn't know how. I've been trying to end it with him, but—" I took a step toward him and stopped, eyeing the throng in the hallway, hoping against hope Adam wasn't in the crush of bodies.

"Not a conversation you want to have here?" Hearing the cynicism in Declan's voice felt all wrong, like a record scratch in my mind.

I deserved it, every ounce of doubt, every verbal jab. "I was trying to find the right time. I didn't expect..." My throat filled, and my voice shook. "I didn't expect... what happened today. I know I didn't handle it right. But please don't go."

Declan looked down at his shoes. "Emma..." He sighed. "Like I said, you don't owe me anything. I shouldn't have assumed—"

The tears that had been threatening to spill over did. "But you didn't assume, Declan, I told you," I said. "I owed you the truth. At least that. After everything you went through with Maeve, I knew better." Through the blur of tears, I saw Declan hang his head. There was no way he'd forgive this. Not wanting to watch him walk away, I closed my eyes and turned back to the pantry, waiting to hear his footsteps recede.

Long moments stretched, and they didn't. Instead, his footsteps shuffled across the kitchen toward me, deliberate and heavy. "Are you all right?" Declan's voice was reluctant but soft as always, a blanket I wanted to wrap around my frayed nerves. My breath caught, and I swallowed past the instant lump in my throat. After everything, it still went against his every instinct to walk away from me when I was in obvious pain. Being around me hurt him, yet he still didn't want to leave me to my own mess.

"I'm fine." It struck me how often I'd lied to him lately, or at least withheld the truth, just to be close to him. It would be only fair now to lie to let him go. The silence spooled out, Declan's presence unignorable, even as he said nothing in response. "Really. You have every right to be pissed. You don't have to comfort me for hurting you. You can go."

When he still didn't respond, I turned around to insist. But the sight of him leaning back against the kitchen counter, leaving me as much room as he could in the cramped space, knocked me off balance. He was hunched forward as always, all six foot five of him trying to crouch within my eyeline. He'd tied his wild cloud of hair back into a low ponytail some-time after our encounter with Daphne, his flannel hanging loose on his lanky frame. I'd had my hands wrapped around him, tasted him hours earlier. No sight could feel more like home to me, I realized. "Is that what you really want?" he asked, anger and want and concern warring in his eyes.

No. It was not what I really wanted, not at all.

I crossed the room in three unsteady steps, burying my face in his chest. He smelled like he always did, woodsy and faintly of a library. It was a risk—he could push me away and had every right to do so. But I couldn't miss this last one if I never got another chance to hold him. After a moment, his arms folded around me as gentle as wings. I couldn't tell if it was forgiveness or goodbye, but it felt like I'd been granted a last-minute pardon while walking to the electric chair. "I am sorry," I choked out, so grateful and so undeserving of his unquestioning acceptance. "I never wanted to hurt you. I was just afraid of losing you." He needed to know that much, even if we never spoke again.

"Shh," he whispered, his chin on the crown of my head, threading his fingers through my hair in long soothing strokes. If these were going to be our last moments, I focused on breathing him in—

inhaling the palpable sense of peace I felt whenever I was with Declan. Whatever he'd decided about us stood on the other side of this embrace. I held on tight so I wouldn't have to find out what it was.

We stood like that for what could have been hours, his tall frame rounded protectively over me, like I was sheltering under the branches of an ancient tree. We didn't say another word, simply basked in the minor miracle of no one else bursting into the kitchen at a rowdy party while Declan drew light circles on my back with his long, delicate fingers. I wanted to learn every line and whorl on his fingertips; no one had hands so exquisite. I felt myself melting into the cradle of his arms, anchoring, rooting. Impossible as it sounds, I could have fallen asleep there in the midst of the party, lulled by the safety of Declan's even breathing and the relief of no longer pretending everything was okay after weeks of fighting for every breath. As long as I stood there, I could revel in the sense of being home inside someone else's skin. As time suspended for us, I thought *oh. He's saying goodbye.*

Our idyll broke apart in the time it took for someone to need a refill. The party was no longer distant background noise as raised voices made their way into the kitchen, and I felt a sudden viselike grip on my arm. I was still on my feet, Declan holding me steady. My mind scrambled to take in what was happening.

"What the fuck is going on here, Emma?" Adam's fingers dug into my bicep, his eyes flashing dangerously with embarrassment and rage.

"Stop shaking her, man," Declan said, an edge of warning in his voice. This gentle giant who carried nuts for the squirrels sounded ready to take Adam outside. Declan was taller, but Adam was stocky and dense, solidly built and angry enough to do real damage. All the emotional equilibrium I'd regained holding Declan leached from my bones, panic kicking my heart rate into the stratosphere. I stepped back from Declan, shifting my focus to Adam before this escalated into a real fight. Losing contact with him felt like severing a limb.

"Adam, hey, we were talking and I was just so tired I must have passed out. So embarrassing," I said to Adam while fake blinking sleep out of my eyes. I reached out to placate him, but he was still zeroed in on Declan.

"What the fuck is your deal, man? Did you roofie my girlfriend?" Adam looked like he wanted to square off and punch Declan right there in the kitchen. The pink of his cheeks could have been protectiveness, indignation—but as I took in the group of onlookers edging in from the hallway, I thought it was more likely embarrassment.

"No, Adam, I just had too much to drink and fell asleep, calm down," I begged, stepping between them to create a barrier, though Adam's grip on my arm was starting to hurt. "See, I'm fine."

"Let go of her fucking arm. I won't ask you again," Declan said, his jaw tensing. I could feel how hard he was working to keep his hands off me and let me handle this the way I wanted to, how much he'd rather handle it himself. Adam looked like he'd be perfectly happy to oblige Declan's wishes on that score. My mind flooded with nightmare scenarios—Declan being charged with assault, losing his visa, and being deported—I couldn't be the cause of any more pain in Declan's life. This had to end now.

"Adam," I said, resisting the urge to snap my fingers in his face to pull his attention from Declan. "I just need to go home. This is stupid. Please just take me home."

If I had to rank the last two things I wanted, going home with Adam would be second only to a fight between Adam and Declan, but taking him with me was the only way I could think of separating the two of them. For an awful moment, I thought I was too late, and the situation would boil over. But after trying to stare Declan down didn't work, Adam huffed a reluctant breath and stepped back, dragging me to the door through the path rubberneckers were hurriedly making for us. If he wasn't going to win a fight, he would at least attempt to regain his dignity by being the one to leave with the girl. I felt Declan's eyes on my back as Adam pulled me away. Every step away from him felt wrong, like another betrayal.

Every step of the walk back to my apartment was painful. Trash skittering on the sidewalk with the wind looked surreal in my half-awake state, yesterday's snow turning to slush making my gait unsteady. I kept up an endless monologue to Adam about how tired I'd been at the party and that I'd just nodded off talking to Declan about my Comparative Fairy Tales class, that I must have just dozed for a second and Declan caught me, that Adam must have walked into the kitchen right after. I tried to draw Adam out by asking him to relay our friends' reactions to his news about Kirkland and Ellis, hoping the subject would dispel the storm cloud over his head, but Adam just grumbled, clearly irritated with the way his night of triumph had ended.

"Thanks for walking me home. I didn't mean to ruin your night," I said when we reached my block, wondering if I could avoid him coming up, but he shrugged it off and let us into my building with his key.

Just do it now, get it over with, echoed in my brain. *Rip off the Band-Aid*. What was with my compulsive desire to please this man? Why was I letting him bully me into a relationship? Was my self-esteem that fucking low? I was starting to wonder if most of our relationship had been little more than inertia. But in the same breath, I'd think how could I possibly break up with Adam after two years on the sidewalk after some shitty party? After all the plans he'd made for our future with me in mind? Didn't I owe him a little more consideration than that?

Back at my apartment, I closed myself in the bathroom, knowing I'd find Adam in my bed waiting for sex, feeling especially entitled to it after his news today. I splashed water on my face, trying to remember the last time I'd wanted to. I could still feel Declan's hands on me, spiking my heart rate and leaving me hot, wet, and frustrated. The apartment was eerily quiet; Anika's and George's doors were shut, so they were either gone or in bed long ago.

As I climbed into bed, Adam pressed up behind me, nudging with his knee to part my legs. "Adam,

I'm sorry, I'm kinda wasted," I lied. "Can we just sleep?"

He sighed and rolled over. "Fine." I stared at my phone on the nightstand, wishing I could email Declan. Tonight could only have been more colossally fucked up if the earth opened up and swallowed me whole.

I BARELY SLEPT THAT NIGHT. Ideas of what I could do to make things right with Declan chased each other around my brain in endless intersecting serpentines. Adam's arm, which he'd slung across my chest in his sleep, felt like an anchor, a brand. I got up at 6:00 a.m., hoping against all reason that I'd find an email from Declan in my inbox, feverish with the anxiety that some cord between us had broken, that our embrace in the kitchen really was his way of saying goodbye. When there wasn't, I tried to tell myself it was too early, especially for a Saturday morning, and spent the next two hours cleaning the kitchen. I knew that if anyone was owed an explanation, it was Declan, but putting it in writing felt impossible.

By the time the clock read 8:00 a.m., I was so frantic to talk to Declan that I left Adam sleeping in my bed and fled my apartment to hunt Declan down and work this out once and for all. I knew from experience that the Reg was my best shot when I needed to find him, and it had just opened for the day. I ran into a bleary George in the hallway, made up a story about a missing reference text, and said I needed to run to the library. I practically sprinted down Ellis to the Reg and up the stairs, where I knew he liked to set up camp most weekend days. I threaded my way between stacks and tables of silent studiers searching for him. I finally spotted him far from his usual spot in a corner, hunched over a stack of reference materials and his laptop.

I rushed to sit across from him at his table, leaning forward to get his attention. "Declan, there you are," I whispered, though it still felt like it echoed in the cool hush of the library. He glanced up, his face inscrutable. There were faint purple shadows under his eyes like he'd gotten as little sleep as I had. I wanted to wipe them away, wrap both of us into a thousand blankets, and do last night over the right way. "We need to talk." The understatement was almost comical at this point, but the look on Declan's face indicated he didn't find it funny.

"I've a lot of work to do. I need to focus right now," he said, turning his gaze back to the notes in front of him. My throat tightened with fear. This was worse than last night when he first found out about Adam. He was doing his best to freeze me out.

"I'm so sorry about how last night ended. I had so much more to say to you, but I was afraid Adam would start a fight. I had to get him out of there." I clasped my own hands tightly in my lap, waiting to touch him until I knew he would welcome it. If I could just keep him looking at me, I might be able to make him understand.

He blinked slowly, his eyes wary in a way that leached all my relief at finding him out of my veins. "You know, I am getting really tired of hearing you apologize," he replied, glancing back down at his books, though I could tell he wasn't reading.

This closed-off version of Declan was so unfamiliar that I stumbled over how to respond. On a normal day, I knew how to cajole him out of a mood or how to distract him from a funk. This was far from a normal day. "I know, but I need you to know how much I mean it. Last night was so terrible—you… meeting Adam, and then he was such an asshole to you and leaving was the only way I could think to stop him. I didn't even think about how different that must have looked to you from how I meant it. I'm really sorry about all of it. I want to fix it."

"He wasn't an asshole to me, really," Declan said. If I didn't know him so well, I would have thought he was calm. "He cares about his girlfriend. He was worried someone was trying to harm her. Nothing to fault there."

"But he shouldn't have accused you of drugging me. He should have listened to me instead of losing his shit. That was awful. He's not usually like that."

"I'm sure he's not. But you cleared it up right away. You told him you were just tired, no big deal, and you left together with no bloodshed. No apologies needed."

I gaped at him, unsure how to respond. Declan had always graciously accepted my apologies, had never asked me for an explanation or pushed them back in my face. This studied indifference knocked me off balance.

"Emma..." Declan sighed and leaned back in his chair, his voice still pitched low, but with a thread of irritation laced in it that told me he was close to snapping. "What would you like me to say? You are obviously still with your boyfriend, or we'd be having a very different conversation right now. We don't need to repeat this pattern, and I—I can't keep letting this happen. Going after you and watching you leave. I can't." He closed his laptop with finality and started gathering his things.

"Wait, Declan—" I reached out for his wrist, my voice rising in desperation. Other tables of students were turning at the disruption, but I couldn't bring myself to care. "I said I was sorry, I'll fix it, it's just complicated—"

Declan gently detached my hand from his wrist. "But that's exactly it, Emma. I don't want all of our conversations to be apologies." He stood and left the library, and this time, I watched him go.

A part of my brain couldn't compute what was happening. Declan was never the first to walk away, never shut down on me. He was always heart-stoppingly open, and seeing him any other way was like a dog standing on its hind legs and starting to talk to you about the stock market. With my legs rapidly liquefying, I ran down the stairs and outside the library to catch him. He hadn't gotten much of a head start, but his strides were so long I was panting by the time I caught up with him outside.

"Declan! Please don't go like this." The wind cut through my jacket, nasty and sharp. Declan stopped where he stood without turning. I watched his shoulders rise and fall with a sigh, terrified to step any closer.

He turned to face me, slow and reluctant. The faint lines that his constantly furrowed brow had etched into his forehead stood out. I had never seen him look quite so tired. "Like what, Emma? I don't know what the fuck is going on with you. Yesterday, I thought I knew who you were. I knew you better than I'd ever known another person. Yesterday, I would've trusted you with my life, could have sworn there was never a secret between us. Yesterday I kissed you for the first time and thought we were on the same page and starting something together. And then, in the course of that same day, I learned I don't have the faintest clue what's going on in your life. This whole time you've been in a relationship that, what, makes you miserable? And you never thought to mention it? You want to tell me it just slipped your mind? You didn't deliberately lie to me?" His eyebrows climbed toward his hairline. "If nothing else, Emma, Jesus Christ, I thought we were closer than that."

"We are," I croaked.

Declan swore, toeing the concrete with his boot. "This is not what close looks like, Emma. Whatever this is, I don't want it."

"What do you want to know?" I asked, holding out my arms. "About Adam?"

He looked at me like he wanted to swear again, but he didn't walk away. "I don't care about him," he said. "I care about why you didn't tell me."

The one thing I didn't know how to answer. "It didn't seem like it mattered," I started, which was only half a lie.

"Well, I have to say I disagree. And I bet he would, too."

"I was afraid if I told you, I would lose you! And look what's happening!"

"Emma, don't you think I had a right to make that decision on my own? You're telling me it's so complicated, it's not what it looks like—you didn't think I cared enough about you to listen and believe you? I can't imagine not believing you, except when you're telling me a blatant fucking lie. You want to stand there and tell me the sky is green, you'd better hope I'm goddamn colorblind. And the worst fucking part is I told you about Maeve—no, you begged me to tell you about Maeve. So you knew exactly what you were doing. I should have walked away the second I saw you in the kitchen last night."

A thousand childish pleas were barricaded behind my tongue—*it wasn't like that, please don't be mad at me, please don't let me ruin this*—but I knew from his face that they would make no difference in what happened next. I had pushed him all the way over the edge to a place he couldn't come back from. "So this is it? You don't forgive me. We'll never speak again." If I framed them as questions instead of statements, I would feel even more pathetically lost than I did, clutching my fists and wanting to wail like an abandoned child.

"Please stop," he whispered, looking down at his work boots. "This is hard enough as it is."

"Declan, I'm afraid if you go now, there is no fixing this," I forced out. It felt like a fist was lodged in my throat.

"How is it you plan to fix this, Emma? I'm all fucking ears."

"I'm going to break up with Adam!" I shouted.

"You're going to," he said, his voice grim and unbelieving. "How long have you been planning to do that?"

"Months," I said, "since before Christmas—"

"But you haven't. Why is that?" I felt like a student being nailed by a teacher who knew I hadn't done the reading.

"I... didn't want to dump him right before Christmas, and yesterday, he found out he got this internship, and I thought—"

"See, Emma, there is always going to be a reason,

and then another reason not to do it." The certainty in his voice was awful.

"That's not true—" I protested.

"What can I do to make you understand, Emma?" he said, raising his voice for the first time. It felt like a slap to the face. "I don't want to be your side fling or your backup plan, Emma. I can't wait around for you to choose me. Let me keep what dignity I have left."

"You aren't my backup plan, Declan. If anything, Adam is—" I said, then cut myself off, feeling the shadow of Maeve and Brian over our conversation.

"Then why, why are you still with him?" I felt every bit of his disbelief and frustration. I didn't know anymore, either.

"I didn't want to hurt anyone," I said, so quiet I was barely audible.

"It's not possible for no one to get hurt here, Emma. You need to figure out what you *do* want—not what you think you *should* do or what anyone else wants, including me. I'm removing myself from the equation." His voice was raw, final. "Until you know, leave me be." When he turned and walked away, I didn't chase him.

This time, I let him go.

SEVEN

I walked back to my apartment on wobbly legs, feeling like my insides had been scooped out and fed to the notoriously aggressive campus squirrels. Climbing the stairs felt like scaling a rock face, my body growing heavier with each step. Reaching for the door handle, I could hear Adam chatting with George inside, and what I needed to do became that much harder.

This wasn't a choice between Declan and Adam. I'd already lost one, and I knew I'd have neither of them by the end of the day.

I let myself in, and George greeted me cheerfully from his seat near the living room window. "Sup, Emma gem," he said. "How was the library?"

It took a moment for me to remember the story

I'd made up to get out of the apartment that morning. The sheer volume of lies I'd been telling made me absolutely sick of myself. It had become such a reflex that I hadn't hesitated to lie to George when there was no reason he would need to know or care where I was going, but I still felt the need to cover my tracks. "Fine," I said.

Adam was still in the sweatpants and t-shirt he'd slept in sprawled on the couch. He seemed to catch that something was off in my voice. "Where's the book George said you needed?"

"It doesn't matter," I said carefully, determined to tell the truth, no matter how this conversation might go.

George's eyes flicked between Adam and me, picking up the vibe. "I'll leave you two to it," he said, slapping his thighs as he stood and beat a hasty retreat. I wished I could follow him, that this next part could happen without me. Even so, it suddenly felt so ridiculous that I'd lost Declan because I was afraid of an uncomfortable conversation. What a waste. I would have given anything to turn back time and do this four months ago.

"What's going on, Emma?" Adam asked. He seemed wary, as if he were waiting for something to detonate. After the standoff with Declan last night, his perpetual optimism about our relationship finally seemed to have worn down.

I walked over to sit next to him, staring down at my hands. "Adam," I began, "this isn't working anymore."

He immediately began shaking his head, settling in for another round of the same fight. "We talked about this—"

"No, you talked. You didn't listen. This hasn't been working for a long time, and I don't want to try anymore." I would have been surprised by the steel in my own voice if I wasn't so bone-tired that I didn't care anymore, couldn't care. It was all too little, too late.

Adam reared back on the couch. This wasn't a version of me he recognized. "What are you talking about? Things are the same as they've always been. Better, even—the internship! What about yesterday? We can stay in Chicago like you want."

I closed my eyes, unable to deny any of what he'd said. "You're right—things are the same as they've always been. I think that may be the problem. I'm happy for you about the internship, but even if you stay in Chicago, it won't be with me."

I opened my eyes to watch Adam swallow, his eyes wide with disbelief. I knew the set of his jaw, and he was preparing his argument. He'd wear me down the way he wore me down on restaurant choices, weekend plans, and even how I felt about movies we'd seen. Our future would be more of the same, smooth and easy when I agreed with him, and arguments with labeled exhibits whenever I didn't. "There's someone else, Adam," I said, cutting off his opening statement. It was the one thing I could say to end all the back and forth, and I'd known it all along. "It's over for me. There's nothing you can say to change my mind. I'm sorry."

"You're sorry," he repeated, disbelief fading into anger. "It's that guy from last night, isn't it? The Irish guy."

"It doesn't matter who it is," I said. "It's my choice."

"Just fell asleep, huh? You weren't cheating on me while I was in the other room at the same party?" I didn't deny it. "Ben told me he saw you with some guy at the Pub, but I thought he was just messing with my head. I've been working my ass off trying to make you happy, and all this time you were fucking around on me?" His eyes glistened with outrage and pain. I hadn't known I was capable of getting that reaction out of him.

"No, it's not like that," I said, though I wondered

if there really was a difference. I may not have slept with Declan, but I told him things I'd never told Adam. I'd felt more alive on casual strolls with Declan than I had when Adam was actually inside me. Of the many possible definitions of fucking around, that was one of them. "We wouldn't have worked with or without him. He just made me realize it sooner."

Adam huffed out a breath, looking at me like he'd never seen me before. "I thought we wanted the same things," he said, and for the first time in a long time, I heard vulnerability in his voice. Underneath all the bravado, he really did care.

"I thought we did too," I said. "I'm the one who changed, not you."

We gazed at each other for a few breaths longer, then he stood, noisily gathering his laptop and study materials and stalking off to my room. I'd finally given him the one reason for our ending he had no counter for. I stayed where I was, listening to him pack his things.

It didn't take long. Adam paused at the door to the apartment, looking around like he didn't under-stand what had happened to his morning. "Bye, I guess," he said, bewildered and harsh. He didn't wait for a response before closing the door firmly behind him.

"Bye," I said to the empty apartment. I had just enough willpower left to walk to my bedroom and crawl back under the covers. It may not have been noon yet, but I was done with the day.

A NARCISSISTIC CORNER of my brain thought that the world would stop turning for a while until I got my bearings in the fallout, but that wasn't the case. Days passed in the same rote manner I'd grown used to from my many years as a student, unconcerned with the fact that I was a bombed-out shell of a human being. I didn't know what else to do, so I got on with it. Every day that winter, I got out of bed, had a bowl of cereal with my coffee while I caught up on emails, and went to class. I took notes, I turned in papers on time, and taught my freshman sections competently. I (mostly) practiced basic hygiene, avoided my mother's calls, and did my share of the dishes in the apartment I shared.

I did all of it, but I felt like I was dying.

When I woke up each day, my first thought was *I miss Declan*. The second was *I don't want to do this*. The third was *But I have to anyway*.

When I opened my laptop to check my email, there was always a millisecond when part of me believed this would be the day I had a message waiting in my inbox from Declan. When that was never the case, swallowing my cornflakes got just a little bit harder. No amount of repetition eased the pang of realizing the past hadn't changed overnight while I slept, that it wasn't all one horrible, long nightmare.

I went through the motions in class. I did the readings so I could contribute to the discussion, but it didn't thrill me like it used to. Even when I said the right things, there was no stirring of satisfaction behind my sternum at having cracked the code. I kept my eyes to the ground when I had to walk through campus, changing my routes as much as possible to avoid the ones where I might run into Declan and see how completely he'd moved on.

I waited to reply to Professor Houghton's emails until I thought she was ready to pull the academic equivalent of an intervention on me. When I finally sat across from her in her office, I didn't wait for the interrogation to begin. "I've decided what my thesis should be on," I said.

Houghton's eyebrows rose a fraction. "And what is that?"

"Yearning in the Romantic Period."

She did not look impressed. "That's very broad. And well-trod territory, as well."

I didn't budge. This decision was the one and only thing holding me together. "That's what I'm interested in writing about."

Houghton studied me, her lips slightly pursed. "Then I look forward to seeing what you come up with. You'll have to work on an accelerated timeline. Can you have an outline for me by next week?"

I would have suffered a coronary if she'd asked me the same thing a month earlier. "Sure," I said. I had nothing else to do.

So I read. I read the Brontë sisters, Lord Byron, and Coleridge. I read Keats, Stendhal, and Emily Dickinson. I read Shelley, Frances Burney, and Austen. I outlined. I started to draft. And it was painful. It didn't feel original or groundbreaking, but it felt authentic, and the raw emotion and even melodrama of the material always gave me an excuse for why I was crying if George or Anika asked. I avoided libraries and coffee shops unless I had no option but to use them, scurrying in to check out the materials I needed or an emergency latte and rushing back out, my eyes on the floor the whole time. I cloistered myself in my bedroom, as isolated as any nun, rarely visiting even the bathroom or the kitchen.

A month passed like this, then two. All my time was spent playing catch-up with my new thesis topic, which elbowed its way into every minute, muscling out the thoughts I didn't want to have and the memories I didn't want to relive. I didn't know what I would do when graduation rolled around, but I decided to finish this one thing to the best of my ability. Maybe doing it for myself, my way, would help me figure out my next steps one at a time.

Charlie booked a flight to visit in March when I told her I'd completed enough of my new thesis to sleep longer than four hours a night. When she walked into my bedroom fresh off the plane, she took in the sight of stacks of crusty cereal bowls and abandoned mugs scattered across my desk and nightstand along with the dirty laundry in plaintive piles across the room with a look that said things were more dire than she'd feared. "I gather you haven't been getting out much," she said, picking a path over to my armchair, also festooned with laundry.

I shrugged, unable to deny it. "Sorry," I said. "I know it's a mess."

"Not at all," she said, delicately lifting a sock off the arm of my chair and dropping it to the floor as she sat. "Start your own personal bacteria lab in here, it's no skin off my nose. What I'm concerned about is you."

I tucked a strand of unwashed hair behind my ear. "What do you mean?"

Charlie gave me a look that said *nice try*. "Call me old-fashioned, but a girl has a right to worry about her best friend in the wake of a breakup and coinciding academic smackdown. You obviously haven't been sleeping. I should have come sooner. I wish you'd called me."

"You've been busy too. It's okay," I said, though I wanted to crawl into her lap and cry while she petted my disgusting hair. I'd texted her the headlines—*I broke up with Adam, I'm tossing out my thesis*—not trusting myself to keep it together on the phone. If she hadn't been juggling her own insane schedule (literally juggling, she was taking a clowning class that she described as "hell on earth"), I wouldn't have put it past her to show up at my door unannounced, ready to nurse me back to emotional health with a bottle of tequila and several bracing speeches about how I was the hottest, most brilliant woman alive and that she'd eviscerate anyone who dared to say different.

She narrowed her eyes at me. "Here's what we're

going to do," she said, a plan formulating behind her eyes. "You're going to take a shower, and then we're going out."

"Out?" The idea of running into Declan filled me with dread.

"Hence the shower," she says. "I love you, but I can smell you from here. Go on."

Seven years of experience with Charlie when she decided to be stubborn meant I knew better than to fight a losing battle. "And do your hair!" she shouted when I was halfway down the hall.

By the time I returned to my room, clean and with my hair blown dry for the first time in months, I was reluctantly grateful for the push. It had been so long since I did more than rinse off and brush my teeth that I felt undeniably refreshed. Even more amazingly, Charlie had spent the time I was in the shower sluicing off my misery dirt neatening my bedroom—laundry in the hamper and the army of dishes disappeared (and I suspected washed and sitting in the dish rack to dry). Charlie had even combed through my closet and pulled out a sundress I'd always liked along with a moto jacket and boots, a combination I never would have come up with, but that looked exactly like the person I wanted to believe I was. It was like she knew the brainpower it would take to pick an outfit was more than I had in me.

"That's better," she said, giving a lock of my hair a tug. "Now you won't embarrass me out in public." She added a wink, and it didn't sting.

"Thanks, Mom."

"I thought we discussed this. I'm a *cool* mom. Call me Charlotte so no one knows how old I am."

I was never much of a hugger (happy to hug hello and goodbye and in extreme situations, but that was about it)—and Charlie had learned to restrain her golden retriever level of physical affection for my personal comfort—but at that moment, I stepped forward as if magnetized and squeezed her to me tightly. I could feel her surprise, but she didn't hesitate to reciprocate, wrapping her strong arms around me and adding enough pressure to crush my ribcage. It was perfect.

"Now, don't think you can get fresh with me without taking me out first," she whispered in my ear, and I laughed, remembering I was still in my towel. "I'm guessing you don't want to run into Adam, so I thought we'd go downtown. When was the last time you left Hyde Park, anyway?"

We took the #6 Jackson Park Express bus to a dark (and packed) wine bar downtown filled with wood paneling and moody candlelight, where Charlie finagled us a quiet table in the corner and ordered us a bottle of Nebbiolo. When it arrived, she thanked the server, dazzling him with her gorgeous smile to such an extent that I suspected we'd be getting some freebies from the kitchen or at least that she would be getting a phone number along with the check. She poured us each a generous glass and turned her mesmerizing, lamprey eel-like gaze to me.

"So. Tell me about it," she said. It felt like she was shining a spotlight on me.

"What, the breakup with Adam? I thought you'd be thrilled." Charlie remained mum. "There's nothing much to it. It had been coming for ages. Just took some time to convince him."

"Not the breakup with Adam, though I'll admit I'm happy to never have to listen to his rants about his contract law professor ever again. Tell me about Declan." Her tone was firm, her blue eyes unblinking. I should have known that she would intuit there was more to my relationship with Declan than I'd told her—she knew me too well. I had to give her something, or she would never get off the subject.

I sipped my wine, first swirling it around and sniffing it like I knew anything about varietals and terroir. Charlie resisted rolling her eyes, but I knew she wanted to. She was in patient mode, and it would take more than that to crack her. "We're not hanging out much anymore. It's not a big deal. We're both just busy," I said.

She didn't have to respond for me to hear the "bullshit" out loud. My eyes suddenly filled with tears. "Goddammit," I whispered, using my napkin to dab them away.

Charlie reached across the table and took my hand. Hers was warm and comforting, the pressure anchoring me to the moment. "Oh, I thought so. Have you been keeping this all to yourself, honey?" Her brow creased with concern, which caused my tears to spill over. I'd always said Charlie had a glass face—every thought and emotion she ever had was legible on it, which made her a hypnotic actor and a terrible liar—and the love written there was hard to take when I'd caused so much pain, made so many mistakes that anyone with a single brain cell could have seen coming.

"I made such a mess," I said, both an answer and not. "I fucked it all up. If I hadn't been such a coward, none of this would have happened."

"None of *what* wouldn't have happened? Drag me with you, Emma. Paint a picture with your words. It's what you're best at."

I took a shaky breath, wiping my tears with my cloth napkin. "I don't know. It's like we walked this line between friendship and something more for so long that I convinced myself I wasn't doing anything wrong. We could just go on like that. Or I was just too scared to break up with Adam and find out Declan didn't want me and be left with no one." I took a gulp of the wine, barely tasting it.

"Emma, you will never be alone," she said, her tone tinged with reproof.

"I know I'll always have you, I don't mean it like—"

"No, you dingus. I mean, you are gorgeous and brilliant and caring, and there's a market out there for that sort of thing. You've simply been trapped in an environment that seems to specialize in men who only know how to interact with mathematical theorems, not women."

"What are you talking about? I've always been terrible at dating."

"I'll grant that you're terrible at *picking* men who will appreciate you, but the Adams of the world are not the best option available to you."

"I've never understood why you hate Adam so much—" I didn't even know why I cared, when Adam wasn't the reason I felt like I'd been stomped on by hobnailed boots every day for the last two months.

"Emma, my heart," she said, putting her finger to my lips to halt my defense of Adam. "I never hated Adam. He's not a bad guy. But I watched you tiptoe around trying to keep him happy, and he didn't even notice or extend the courtesy to you. So yes, I thought he was a waste of your personal time. But that's not what we're talking about right now. We're talking about what happened between you and Declan."

"We..." I searched for the words that could convey what our kiss on my living room floor was. "Crossed the line, I guess. And then he found out about Adam, so he knew I was a coward *and* a liar. His ex left him for a friend last year, and that didn't help. So. No surprise I haven't heard from him."

Charlie nodded like it was all adding up. "Have you tried talking to him? Explained, apologized?"

"I did, I mean, I tried to right after it happened. But he was angry and didn't want to hear it. I don't blame him. We haven't talked since then." Two months without our walks, his smile, the way he'd look at me when he was listening intently. Two months in which every day without him in it felt more like a permanent separation, an irrevocable loss. I swallowed.

Charlie refilled my glass. I was surprised to realize it was empty already.

"Like I said, it was never a secret that Adam wasn't my favorite. But I know you cared about him, and you were with him for a long time. It's understandable that you'd be hesitant to break up with him —you've always gone for the guys who are good on paper, and you've never been a bed hopper." Charlie paused, like she was debating the best way to say what was coming next. "And Emma, it's not that I think you weren't yourself with any of your boyfriends—but I don't think they ever got the whole you. I think they may have gotten the whole pre-packaged Emma, the put-together, low-maintenance, high-achieving, and perfectly understanding Emma. But how much did they know of *Emma*, even when she's messy or unsure or louder than is considered polite in a public place? That's my favorite Emma— the one who isn't calibrating everything she says to please whoever she's talking to. But when I talked to you about him last fall—it sounded like you were that Emma with Declan." My throat tightened. I nodded. "So I think you've got to be brave and try to talk to him again. No matter what the outcome might be. By avoiding him now you're being just as cautious as you were by not breaking up with Adam, and either way you don't have Declan."

I huffed out a breath. "I hate it when you're right."

"I know," she said. "That's just a fringe benefit." I gave her a watery smile, which she returned. "Drink your wine, chickadee. We'll figure it out together."

MY WEEKEND with Charlie passed too quickly, as they always did. We slept cramped together in my bed with our heads turned toward one another so we could keep talking until one of us passed out like a childhood sleepover. She didn't bring up Declan again, seeming to know that if she did, my delicate grasp on functioning might crumble. Instead, she regaled me with horror stories from the run of *Comedy of Errors*, coaxing giggles out of me at her own expense.

"Did you ever hook up with that fight coordinator? You never told me," I said, kicking her shin so she'd stay awake long enough to tell me.

"Ugh, it was not worth the telling. You'd think someone who teaches choreography would have some sense of rhythm," Charlie said, and I laughed out loud for the first time in what felt like years. There was a hint of something I couldn't read in her tone, but she moved on so quickly I didn't get a chance to dig deeper.

She didn't insist we go out again, either, instead ordering in Thai and Indian food in rotation, claiming that spicy food would help with balancing my humours. I reminded her that she was an actor and not a medieval doctor, but she just told me to shut up and eat my vindaloo. We binge-watched bad reality TV while Charlie busied herself with cleaning the bathroom, organizing the kitchen cupboards, and dusting the baseboards.

"If you keep this up, my roommates will kick me out so you can move in instead," I told her, admiring the newly pristine shine of our bathtub.

"No they won't. I'm really loud in bed."

"Charlie, you're really loud *everywhere*," I corrected her.

"Hush, you," she said, swatting my butt with the bleach bottle she was holding. "Are you sure you'll be okay when I leave?" Charlie was slated to start rehearsals for *The Seagull* that week. She'd been cast as Nina and was aglow with excitement. I was thrilled for her, and gutted that she had to leave. A few days with her had brought some color back into my black and white world, and I realized I had missed it. When she left, I was afraid I'd lose the sense that it wasn't so hard just to breathe.

I leaned against the bathroom sink. "I'll be fine. I'll be busy with work. And now my bedroom no longer resembles a nuclear testing site, so thank you for that."

"I mean with everything else," she said. "What do you think you're going to do?"

I sucked in a breath. "Try to work up the nerve to get my heart stomped on again, I guess."

"No," Charlie said. "To ask for what you want." She said it so tenderly that I was afraid I might cry, so I punched her in the arm.

"Sure," she said. "But I'd recommend using your words instead."

CHARLIE'S ADVICE TO use my words and ask for what I want pinballed around my head in the days that followed, aided by the many texts she sent saying the same thing during her breaks from rehearsal. If I was going to attempt it with Declan, I needed to work my way up to it. I had a longer-standing source of tension to address, anyway.

This led to me pacing and fidgeting on my balcony on a brisk spring afternoon, waiting for my mom to pick up the phone. It hadn't been complete radio silence since Christmas, but our contact had been sparing and mostly filtered through my dad. He did his best to make it seem like this was totally normal through his obvious discomfort, but I didn't have the energy to tell him he could drop the act. For her part, my mom played the same strategy that worked for her in the rest of her life: remain as immovable as a boulder, and eventually, I'd have to come to her.

I'd planned this call when I knew she wouldn't be in class, have office hours, or be commuting back to Framingham. I even had a piece of paper with talking points crumpled in my hand, knowing how skilled she was at manipulating conversations to her advantage. This time, I was determined to have my say, no matter how she reacted. I forced myself to lengthen my exhales to signal my nervous system that I was not being chased by a lion, just calling my mom.

After what felt like a thousand rings, she picked up. "Hello Emma," she said, sounding unsurprised that I'd called. Considering I hadn't done it in months, and I used to call at least weekly, I had to bite my tongue. She wanted me cowed, and I wasn't going to give it to her.

"Hello Mom," I echoed her. "I thought it was time I gave you an update on my thesis and my future plans."

"I'm all ears," she said. I could picture her relaxing back into her leather office chair, waiting to hear that I'd completed my thesis on gender representation in the gothic novel and was applying to a PhD program at Swarthmore, ballooning student loan debt be damned.

"I changed my thesis topic. I'm turning in a draft to my adviser next week."

I heard her gasp through the line as clearly as if she were sitting beside me. "Emma. You didn't. This late in the year? That's suicide!"

I drummed my fingers on the balcony railing, gazing down at the pedestrians on the sidewalk below, wishing I was with them instead of having this conversation. Again. "Actually, Professor Houghton made it clear that if I continued with my original thesis topic, I was in danger of failing my thesis defense. So I took her advice and changed my focus to something that actually interests me." I felt a little breathless, like I'd been walking uphill and couldn't get quite enough breath in my lungs.

"What an asinine piece of advice. This is why I didn't want you to pick an adviser with all this Iowa Writers' Workshop impracticality. A thesis isn't something you write for pleasure—" she started, but I cut her off.

"Mom." She stopped talking. "I need you to listen to me right now." I tried to disguise the slight shake in my voice, realizing I may never have demanded her attention in quite this way before and that it scared me. I took her silence as assent and went on. "Writing something that *I'm* interested in, that *I* picked—it's been easier, and better, and I've been happier." I couldn't exactly claim to be *happy*, but that I had been *happier* in my work since the change was undeniable. "Maybe it's not as original or publishable, and it's not what you would write, but I can stand behind it and be proud of my work. That means a lot to me. I think I've been trying to make you proud for so long that I forgot I should be trying to live up to my own standards. Making this change was a step in the right direction." I took a breath, waiting for her reaction.

"What's your new topic?" She sounded like her jaw was clamped in a vise.

"Yearning in the Romantic Period." I braced myself for the impact.

"Jesus, Emma, could you pick anything to make you look more like a lovesick teenager and less like an academic?"

"Mom! Enough!" The uncharacteristic firmness of my voice stopped her. "This can't be the way things are with us anymore. I don't want to be your student, or your advisee, or your protégé. I want to be your daughter. And I deserve your support, regardless of whether you agree with all of my choices. And until that's something you think you can do, we won't be talking very much."

The silence between us stretched out, my heart in my throat and dying to backpedal while at the same time exhilarated by my own daring. I realized how long I'd been wanting to say those words but was too afraid to risk them. There was relief in letting them out, in knowing I couldn't take them back.

I took a shaky breath. "I know this is a lot to digest, so I'm going to say goodbye for now. When you've had some time to consider what I've said, let me know what you think."

"Emma, I'm worried about your choices. If you don't stick to the path now, it will be very hard to course correct in the future—" It felt like she was reaching through the phone to grab me and shake some sense into me.

"Goodbye, Mom," I cut in. "I love you." I hung up before she could work her usual magic, spinning a horror show future in which not fulfilling every one of her ambitions for me led to regretting my petty rebellion in a dingy studio apartment while living off government benefits. I had to protect my own nascent belief that there was more to life than avoiding disappointing others, it was too new and fragile to survive a Geraldine Brice scolding. It didn't feel like it right now, but I knew I wanted to try.

EIGHT

Two weeks passed without a word from my mom. I kept writing, turning to my new source material for comfort. I started trawling job sites looking for writing positions at universities, which would take me out of the teaching field but still allow me to write and stay in the academic world at least tangentially. I knew my mother would be aghast at the thought of her daughter as a content writer, and as the time without a response from her lengthened, that only became an added benefit. I applied sporadically, just to universities in Chicago, holding on to hope that I might be able to keep some sense of home.

My life, which had never been particularly varied or raucous, had gotten very quiet. It was lonely, but for the first time in a long time—maybe ever—I felt like I could hear myself think without the clamoring of others' expectations. I decided I would get to know myself and do it on purpose. I bought a blank notebook and used it as a journal, turning to it whenever my mind got too loud or crowded to focus on my work. It felt like I was unpacking my brain like a suitcase, pulling out random, unpaired socks and wondering where they came from in the first place, deciding whether they were worth mending.

I didn't know exactly what my life would look like moving forward, but at least I had a better idea of what I didn't want, and more confidence that I'd be able to figure it out. Declan visited me in my dreams most nights, and the relief of seeing him flooded my chest every time, only for me to wake up reaching for him alone in bed. Still, I was grateful for whatever fragment of him I could have, even if it was only somnambular. I hoped I could keep this piece of him, even if it was only my subconscious trying to reconcile his absence. I liked to think that when I dreamed of him, he was dreaming of me too.

My silent phone and empty social calendar meant I was able to complete my new thesis in record time. Instead of dragging every sentence out of my reluctant, waterlogged brain, connections and insight sprang out of my genuine joy in spending time with the material. Whether or not it was "well-trodden territory," as Houghton said, I was proud of it, and not because anyone else had decided it was worthy. I felt real pleasure in a job well done that I had chosen to take on myself.

The night I emailed the final draft to Houghton prior to my thesis defense, I got up from my desk, bleary eyed, and toddled to the kitchen for a celebratory glass of wine. I still had the bottle of Jameson that Declan brought me months ago, but I didn't like thinking about it being gone, so I left it untouched. Instead, I poured a healthy slosh of red wine into the one unchipped wineglass Anika, George, and I had between us and went to sit by the window in the living room.

It was past two o'clock in the morning, and my roommates were asleep. The only sounds came from the muffled traffic on the street below. It was a beautiful night, and the moon was bright in the sky. Charlie's words hadn't stopped rolling around my mind since her visit, that I needed to be brave, that I was my whole self with Declan. That was worth possibly embarrassing myself and breaking my heart even further, if there was a whisper of a chance that we might save what we'd once had.

I opened a new message in my email browser and stared at the screen, clutching my wineglass. *Hi* I typed, then immediately deleted it. Nothing I could say would be adequate or undo the mess I'd made. What was the point?

I leaned back in my chair and took a deep breath. Maybe I would never press send. Maybe I could write this just for myself, like the journal entries I'd been scribbling in my notebook.

I have no right to say it, but I miss you like a phantom limb. I dream you're there and wake up feeling pain where you're supposed to be.

I've thought a lot about how I treated you in the past few months, how I could apologize, how I could explain so you would forgive me and we could go back to the way things were before. I don't have any excuse for why I wasn't honest with you, and even if I did, it wouldn't matter. What matters is the impact, and in trying to keep you, I hurt you. I know you don't want to hear any more of my apologies, but I am more sorry for that than I could ever say.

The truth is that finding you felt like the most incredible miracle, and one that could have been taken away at any time. No one could possibly be so kind, so interesting, so gorgeous and unique and gifted. No one could make me feel like they held the key to me being my fullest self, not just Emma the student, Emma the quiet one. It was hard to believe sometimes that you were real. Reading that back, that's a lot of pressure to put on you. Another thing to be sorry for.

I know you said Adam doesn't matter, and you're right. But since you shared what happened with Maeve, I figure I owe you at least the broad strokes. I was with Adam for a little over two years. They were mostly inertia and me thinking there wasn't much more to a relationship than two people who liked spending time together and had similar plans for the future. He fit in a neat corner of my life, and nothing really changed from the day we met until the day we broke up. Once I met you, you bled into everything. My time, my thoughts, my routine, my plans. It felt messy and scary and wonderful, and I thought if I just had enough time to figure out if it was real, I would know what to do.

And then we kissed—or, to be fair, I kissed you. I knew it was real, more real than anything else I'd ever felt. And that even if being with you meant I would have to confront all the things in my life that didn't fit me anymore—not just Adam, but grad school and whatever professional future I'd been making my way toward for the past seven years—and

I knew that even if we fell apart, I wanted to do it anyway.

I could tell you that I knew I couldn't put off breaking up with Adam any longer the second you left my apartment that day, which is true. I could tell you the reasons I chickened out, why I decided I needed to delay a little longer, but it doesn't matter. Because the choices I made were selfish and guaranteed to hurt you again, and they did. After what happened with Maeve and Brian, I know how that must have felt. I hate that I broke your trust in the same way she did. You deserve so much better. Nothing she did, or I did, was because something was lacking in you, but lacking in us.

What you do need to know is I broke up with Adam three months ago, right after the last time I saw you. It was a relief and probably should have happened long before I even met you. But I put it off, and he was one more person who was collateral damage to my selfishness because I couldn't bring myself to make him angry with me. I wasn't kind enough to be the bad guy.

I've wanted to talk to you every day since then about things big and small. When George makes a malapropism that's actually better than the word he really means, or I've had another draining marathon meeting with Houghton. I changed my thesis topic, by the way, which is certifiably insane this late in the game. But like we talked about, I've spent enough time doing what I thought I was supposed to instead of what I wanted. I haven't had many people in my life who cared about that, but you were one of them, and it was a bigger gift than you realize.

The last time we spoke, you said I needed to figure out what I want. There's a lot I still don't know. I don't know what I'll do when I finish my master's, I don't know where I'll live. But wanting you and missing you remain the only things I'm sure of. I don't know if you feel the same way you did three months ago—it seems impossible that you could, after everything—but even so, I want you to know. My time with you is something I will always treasure, and if there's no more of it, I remain grateful for and undeserving of the time I did get.

If you think you might be able to forgive me, come here to me.

I stared at the words on the screen for a long time. They were only a fraction of what I wanted to say to Declan, a faint shadow of how I felt. All the same, I decided to make Charlie proud and pressed send.

. . .

I WOKE the next morning unsure if I'd actually written that email to Declan or dreamed it in a red wine haze, but a quick perusal of my outbox confirmed that I did, in fact, send it at 2:13 a.m. I swallowed a groan of reflexive embarrassment, closing the browser before I could reread it and castigate myself over each word. Even if what I'd written was cringe-inducingly vulnerable and too little too late, I still wanted Declan to know how I felt. Maybe this way was better; it gave him the option to ignore me if he didn't want to hear it. As much as I wanted him to respond, I would have to respect it if he didn't. A lack of response was still an answer, after all.

I knew that if I stayed in my apartment, I would continue to stew over my late-night wine-fueled choices and re-litigate the choice all over again. I pulled my hair into a ponytail, threw on jeans and a striped tee, and rifled through my dresser for a light layer. Declan still had my favorite UChicago hoodie —as far as I knew, anyway. Maybe he'd burned it. I wouldn't allow myself to stew any longer; I would go for a walk, go downtown, do *something*.

When I emerged from my room, I ran into

George in the hallway. "The Unabomber has left her bunker!" he cried with glee. I rolled my eyes but smiled. I remembered meeting him at the Pub after taking his number from an "ISO roommates" flyer on a campus corkboard, how bubbly and endearing he was right away. I'd assumed he would find me boring, but by the time we'd reached the bottom of our pints, he offered me the room. ("Our last roommate was an honest-to-god Druid," he'd whispered to me. "I just want to wake up in the morning without fearing I'm sharing a wall with someone who wants to turn me into a toad.")

"Good morning to you too, George," I replied.

"Off to enact your devious plans on humankind?" he asked, leaning against the hallway wall. George rarely stood up straight—instead, he flopped onto or propped his limbs on the nearest sturdy surface, holding his chin in his hand as if he were a boneless rag doll. On someone else, I would have found it an exhausting affectation, but on George, it made me feel ten pounds lighter.

"Just need to get away from my computer," I said. "I sent my revised thesis to Houghton last night, and I don't want to stare at my inbox until she replies." There was truth to that, if not the whole truth. I hadn't confided in George about the root cause of my months of hibernating misery and let him and Anika think it was because of my breakup with Adam.

He nodded knowingly. George was as playful as a gamboling puppy, but he was no dummy. His Master of International Policy had been no cakewalk, and he knew the anxiety of thesis defense well. "You should probably throw your phone in the lake as well," he advised.

"Noted," I said. George ushered me out our door with a flourish and an admonition to steer clear of campus.

My first thought was an aimless ramble around the neighborhood, but I found my feet leading me back to Viva Coffee, site of my first meeting with Declan. I didn't know how many more opportunities I would have for lazy afternoons there as graduation loomed mere weeks away. *I should have at least one more chocolate croissant*, I thought. Polishing off my thesis and sending that email must have jump-started my dormant nostalgia.

The bell jangled to announce my entrance the same as always, but no feeling of peace descended. The same scattered assemblage of tables and armchairs filled the space, a low murmur of chatter permeating the air, and somehow it felt like a place

I'd never been, just a scale replica of the coffee shop I'd spent all those days in over the past seven years. Defeated but with no better plan in mind, I approached the counter to order. To go.

Out of the corner of my eye, a tall figure rose from the armchair next to the fireplace. My heart juddered to a stop. I stared resolutely at the baked goods in the display case, telling myself it was not who I hoped and feared it was. I was just thinking of him because of the email and that first day next to the fireplace. I would not fall prey to my own imagination.

"Hi," I said to the woman at the counter. "Could I have—"

"—a medium latte and a chocolate croissant, please? I'll pay."

I turned slowly, unprepared to face Declan in person after all this time. "Hi," I said, at a loss for any other words in the English language.

"Hello, Emma," he said. We both struggled to make eye contact, as embarrassed to face each other as shy kids on the playground, but my heart ached to see him. His hands were pushed into his pockets, his chin tucked close to his chest.

"You don't have to pay for—" I started.

"I think we need to—" Declan said at the same

time. We both quieted as the scream of the milk being frothed for my latte filled the café, making further conversation pointless for the moment.

I stared down at my shoes, wishing I could evaporate on the spot. What had possessed me to send that email *now*—couldn't I have waited until after graduation, when I would already have moved away and wouldn't be risking this excruciating encounter? Inwardly, I berated myself for my absolute lack of self-preservational tendencies.

The barista flipped off the steam wand, and the high-pitched whistling stopped. We waited in awkward, painful silence until she brought my latte to the bar along with my croissant. "I've got it. Please," I said as Declan reached for his wallet. If he was about to shatter my heart, I couldn't stomach him paying for my coffee as well. Not that I'd be able to swallow it. He stepped back while I paid and tipped.

When I turned back to face him, I asked, "Should we go somewhere? Take a walk?" The thought of sitting down at Viva for this conversation, where everyone in the café would hear what we had to say whether they liked it or not, made me feel like I was breaking out in hives.

Declan nodded and went to gather his things

from his place next to the fire. I tried not to remember how he looked the day we met as he thawed out from the cold and wet, and the way his hair curled into little tendrils around his face. How something in me had thrilled to the sight of him, a gift and a surprise just for me, all its riches yet to come. It reminded me that all of it might be coming to an end.

Without discussing it, we both headed in the direction of the lake, away from campus. It was a beautiful day; the sky a bright blue with puffy, perfect clouds scudding across it. The wind tugged sweetly at our hair and clothes without gusting so hard that we'd have to shout to hear each other—if we ever gathered the courage to speak again.

When we could walk no further east without having to swim, I gestured to the grass next to the lakefront trail, looking out over Lake Michigan. We plopped down on the ground, no benches in sight. I tore off a piece of my croissant and popped it in my mouth to have something to do. My mouth was so dry I couldn't taste it.

"I got your email," Declan started.

I nodded, unsure how to react. My heart was racing and I thought I might vomit. I put the croissant down. "I figured," I said, resisting the urge to apologize.

"I've been meaning to call you—got an international phone plan worked out after all that," he said, sheepish. "But we never got around to exchanging numbers."

"No, we didn't." I wondered what he'd felt the urge to tell me after insisting I leave him alone until I knew what I wanted. My mind flipped through possibilities like a Rolodex—he'd found someone else, he was moving back to Ireland, he'd gotten over whatever it was he'd felt for me. That he still wanted me.

Whatever it was, I was going to hear it now. I wasn't sure I was ready.

"I wanted to say I'm sorry too." Declan held up a hand to forestall my protests. "It wasn't fair of me to bring the baggage from my last relationship into what was happening between us. We weren't together, and you aren't Maeve."

"I think the general sentiment of 'make up your mind' was pretty fair," I murmured.

He looked like he couldn't argue that point. "But I didn't give you very much time to do that. I told you how I felt for the first time, and then I fucked off the next day."

"I knew how I felt. And four months is plenty of

time, Declan." I thought of all the evenings I'd spent biting my tongue when Adam came over, thinking our relationship would just run out of gas and I could avoid being the bad guy. If only I'd said something, if only I'd been willing to tarnish Adam's image of me, Declan and I wouldn't be here now with grass tickling our ankles and ants making a play for my croissant.

"I don't think either of us was certain of what we were to each other all that time," he said. "Sometimes I was so sure we were on the same page, and other times, I couldn't get a read on you, so I figured I needed to wait for you to catch up. And our friendship had become so important to me I was afraid to risk it as well. I felt like you were all I really had here. It was a lot for me to ask certainty from you when I'd been struggling with it too."

"I wanted you to ask a lot of me," I said, sniffing back my omnipresent incipient tears. I still did want him to ask a lot of me, but saying it felt like one more selfish thing I should avoid. Whether this was our last conversation or there was a chance we might be able to repair what I'd broken, he deserved more thoughtfulness from me than he'd gotten the first time around.

"I'd come to rely on you too much. I'd structured

my whole life in Chicago around you and never considered whether that was something you wanted or whether it was becoming too much. And knowing you as I thought I did, I wondered if you even would have told me if it wasn't. I knew you wouldn't want to disappoint me."

I caught it, his doubt—*as I thought I did*. This would be our last conversation. "I loved it," I said. "The time I spent with you was when I was happiest." *I'd do it again*, I thought.

We both continued to stare at the grass, afraid to face each other. I'd already laid myself bare in my email, so why was he hesitating? He had to be about to let me down gently. It was what I deserved.

"I want to believe I *know* you," he said, so softly it was almost a whisper. "When I thought that maybe I'd never known you, that I'd gotten you wrong, I thought I was going crazy. If, again, I couldn't tell what was right in front of me."

I wanted to tell him that he did know me, maybe better than anyone, and never to question that. "Like I told you about Maeve—you didn't know about Brian because she didn't want you to know. I didn't want Adam to know about you or you to know about Adam because I didn't want to lose you. So I split myself in two—like I had a real life and a pretend one. The one with you was real to me," I said. "I know how selfish that was. I don't want you to doubt what you felt." Using the past tense was taking it out of me, word by word.

"It killed me to walk away from you, but I had to do it. I needed to be the one *someone* chose." My heart broke at him thinking he could ever be my second choice. *You know when there's a first and second place,* he'd said. "I was angry, and I had reason to be, but I thought with enough time I'd be able to sort it out. Either how to forget you or figure out what I was doing wrong so this wouldn't keep happening to me. But the longer I went without seeing you, the more real it all felt to me. There was no forgetting that. I wanted you to have what you want, even if that wasn't me. And when I didn't hear from you, I figured that was your answer."

I shook my head. "I didn't think you'd want to hear from me. I thought you deserved your space." I didn't say how I'd imagined him in all the places I'd come to think of as ours—by the fire at Viva, at a rickety table in the Pub, perusing the shelves at 57th Street Books. How the thought of him seeing me in any of those places and choosing to walk away might kill me, so I'd steered clear of them instead.

"But I still wanted to believe that I was wrong or

that you just needed more time. I went to Viva Coffee almost every day, the Reg every other day, always hoping you'd be there. When you weren't, I..." he trailed off. "I tried to move on."

I swallowed around the lump in my throat. There it was. "I get it, I do." He'd found someone who didn't take him for granted. I hoped to god it wasn't Daphne. "I *was* avoiding you. But it wasn't because that was my answer. I didn't think I could stand seeing you and not touching you or you walking away from me again," I said, my voice wobbling. "And you were right—I'd spent so much time trying to do what I was *supposed* to be doing, pleasing other people, that I didn't want you to think that choosing you was just—a reaction, or that I thought it was just the right thing to do after everything that happened." I took a deep breath. "It took a while for me to realize it while we were apart, but I've only ever really been myself with a few people. The rest of the time, I've been sharing just the pieces that fit with who I think they want me to be, and it got comfortable because I knew what to do. I knew what role I played what was expected of me. If I ever got to be with you for real... I knew I'd have to change my whole life, that I couldn't go back to being the person I knew how to be, and that scared me." I wiped away a tear with an impatient hand. "I said all that in my email, but I know that I have to change my life with or without you. But I'd rather it be with you."

I steeled myself to actually look at Declan, to face whatever he had to say even though I was afraid that he would finally turn me down—all his explanations about our time apart felt too much like the prelude to letting me down easy. The compassion in his eyes was painful. I looked away, but he reached over to take hold of my chin and force me to meet his eyes.

"Emma," he said. "You terrify me. But I said it before and I still mean it. I'll take you any way I can have you."

With an audible sob of relief I threw myself onto him, crying snottily into his shoulder while his long arms folded around me, gentle as gossamer against my shoulder blades while somehow still adding enough pressure to anchor me. My body seemed to release all its accumulated tension and misery in the comfort of being able to touch Declan again, to feel his hair tickling my face in the breeze and to smell his particular unnamable scent. I dug my fingers into his shoulders, seeking reassurance that he was real, that this was real, while he rested his chin on the crown of my head. I felt his own shuddery breaths against my chest and realized he was crying too, so I nestled closer to provide him the same sense of safety he was giving me. It was completely unsexy and profoundly joyful.

We stayed like that, clutching each other next to the lake like we were afraid the other might blow away, for what could have been hours. Not much was said in words, but instead by touch. *I'm sorry* by tucking a strand of hair behind an ear. *I missed you* with a thumb running across the back of a hand. *I never want to be without you again* with each synchronized breath, each brush of lips against skin. You couldn't call what we were doing kissing—more inhaling each other, searching for tactile reassurance. It was our most honest conversation to date.

When even the late spring warmth of May and the bliss of our reunion couldn't protect us from the chill of the wind off the lake, we started walking west again. I was going back to Declan's apartment for the first time since that day in January, when his hand slid to my waist and my brain short-circuited.

"I always wondered why you never came over," he said, twining his long fingers around my hand. It was strange to realize that this was the first time we'd ever held hands, how oddly intimate it felt, and how right.

"I couldn't handle the temptation." Thinking back to the only times Declan and I had been truly alone together, I said, "Clearly."

He squeezed my hand, the memory alive between us. "Tell me what you've been up to. You said you changed your thesis topic?"

I nodded, and we spent the duration of the walk filling in the gaps of the past three months. My update was elliptical, full of empty spaces where I still had decisions to make. Declan beamed as I told him about my new thesis.

"Only you would have the absolute gall to write about yearning in the Romantic period and call it scholarship," he grinned. "I adore you."

"Please, you sound like my mother. I was really feeling connected to the subject matter," I deadpanned, elbowing him. "All that lyrical moping."

"Darling, I've felt connected to that subject matter since the moment you waved me over to that fire, like a nymph out of myth. I was lost."

I colored, remembering how he'd struck me as a fantastical creature that day, beautiful and mysterious, arriving fortuitously in a perfect storm. Maybe that's what falling in love is—ridiculous and hard to believe but something you feel in the part of you that's still primal, that needs mythology to understand a dark and frightening world.

We arrived at his building, the courtyard bursting with green in a way it hadn't back in January. He held tight to my hand as we climbed the stairs, both of us nervous and quiet once again.

Declan unlocked the door to his apartment and let me walk in first. As he closed the door behind us he smiled at me, running an anxious hand through his hair as he watched me take in the space. I wondered if he was also thinking of that moment on his couch, when we might have crossed the line if we'd dared. "I'd have tidied up if I knew you were coming."

"I don't think either of us knew what was coming today," I said, taking a tentative step toward him. He stepped forward to close the gap between us, the air crackling with what was about to happen.

"Wait," I said, though I had to hold my own hand behind my back to keep myself from reaching for him. I had to know if he'd truly forgiven me or if he was just lonely. "We need to talk about this."

"I thought that was what we had been doing," he said, aiming for jocular but missing the mark. It was killing me to think he would hide the pain I'd caused him from me out of deference for my feelings.

"Declan," I said, placing a hand on his chest to keep him at bay, his heart beating faster than climbing the stairs could justify. He stilled, though I couldn't tear my eyes from his chest right at my eyeline. "I hurt you," I said. "I don't see how you can trust me again."

He inhaled, the breath full of things he could say, then nodded. "Yes," he said, and though I knew the truth of it down to my bones, it stung. "But that happens. We are going to hurt each other, many times if we're lucky. It's the putting back together that matters, Emma. You're worth the pain of it."

The air left my lungs in a shaky, tearful sigh of relief.

"Come here to me," he whispered. I walked into his arms. My shelter, my home. I felt his deep inhale with my ear pressed into his chest, my arms wrapped so tightly around him I was surprised he could breathe at all. Declan pressed his lips to the crown of my head and I felt his gratitude down to my toes. "I didn't bring you here to sleep with you," he said. "Sex isn't an apology and it isn't something you owe me. If you want to be just friends, I'd rather that than nothing."

I laughed against his chest. "You're a wonderful

man, Declan, but our friendship was killing me." I looked up at him. "I want it all."

He let out an incredulous breath of relief and walked me backward toward the door to his bedroom, step by agonizing, exquisite step.

ME, Declan, and a bed all in the same place, with nothing left to keep us from each other. I reached for him, my hands shaking with the disbelief that this was finally happening. Declan bent down, cupping my face between his hands like water, his lips a hair's breadth away from mine. I swallowed his shallow exhales, exhilarated to realize he wanted this every bit as badly as I did. I closed the distance between us, our kiss sealing us together in an electrifying moment.

It started gently, a test and a taste of a kiss. We were tentative with the shared fear that this moment might dissolve like smoke, a mirage we'd imagined because we wanted it so desperately, shy with each other after so long apart, but we quickly lost control. I drew his lower lip between my teeth in a teasing bite, challenging him, and he groaned, sweeping his tongue into my mouth. My hands snaked up his back, clasping behind his neck in my desire to pull him closer, down within my reach. I wanted to climb him like a goddamn redwood. With a noise of impatience, Declan reached down and lifted me against him, chest to chest, my feet leaving the floor with an ease I wouldn't have believed. I twined my legs around his hips, crossing my ankles behind his back and grinding against him, tugging on his hair and leaving absolutely no doubt where I wanted this to go.

Declan walked us up against the bedroom door (though it was more like a stagger—we were already drunk on each other), closing it with our weight, his hands traversing my ribcage as attentively and reverently as if they were reading braille. My head dropped back against the door like a puppet with its strings cut, breaking the contact of our lips but exposing my throat to him. Declan took the invitation and buried his face in my neck, his breath feather light against my clavicle as I felt him fighting for control. "Okay, okay," he said, his voice shaking, "we have to slow down..."

"No we don't," I said, leaning forward to tease his earlobe with my teeth. His skin was honey, it was wine. I wanted to swallow him whole.

Declan laughed low in his throat. "You're used to getting what you want, aren't you?"

"Not when it comes to you," I answered honestly.

He stilled. His eyes met mine, searching and deadly serious. "Is this what you want?" He'd asked before, but it didn't surprise me that he would ask again. Declan would always want more than acquiescence or ambivalent consent. He wanted enthusiastic, wholehearted desire, and he wouldn't take his own pleasure without it.

With anyone else, I would have joked that it was obvious what I wanted writhing against his cock like I was a cat in heat. But there was something so rare and precious in how Declan had always wanted to know my truth and taken me at my word. I didn't want to diminish that now, in this fragile moment.

"I have always wanted you, Declan." Saying it out loud made me feel more naked and vulnerable than everything we'd done up until this moment, everything I could imagine doing with him.

I watched the words root in him, washing away his fear and hesitation. Never breaking eye contact with me, he carried me over to the bed, laying me down with infinite gentleness. The intimacy of it took my breath away. Declan knelt over me on the mattress, caging me between his legs and began slowly kissing his way down my neck, leaving a trail of heightened awareness where his lips, teeth, and tongue had been. While his mouth was busy, his hand slipped under the hem of my shirt, his broad palm spanning my stomach and feeling my every shaky breath. When his fingertips reached my breast, teasing just inside my bra, I felt like I'd been hit by tranquilizer dart to the point that I stopped breathing.

"Emma?" He paused, pulling back to read my face. Impatient with any delay, I grabbed his ass and pulled him flush against me, feeling both of our pulses pounding with need. I felt him grinning into my neck. "We've always had to steal our time, Emma." He brought one and then both hands over my head, a loose clasp on my wrists I could easily escape. "I intend to take my time with you now."

Suddenly near tears, I nodded. Declan, being Declan, noticed and released one wrist, tenderly stroking my cheekbone with his thumb, then kissing a tear that escaped down my temple. We locked eyes and felt in the moment that what we were about to do was going to matter to both of us in a way we'd never experienced before, and might never experience again.

I hooked my leg behind his lower back, pulling him close enough to feel his weight on me. I dragged my free hand down his chest, thrilling to the path of goose bumps I left along his skin, all the way to the trail of hair leading to his groin. Declan nipped at my mouth and evaded my searching grasp. "We have time," he whispered, sliding down my body to kneel at the edge of his bed, gently unbuttoning and then sliding my jeans off. Even that friction was a tantalizing form of torture. Missing contact with his skin, I tried to sit up and pull him back into bed with me, within comfortable mauling range, but he braced his forearm across my hips to hold me down, planting delicate kisses up my inner thigh that had me squirming at his breath so close to my core. With the hand that wasn't holding me still, he grabbed my ass in a greedy handful and toyed at the hem of my underwear with his thumb. My brain, as well as the rest of me, was quickly liquefying.

When it became clear that I no longer had command of my muscles, Declan kissed his way up the seam of my lips through my dampening underwear, ending with a torturous nibble at my clit. I almost screamed at the intensity of the sensation, clutching the sheets in my frustration. "Declan, are you trying to kill me?" He chuckled. "Keep in mind if you make a joke about 'le petit mort' that turnabout is fair play," I panted.

Declan nodded, hooking his thumbs in the elastic of my underwear. "Poor darling," he murmured, pulling them off and breathing into me. "Do you think you can wait a little longer for me?" He swiped his tongue up to my clit, the pressure firm, simultaneously tapping at my entrance with his middle finger between circular licks of his tongue.

I moaned, giving up on the sheets and grasping my own breast. Declan jerked forward, watching as he worked. "I cannot believe you are real," he whispered. "Tell me what you like."

I wasn't sure I knew my own name, let alone enough English to string together a coherent sentence. "More." That was all I could manage.

At that, he slid his index finger inside me, working in rhythm with his tongue, driving and curling upwards, then added his middle finger. I wrapped my thighs so tightly around his head that I worried I would hurt him, clenching around his fingers as I felt the pressure building. "Declan, I need you," I said.

"You have me," he replied, and I came harder than I'd ever come in my life.

He stayed with me through the cresting waves of my orgasm, which went on longer than I would have thought possible, gradually diminishing pressure and slowing his movements as my pussy spasmed around his fingers. My clit sent spirals of pleasure down all my nerve endings. As I finally came down, Declan leaned back, and I managed to reach for him, landing clumsy pets on his hair and face, which made him laugh. I felt boneless, spent, and somehow more alive than I thought possible.

"Jesus," I panted.

"I've always admired that about you, you know." He smiled. "So eloquent, such a nuanced vocabulary." The corner of that talented mouth tilted up, and just like that, I was ready to go again.

I sat up, fisting my hands in the neck of his shirt. "How is it that you are still completely clothed?" I asked, burying my face in his neck. I wanted to bottle the way his skin smelled.

"I suppose my hands were busy," he murmured, walking his fingertips down each vertebra of my spine. With my grip on the fabric, I pulled us both to stand and began walking him backward toward the armchair in the corner of his room, pulling his shirt over his head as I pressed him down into a seat. I straddled his thighs, leaning back to take in the view. My gaze must have been ravenous, taking in every square inch of skin that had been denied to me when he was just my friend. I hummed with appreciation as my fingernails traced his pecs and down his abdomen.

"Just your standard-issue scrawny Irish boy," he said, clearly uncomfortable with being scrutinized so closely.

"Stop," I said, pressing my hand to his heart. I could feel the frantic beat of it under my hand. "You're perfect." Once again, I cursed whatever made men believe they needed to be mountains of sculpted muscle to attract women. I had never found the appeal in the gym rat type, but I'd always been a sucker for lean and bookish. Delicate but strong with intellect and attention sparking in their eyes. "And as far as nudity goes, I believe I'm still at a disadvantage here."

I reached between us for his fly without breaking eye contact. Declan huffed a shaky breath but let me do it, eyes on my mouth. I had to climb off his lap to slide his jeans down, and as I did, his erection sprung free, tenting his boxers. I remembered its pulse against my core and shivered. I peeled off my shirt and dropped my bra behind me so he could see all of me. Then I spread his knees wide and knelt between them, scraping my teeth down his abs. Declan gripped the arms of the chair. "Emma, you don't have to—"

I wrapped my hand around the base of his cock through his boxers, feeling its satisfying girth twitch in my palm. "Have to? I've been dying for a taste." As long as no one was trying to force my head down his shaft and gag me in the process, I'd always liked giving head—the heady power of reducing a rational human to a wordless puddle of pleasure with nothing but my mouth. "Come on, lift that scrawny Irish ass so I can get these off."

Declan obliged, and there he was, finally, glistening at the head. I leaned forward for an experimental lick of the tip, salty with pre-cum. "Oh Christ," Declan muttered.

"So eloquent," I teased, "such a nuanced vocabulary," then drew him as far into the back of my throat as I could. Declan swore. I drew back on a long suck, wrapping my fist around his base and pumping slowly as I bobbed up and down, circling the head with the tip of my tongue. The noises coming out of him were making me so wet I had to squeeze my thighs together, chasing the pressure I needed.

Suddenly, Declan grasped me by my shoulders and pulled me off him with a loud pop. "Jesus Christ, darling, please stop. I'll never last."

I was tempted to argue, enjoying the taste of him as well as wanting to torture him a little longer, but I wanted him inside me so badly that I decided we could experiment with leisurely oral sex at a later date. "Condom?" I asked, leaning back on my heels and trying not to squirm with impatience. Declan stood and stumbled over to his nightstand, scrabbling in the drawer, and was already on his way back to me as he tore open the foil. I was so done with every moment that we weren't touching.

Declan's hands were shaking with anticipation, fumbling a bit as he rolled the condom onto his shaft, so I pushed him back into the armchair and added my grip into the mix. I straddled him once again, my hands on his shoulders as he nudged against my entrance, hissing breath between his teeth. I held the base of his cock with one hand as I slowly worked him inside me with little shifts forward and back, easing his length deeper in delicious rocking motions. I grew slicker with each teasing thrust, my body dying to feel every inch of him. Especially at this angle, I couldn't take him all at once, even though I was wet as a Slip 'n Slide, but I loved it— getting to see all of him, him seeing all of me, that he was still close enough to lean in and kiss.

He still wasn't fully seated inside me when he reached up to cup the side of my face, wrapping his other hand in a gentle grip on my hip, helping to rock me gently further down. I pressed my forehead to his, our open mouths touching, but we were too far gone for kissing. I breathed the heat of his breath and gave mine back, sharing whimpers and groans until he bottomed out. I was so far gone I felt drugged.

For a moment, neither of us moved, and still our nerves jumped and danced. I was so exquisitely full I could have come again with a single thrust, delicately balanced on the knife edge of my second orgasm. But then I tilted my pelvis back and around, feeling his hardness against all my soft walls, and Declan's hands clawed my back, his breath suddenly harsh. He began to roll his hips up, matching the cadence of my thrusts, and the coil of it connected with my G-spot and allowed me to grind my clit against him simultaneously. I almost lost control of my rhythm immediately, the pleasure crowding in from all directions too much for me to handle, but Declan bit my collarbone and whispered "Please don't let this end." I wasn't sure how long I could withstand the intensity, but I nodded, feeling sweat begin to bead between my breasts. Declan leaned forward to lick it. "I love every inch of your body," he said. I rewarded him with a tight squeeze that made him suck in his breath. "Wicked woman," he chided, half laughing, increasing the speed of his thrusts, holding me steady with an arm wrapped around my hips as he fucked up into me.

I would have teased him back, but I was swept out further and further beyond words with each punch of his hips. My head tipped back. "Declan, I can't—"

"Yes, love," he said. "Show me."

My orgasm felt like a detonation, spreading warmth and an exquisite ache through every molecule of my body. Declan finally released his relentless control and tipped over the edge with me, his fingers digging into my ass in a way I knew would bruise, a love bite, an ache that would bring a blush to my cheeks each time I brushed against it.

We came down together, our breath mingling in the little space between us. Declan pulled me to his chest, leaning back in the armchair, skin against skin sending perfect chemicals showering through my brain. The aftershocks of our climax rioted through us both, shivery and beautiful. He kissed my temple. "Thank you, darling," he whispered.

"I will never get tired of 'darling' in your accent," I said, my voice gravelly after my earlier screams.

He smiled, a world of tenderness reflected in it. "Then I regret to inform you, darling, that I need to dispose of this condom."

"No," I said, clinging to him. Now that I knew how my skin felt next to his skin, I was uninterested in any activity that didn't involve us touching.

"Oh, all right then." He laughed, his hand stroking up and down my back. "For at least another thirty seconds."

"I'll take it," I whispered, and once again, I was near tears. When he did pull away from me and I had to give him up, I immediately regretted the loss of him inside me.

"Emma," he said, grasping my hand, "it's not the last time. I promise." His voice held joy and awe and reassurance. I nodded, curling my knees into my chest now that I didn't have his body heat to warm me.

When he returned from the bathroom, he bent over to scoop me up in his arms. "Come to bed," he said. "Stretch out. Let me look at you." He laid me down and crawled in next to me, tracing a finger along the scar I got from my appendectomy. "There's so much still to learn about you." I felt it as he meant it: a promise. He pressed a light kiss on the scar, which made me squirm. "That's right," he murmured, an evil glint in his eye. "She's ticklish."

"Don't you dare," I warned him.

"Wouldn't dream of it. Don't want to scare you

away." He rested his head in one hand, propped up on his elbow.

The thought made my throat tighten. "I think we're past that now," I said.

"Since we broke up before we were ever together?"

I winced at the accuracy of it. "That may be true, but that also means now we can have the honeymoon period. And appreciate it all the more since it almost didn't happen."

Declan nodded, but I could see he was holding something back. I propped myself up on my elbows, zeroing in on his conflicted face. "Declan, what?"

He licked his lips, looking like he was measuring how to say whatever came next. I held my breath. "I applied for a transfer to UCD in the fall," he said, his gaze still on my appendectomy scar.

I felt like I was in an elevator that had just plunged thirty floors. I wished I could be angry, that he would take it back, but I knew exactly why he'd done it. I understood it. "Oh," I said, my voice small and thin as a child's.

He leaned over and kissed my temple. "I think I can still get out of it," he whispered, forcing hope into his tone. "I don't think I've missed the deadline to withdraw without penalty." I didn't know if he would deliberately lie to me if that wasn't the case, but he sounded far from sure.

"You can't afford to withdraw if you missed it, Declan," I said. Let alone the expenses associated with moving across the Atlantic *again*. I felt sick, stuttering over my inhales.

"Shhh," he said, melding himself to my side and pulling me close. "I'll figure it out. Please don't worry, darling. I just didn't want to keep it from you."

I clutched his shoulders and inhaled deep lung-fuls of his scent, whatever unnamable pheromone of his that had ruined me for anyone else. I would suck the marrow of every second of our time together; take nothing for granted even as my mind spiraled into a future with an ocean between us. I'd set us on this course with my own secrets and indecision. I couldn't blame him if it ended in our separation.

He kissed his way from my clavicle to my navel, the softness of his lips almost too much to bear. My body was a riot of sensation, arousal and heartbreak and shock. Our second time was slower, reverent, even a little fearful—a clear attempt to stop time, to deny the crushing reality of finances and obligations. For a few minutes, at least, we held the future at bay.

Afterward, Declan pulled me into his embrace,

both of us on our sides, face-to-face in the bed. I wrapped my leg around his, twining him closer to me, placing a hand on his chest while he wound his arm around my waist. Just feeling his skin on mine sent joy and belonging sparking through my veins, a joy that was complicated by the looming possibility of losing each other again. We breathed in each other's shallow exhales like ex-smokers trying to catch a whiff of someone else's passing cigarette.

"So we finally made it here," he said, planting a kiss on my forehead. "I was afraid we wouldn't."

I didn't know how to reply with all the unknowns crowding my mind, and he seemed to know it.

"Emma, I promise you I won't let this be the end," he said.

It was enough to loosen the band tightening around my lungs and allow sleep to pull me under, drugged by Declan's smell and the treacherous hope that somehow everything would be all right.

NINE

Morning came and I awoke to Declan's head next to mine on the pillow, his hair a wild cloud behind him. It wasn't a dream: he really was mine at last—at least for now. I was enthralled by his face in sleep, the soft blue undertone of his eyelids, the rise and fall of his chest with his breath. I couldn't resist nuzzling my way closer to him, pressing every inch of skin I could against his. Declan's eyes opened, a little bleary but infinitely dear. "There she is," he said.

"Another squirrel for you to feed."

His early morning laugh was more of a rumble in his chest. I loved the vibration of it against my skin. "Don't knock it. Without you around, they've been my only social outlet."

"If that's true, you've been dodging women all

over campus. Daphne Vega wants to lick you like an ice cream cone."

Declan's eyes widened cartoonishly. "Daphne from my building? The first floor?"

It was my turn to laugh. "You are oblivious, and I love that about you." I bit the inside of my cheek, worried that I'd revealed too much. I fought the urge to burrow under the covers and avoid his eyes.

"I'm not that oblivious," he whispered. I felt a mysterious pressure against my hip and didn't get out of bed for another hour.

By the time I did, the sun was high in the sky, and my phone battery was dead. "Shit, I have a review session with my undergrad Poe students," I said, pulling my shirt over my head, the static making a fright wig of my hair. I ran my fingers through it like a comb in a futile attempt to look like I hadn't had more orgasms in the past 24 hours than in the previous six months, but Declan just smiled and handed me a hair tie. One of the perks of loving a man with long hair.

"I've always liked your hair pulled back," he said dreamily.

"Why, can't take a little competition?" I asked, gesturing to his much more impressive bedhead.

"No, you wagon. Because I like to see your pretty

face. Now be on your way or you'll be late." I leaned in for a kiss goodbye, a long lip lock to breathe each other in. "But don't forget your jacket."

"I wasn't wearing one—" I started to say but cut myself off when he gestured to the bed. I thought he'd been pulling out his own clothes to dress for the day, but there was the hoodie I'd loaned to Declan to dry his hair the day we met, clean and meticulously folded. "You kept it," I said.

"Like I said, fits a dream."

My smile went a little wobbly at the idea of losing any of the time I had left with him. "What will you do while I'm gone?"

As ever, my attempts to hide my feelings from him were futile. "I have some calls to make. My adviser, admissions at UCD."

"You don't have to do that. If that's not what you want." I swallowed past a golfball-sized lump in my throat.

"You're what I want, Emma," he said as if stating he wouldn't mind having air to breathe.

"You have me," I answered honestly. "Even if you go. We could do long distance. Or maybe I could get a visa and go with you." I had less anchoring me to Chicago than he did at this point. "We have options. I don't want to dictate your life for you."

Declan crossed the room and wrapped me in a viselike hug. "We're two very resourceful people, darling. We'll sort it. Go find your undergrads, and I'll start working on my end."

I nodded against his shoulder and took a deep breath. Maybe that was another thing love did: helped you access the strength you needed to do the right thing for the person you love, even when you were certain you didn't have it in you.

As I speed-walked my way to campus, it was hard to believe these were the same streets I'd walked every day for the past three months. I'd felt nothing but achy sadness and regret so unrelentingly that it was a sweet surprise to feel anything else, even if my uncontainable joy warred with the unknowns of the future. At the moment, it felt like even the wind was on my side, pushing at my back to get me to my review session on time. Each crosswalk signal turned to walk as I approached, seemingly as gleeful as I was that Declan and I had finally come together. I found myself moved by all of it, as if Hyde Park itself were offering us a benediction.

Or at least that was how I felt until I rounded the corner outside the English department's building on the quad and recognized a very familiar silhouette. There was Adam, not neat and tidy as usual but tousle-haired and glasses askew, walking hand in hand with a petite Asian woman. He was beaming at her in a way I could never have imagined him looking at me.

I stopped in my tracks, wondering if it would be childish to hide from him or kind to give him the opportunity not to acknowledge me. It was a moot point since we were out in the open on the quad with nowhere to hide, but the impulse was there. I felt naked, like the last day and night with Declan in all its detail were tattooed on my face.

Adam looked up and clocked me where I stood, taken aback for only a moment. He kept walking toward me, holding tight to the woman's hand, and I plastered something approximating a smile on my face, unsure if reprisal or awkward pleasantries would come next.

"Adam," I said, "hi." I had the insane thought that I should offer him my hand to shake but thankfully suppressed the impulse.

"Hey, Emma," he said. His companion whipped her head to take me in and then looked straight back at Adam while plastering herself to his side. So we were all great with subtlety. "Nice to run into you."

"Yeah, you too," I echoed, at a loss for the etiquette for this situation. When I hadn't been thinking of Declan over the past few months, I'd been imagining Adam throwing flaming darts at my picture, so his amicable tone threw me off.

"Sorry, this is Tiffany." He gestured toward his companion. "My... girlfriend," he added, side-eyeing me for my reaction. He looked like he was afraid I might start yelling.

"Wow!" I cried, startling myself and them. I was so surprised at my genuine happiness in hearing that Adam had moved on that I was dangerously near tears. Clearly my body, so used to containing only moderately sized emotions, had overheated and was now spewing giant feelings at any and all targets. "That's so great! I'm so happy for you!"

Tiffany looked dubious, and Adam seemed somewhat alarmed by the sheen of tears in my eyes, but my smile was real. "Yeah, we met at a mixer the law school set up with the business school. We got into an argument about the case against Microsoft acquiring Activision, and that was it." He glowed. She glowed. I glowed back at them. I couldn't imagine a more perfect meet cute for Adam. I could picture him telling this story at parties for decades with the same gleam of satisfaction in his eyes, Tiffany's arm coiled around his waist while she looked up at him with pride.

"I love that," I said. "I'm so glad you went to one of those mixers. You were always meaning to."

He ducked his head, remembering the nights he'd end up at my apartment, too tired to expend any social energy beyond maintaining this one relationship outside of law school. "Yeah, I'm glad too. Where are you off to?"

"Oh, I'm late for a review session with my undergrads," I said, suddenly aware of the time, but my feet were glued to the pavement.

"That's right, you always help your students study for the final," he said with true warmth in his voice. At that moment, I knew I couldn't regret my time with Adam. We may not have been right for each other in the larger sense, but he was a kind person, and I was grateful to get a glimpse of him happy. It was a gift I didn't deserve, knowing that letting him go hadn't been the right thing for me alone, but it also freed him to find greater happiness than I'd been able to give him.

"I do have to go," I said, "but Tiffany, it was so great to meet you!" She nodded warily, unsure what to make of this effusive ex she'd been blindsided with, but I meant it. I saw Adam squeeze her hand in reassurance, and I felt as comforted as if it had been my hand. "Adam, if I don't see you before then, go kill it at Kirkland & Ellis. You worked so hard for it."

He nodded. "Thank you. What about you, what are you up to next?"

I smiled even bigger. "I have absolutely no idea."

He seemed startled, either by the statement itself or the ebullient smile that accompanied it, but he waved goodbye as I rushed off to meet my Poe undergrads.

As I sprinted the rest of the way across the quad, I sent a fervent wish into the universe that Adam and Tiffany—or Adam and whoever, the whole world while I was at it—would be outrageously happy and that none of us ever stayed in a relationship that resembled treading water. I wished for all of us to float.

THE DAY of my thesis defense arrived a week later. It was a lucky thing that I'd already finished my final draft since Declan had been a near-constant presence in my apartment since our reunion, and I was at his apartment every night that he wasn't at mine. I managed to be late to almost every class and commitment on my calendar when I was typically the first to arrive, unable to tear myself away from his sweet whispers and strong hands after missing them for so long. I startled my professors and students with my breathless, windswept appearance, but I had never felt more beautiful or more alive.

I had emptied the contents of my dresser and my closet looking for the most professorial ensemble I could assemble for my thesis defense. Skirts and button-downs and cardigans designed to look like blazers were strewn across the floor, but I couldn't settle on anything, my nerves tuned to a high pitch. This was the first and only thing in my life to drag my attention away from Declan in a week.

Declan watched my indecision with amusement from my bed. I knew if I turned around, I'd be distracted by the vision of his bare chest, the blankets tangled around his waist, and I'd risk being late for an entirely different reason.

"You wouldn't happen to be displacing your anxiety about defending your thesis into a sartorial crisis, would you, darling?" he asked.

"If we've reached sartorial crisis level, I may need to cancel the entire thing and go shop," I muttered, thinking wishfully.

"Here," Declan said, and I heard his feet hit the floor as well as the sound of friction against fabric as he knotted the top sheet around his hips. He grabbed a pencil skirt, short-sleeved white button-down blouse, and tailored blazer out of the pile at my feet. "This screams 'thesis defense.'" He laid the items out on my newly vacated bed.

It was perfect, but acknowledging that would mean I'd have to actually get dressed and go do the damn thing. "Does it actually scream? I think that might give me an edge." I looked him up and down. "I like your outfit better," I said, gesturing to the sheet. "Very Socratically inspired."

"You cheeky thing," he said, planting a kiss on my forehead. "You're trying to distract me, and I won't be the downfall of your thesis defense." His tone was teasing, but I knew he hadn't missed my real fear that I was about to fail in a way I never had.

"I suppose my thesis itself could be its own downfall," I murmured, turning my face into his chest, taking in soothing lungfuls of his smell with each breath. "It may not need any help."

"You said you were proud of it, no matter what happens today," he reminded me. "Nothing can take that away from you."

"You know, it's unfair to use something I said in bed against me."

His mouth quirked at the corner. "Would you like me to come with you today? As moral support?" I pictured it for a moment, him sitting silent in the audience while committee members fired questions at me. He'd defended his own thesis, so he knew what I'd be facing today, and while my department didn't have a strong culture of guest attendees for thesis defenses, they were allowed as long as they didn't interrupt or ask questions. The thought of looking out to see Declan in the auditorium during uncertain moments was tempting, but some self-reliant instinct in me pushed it away.

"I think I have to do this by myself," I said, my hand lingering on his chest, almost nose to nose with him. I didn't know the words were true until they left my mouth. "But thank you."

He nodded, unsurprised and unoffended. "Then you'll just have to know that I'm proud of you," he said.

"Hopefully you still feel that way when I fail my thesis and have to flee Hyde Park in disgrace."

"We talked about these jokes at your expense. I don't care for them."

I sighed, ceding the point. "You're right. Bad habit."

"And you said the interview with DePaul went well. So I doubt we need to worry about fleeing the city." I heard the *we* like a promise and my heart rate slowed just a little.

I'd gotten word the day before that I'd been passed on to the second round of interviews for a content writer position at DePaul University. If it worked out, I could even stay in Hyde Park—the commute to their downtown campus was more than doable, and the thought of not having to leave the life I loved and all my favorite haunts behind felt almost too good to be true. I was trying not to think about whether I'd actually get an offer. One week was far too early to discuss it, especially considering the very real possibility of Declan not being able to withdraw his enrollment at UCD, but I'd been imagining a one-bedroom apartment in Hyde Park with him; just enough space for both of our books but not so much that I couldn't spend the rest of my time on top of him. I could love that even more than the apartment I was leaving. "I should just get this over with."

He nodded. "You can do that. But also, if you think you can, you should try to enjoy it just a little. You made a bold choice and you've worked hard— not just on this version of your thesis but for your whole academic career. See it as the victory lap it is." He rubbed his hands up and down my arms in reas- surance.

I swallowed hard, Declan's earnest and unconditional support still a little hard for me to accept, and picked up the pencil skirt. "Don't think I didn't notice that you chose the tightest item of clothing I own that could possibly pass as professional."

He shrugged, letting the sheet dip low enough to reveal his hip bone and the mouthwatering V leading to his groin. "I want to be able to picture your ass in that skirt while you use words like 'translanguaging.'"

"You clearly haven't read my thesis. I'm more likely to disparage mannered formalism," I said, a little out of breath at the sight and the heat of him so close. I was still sore from the night before—and the night before that—but his proximity worked on me like a drug. My knees were wobbly, and it wasn't just from my impending thesis defense.

"Well, the *form* of your ass is unimpeachable," he replied smugly, nipping at my collarbone. I'd never experienced a connection so greedily tactile as ours, so embodied. I wanted to eat him alive, to feel the scrape of his teeth over every inch of my skin. If I didn't disentangle myself from him now, I'd never leave.

I peeled myself off him with regret. "You can admire it tonight. Will you be at your place?" I asked, hoping I'd sufficiently masked the pleading in my tone. We'd already gotten into the habit of trading nights at each other's apartments, which made it easier to grab fresh clothes and swap out reference materials, but whatever we were to each other now was so new I didn't want to jeopardize it by making assumptions. And more than that, if my thesis defense went badly, I wanted to know I'd be able to burrow under the covers with Declan wrapped around me like a protective shell, safe from the world outside.

"I will be wherever you need me," he answered simply. "Call me if you change your mind about me coming. It can help, knowing there's at least one friendly face in the audience."

I left my apartment twenty minutes later, running through my prepared answers for the questions I thought most likely to come up from the committee, but threaded among them was Declan's promise: *I will be wherever you need me.*

THE ENGLISH LITERATURE department had decided to hold their thesis defenses in a small auditorium that would seat 200, probably because the idea of forcing their master's candidates to sweat through their clothes under the harsh stage lights appealed to their collective grim sense of humor. Other than the committee seated at a long table in the front row, no more than a dozen people were scattered throughout the auditorium. They were likely all other English master's candidates, looking to gather a sense of which committee members were the interrogators and what lines of questioning they could anticipate before their own defenses. I stood center stage, trying to ignore everything other than the panel in front of me and pretend I was Charlie and this was just one more performance.

Professor Houghton sat at the center of the table facing the stage, her colleagues flanking her. I could just see the reflected light from the stage glinting off her glasses, the rest of the audience mostly obscured by the brightness of the lights. I'd finished my presentation with minimal stumbling, laying out my topic and its significance, and now I was waiting for questions from the panel, trying to excise the image of standing before a firing squad from my mind.

"I must say that I'm impressed with what you've been able to accomplish in such a brief period since changing your thesis topic," Houghton said. It may have been muted praise, but I was willing to take it. The longer I'd spoken as I shared my presentation, the more my nerves had fallen away, and my excitement about my research carried me for the first time. I'd forgotten to scan faces for approval or censure, to recalibrate my approach based on minute changes in facial expression because I couldn't wait to share what I'd learned. It was an out-of-body experience, a revelation.

"Thank you," I said, noting that my feet felt solid on the ground, that I no longer needed to hold my hands behind my back to hide their shaking the way I had when I first stepped on stage.

As Houghton launched into a question about how my thesis contributed to the "crowded" literature surrounding the Romantic period, I noticed a figure in the audience shift in discomfort. Something about the gesture was so familiar I couldn't shake it.

After a beat, I launched into the answer I'd prepared—I would have been foolish not to anticipate it, especially the dry implication that there was no new ground left to cover. The gears of my mind turned at double speed, telling me there was no way that figure in the audience was who I thought it was, resolutely training my eyes on the glint of Houghton's glasses.

Houghton seemed to find my answer adequate because she allowed another panel member to jump in and ask a question about my background research.

I made a quarter turn to put the figure further into my peripheral vision, focusing intently on my answer —I'd anticipated this one as well. I was hell-bent on making it through this cross-examination without adding the emotional high and accompanying crash of realizing I was wrong about that figure in the audience.

"If given the chance, what would you do differently?" This question was from Houghton. If I didn't know better (and if I wasn't effectively blind), I would have said she was almost smiling.

"As you know, Professor, I was given the chance to do things differently," I said. "I spent the first several months of the year on a different thesis topic. It was not going well," I said—a cataclysmic understatement, but what the hell. "Considering the state my work was in, you were kind enough to advise that I choose something that I was more interested in examining. Given the chance, I would take advantage of that opportunity again—and advise anyone else to do the same."

She nodded, and my pride in myself didn't preclude a bloom of pleasure in my chest from knowing that she was proud of me too.

When all was said and done, the cross-examination complete, the committee approved my thesis. I was pleased and proud, relieved to know that the consuming effort of producing a thesis was behind me. But more than anything, I was looking forward to the unfettered future, however nebulous that may be. When I exited the auditorium, the figure I'd seen in the audience waited for me in the hallway. I'd known all along.

"Hi, Mom," I said.

She looked like she was preparing for a root canal. She stepped toward me, though she stopped short of offering me a hug. "Hello, Emma," she said. "That was... very well done."

I looked at her, scanning for the polite lie. I couldn't find it, just obvious discomfort. "Thank you for coming." Declan was right. A familiar face in the audience could mean a lot—I hadn't been prepared onstage to grapple with how desperately I wanted the figure in the audience to be her. After everything, I wanted her pride and acceptance—not because she was a respected scholar, but because she was my mom, and I wanted her to tell me I did a good job. Now that she was here, something I hadn't truly believed was possible, I didn't know what our next step was.

She nodded. "I wasn't sure if you wanted me to—but I thought..." She looked distinctly uneasy. My mother was not a person who apologized or admitted uncertainty, and the experience looked to be an uncomfortable one. She took a breath and threw her shoulders back, as ever, one to rip off the Band-Aid. "Watching you today... I've never seen you like that." She irritably blinked back tears, a bewildered grief in her tone. "So passionate. It lit you up. I think... I think in trying to help you succeed, I may have dimmed your light." Her voice wobbled ever so slightly, and my heart cracked.

"Mom—" I started, but she held up a peremptory hand, much more like the mother and professor I knew.

"Let me do this." She took a bracing breath. "Emma, I'm sorry. I've always wanted the best for you—at least what I thought was the best—but I can be a bit of a steamroller once I get going, and things... got out of hand."

A grin twisted my mouth at my mother's characterization of herself as a "bit" of a steamroller. I imagined my dad, her students, and her colleagues all screaming with laughter, but I held my own back. If she was a bit of a steamroller, I was a bit of a pushover. We were both trying to do better.

"A good teacher is supposed to nurture and shape the talent inherent in the student and equip them to express their own unique insights, not force them into whatever shape suits the teacher better or to parrot the teacher's point of view. I should have known better with my own daughter." It was Geraldine's MO to castigate rather than make excuses, so it shouldn't have surprised me to see her be so hard on herself, but I found I didn't need her bitterness. It didn't make me feel better.

"It's okay, Mom."

"No, Emma, it's not, and no matter what you do with your life, you can't go around telling people things are okay when they aren't—" She caught herself, a dry laugh escaping her thinned lips. I smiled at her glimmer of self-awareness.

"Never mind, then," I said. "Thank you for the apology. But what I mean is I'm okay."

"Congratulations on your thesis approval," she said. "It was a brave thing to do, choosing your own path despite my... strongly worded concerns, and it suits you. I know we have a long way to go in reframing our relationship—but I want you to know that I love you, and I'm proud of you. I'm sorry if I ever made you feel that you had to be my carbon copy to have my support."

I nodded around the lump in my throat. Then she stepped forward and hugged me. Stiffly, at first—

she'd never been a particularly demonstrative person. The fact that she'd even shown up today had already bowled me over—but as I hugged her back, we both softened into an embrace that was more peaceful. It felt like forgiveness.

AS PROMISED, Declan was waiting for me when I got to his apartment that night. I could tell by the disordered state of his hair that he'd started to get anxious about the delay in my return; he must have been running his hands through it nonstop if his slightly electrocuted look was anything to go by. He was wearing his glasses, the sleeves of his ratty, beloved green cardigan pushed up to his elbows, and I'd never seen a dearer sight.

He had shot to his feet when I opened the door (he'd already made me a key), the question unspoken but clear in his eyes. *How did it go?*

I'd left him in suspense long enough. After our reunion in the hallway, Mom had taken me to the Drawing Room, one of the bars in the hotel she was staying in downtown, for a celebratory drink. It had the kind of simultaneously glamorous and cozy vibe that I loved, and I'd been so enraptured by the ornate details in the room and my joy at reconciling with

Mom that hours had passed before I got on a bus back to Hyde Park. I'd thought about texting him that I was on my way—wonder of wonders that I even could, how beautifully banal that he would want to know—but wanted to give him my news in person.

I closed the door behind me, nodding, and Declan swept me into a vertiginous hug with a whoop. I wrapped my legs around his hips, twined my arms around his shoulders, and gave him a sloppy kiss, which he returned with enthusiasm. Those were things I could do now. I couldn't imagine it would ever get old.

"Tell me everything. I was going spare thinking of you all day, wishing I was there with you." I noticed the absence of the question—"where were you?"—or any reproach, and was filled with awe once more that he existed, and I was lucky enough to find him on a rainy day in a coffee shop.

"I can barely remember it," I said, still secure in my perch wrapped around Declan. I loved looking at the world from this angle. "It all went by so fast." He started walking toward his kitchen, still holding tight to me.

"That means it went well. If you remembered all the details, that would mean it was a struggle. It sounds like it just flowed out of you," Declan said, not even out of breath after carrying me across the apartment. He set me on the kitchen counter like I belonged there, opening cupboards and rustling for glasses before opening the fridge with a flourish to reveal a bottle of Dom Perignon waiting for my return.

"Declan," I breathed, knowing all too well that was no small purchase on a PhD student's budget. "What if I'd failed?"

"Then we'd toast your next adventure," he said and opened the bottle with a pop. I grabbed it from him and took a swig straight off its neck to catch the wine as it bubbled over, the carbonation tickling my throat and making me cough. I didn't care. I handed the bottle back to Declan, and he did the same.

"I know you needed to do it on your own, but I wish I'd been there all the same," he said a little wistfully, wiping his mouth with the back of his hand, grinning at me while he poured and handed me a glass.

"Much more civilized like this," I said, clinking my glass against his. "I missed you too. But you were right, though, about it helping to have a friendly face in the audience."

Declan paused, his glass halfway to his lips.

"Who was it?" he asked, without a trace of jealousy, just curiosity.

"My mom," I said, unable to disguise how surprised and touched I still was by the gesture.

"Oh darling," he said. He didn't say more—that it was amazing, or ask how I felt about it, because it was written all over my face. He'd heard enough about her expectations of me and my recent struggle to divest myself of the need to meet them to know the weight her presence had carried for me today.

"I know," I whispered. "She said she was proud of me. And she *apologized* to me. I don't think she's done that since—you know what, I don't think she's ever done that." I took a sip of the Dom Perignon, trying to savor it after my first wild swig. "And then she took me out for a celebratory drink, which is why I was so late." It was also part of why I felt so loose and warm, like all the years of tension had leached out of my body into a puddle on the floor—but only partly. The rest was the high of knowing I'd done what I set out to do, and Declan.

"I'm so glad," he said. "You deserve that."

I'd spent so long thinking that love or even acceptance was something I had to earn that the thought I deserved it just as I was brought a lump to my throat. My achievement today wasn't a prerequisite for the person standing in front of me to support me. "Declan?" I said, scared again for the first time since I stood in the wings, waiting for my thesis defense to begin.

He gave me his complete attention, setting the bottle down and stepping between my legs, where they still dangled from the kitchen counter.

"I love you," I said.

It felt like I'd loved him since before we'd ever met, possibly before time had been invented, but it was the first time I'd said it out loud. The daring of it, the risk of this thing we say so casually took my breath away. Also, the inadequacy of the word to contain everything Declan made me feel. Still, it was the best one available until we came up with something better.

Declan's hand slid behind my neck, stroking the base of my skull. "Oh, Emma," he said. "I tried so hard not to love you. I couldn't do it." The shape of his island o's, the weight of the word.

With that, he captured my mouth with a kiss like the seal of a promise or a prayer. I wrapped my legs around him again and pulled his body flush with mine against the counter, hungry for more. It was warp speed, as far as relationships go—we'd been together a week, hadn't even been speaking for the three months leading up to it—but I knew in my bones I would never feel like this for another person as long as I lived. I held the knowledge tightly, comforted by its finality.

I could taste the champagne on his lips and smell it in his newly rapid exhales. It felt like I was getting drunk secondhand, even as the champagne I'd drunk had already gone to my head. That one heady swig was enough to unlock something in me, when even with Declan so far there had been a part of me that felt shy and insecure during sex, worried my unguarded desire would reveal something about me he didn't like. I slid my hands underneath the hem of his shirt to find his back and raked my fingernails down his skin, reveling in the hiss of his breath. He pulled me closer to him, if such a thing were even possible. The hand that had been cupping the base of my skull so gently coiled in my hair, giving it a delicious pull. With a clumsy hand, I snatched his glasses, pulling them off and dropping them to the counter, resisting the urge to chuck them across the room. I wanted nothing between us. Less than nothing.

Declan used his free hand to unhook and pull at the zipper of my skirt. "This fucking thing," he murmured against my mouth, releasing my hair to lift my ass off the counter with one arm while tugging my skirt down inch by inch with the other hand.

"You liked it this morning," I said, putty in his embrace. For such a slender, almost willowy man, he kept surprising me with the strength he'd hidden away.

"This morning it wasn't keeping me from getting inside you," he growled, finally getting the tight fabric over my hips. I gasped at the coolness of the counter as he set me back down and dropped to his knees on the kitchen tile, taking my skirt with him.

He tossed it aside so quickly his hands were back on me before I had a chance to miss them. He pressed his forehead to my stomach, hooking one of my knees over his shoulder. I gasped as he propped it higher, angling my pussy toward him and leaving me at his mercy. "Show me," he said, and I could feel the rush of liquid heat to the exact place he was training his eyes. My hand shaking with want, I hooked my fingers around the meager fabric of my thong and pulled it to the side.

If my brain had been online, I would have been squirming with discomfort at the exposure, worrying that he would find me ugly or gross (I'd had some boyfriends who were vocal about disliking giving head), pulling at the fabric to cover myself once more. But all I saw in Declan's eyes was naked hunger, pure worship, and I felt giddy and powerful. I slid my knees open wider to give him a better view.

He nipped my inner thigh appreciatively. "Good girl," he murmured, one thumb circling my entrance, which was growing more slippery by the second. I should not have been surprised to discover I had a praise kink, my pulse throbbing with excitement.

The heat of his breath against my clit had me quivering while he was still inches away from making contact. I clutched at his shoulders, furious that I couldn't reach *more* of him. He hummed softly while he kissed his way up my inner thigh, taking a lingering path deliciously and torturously closer to where I wanted him.

"Declan," I begged. "Please don't make me wait."

"But I need more of you," he protested, the vibration of his low voice winding me even tighter. My thighs shook. "You're so beautiful, let me look."

I thought of all the ways I'd tried to be merely acceptable—the right weight, the right grooming, pleasantly pliable—and how in all that time "beautiful" had always felt out of reach. The best I felt was unexceptional—nothing much to praise, but at least hard to criticize. But here, half naked on Declan's kitchen counter, mussed and imperfect and in my own complicated human body, I felt beautiful, and he saw beautiful.

When Declan's mouth first made contact with my clit, a shock ran through my body. I was too turned on, too eager, for this to last any amount of time. I was ready to go off like a firework, my mind inescapably drawn back to the day I took him to Valois and wanted to set Declan tasks with a stopwatch. When he added a finger, then two, and curled them inside me without losing the pressure and delicate friction against my clitoris, I screamed, my hips almost bucking me off the counter as I spasmed around his fingers. He caught me around my hips with his free arm, holding me in place while he gentled his efforts, keeping me steady through the long comedown from the peak of my orgasm. When he'd wrung every last ounce of pleasure from my body—along with the certainty that no one else could ever compare with him—he withdrew and stood, cradling me in his arms and kissing my eyelids.

"Jesus Christ," I whispered, sliding boneless arms around his waist. I was a puddle, both literally and figuratively.

"Nah, just Declan," he said. "Don't let the hair fool you."

I laughed. "I think it's pretty miraculous that you just set a land speed record for fastest orgasm. I'm even still half dressed," I said, indicating my fully buttoned top and blazer.

"Is that a challenge? We could try to beat that record if you want more." His lips were against my temple now, soft and whisper light.

I snaked my hand lower, reaching for his cock, but he caught my wrist. "More to come for you, I meant. If you want it."

"What I want is you," I answered. We'd spent most of the last week in bed, ecstatic with wonder that we could finally get our hands on each other, but I was surprised to find myself still eager for more. I'd never spent this much time horizontal—not with Adam or anyone before him—but I'd also never been with anyone so attuned to my every reaction, someone so intent that I did not feel the need to meet his appetite. I was having two or three orgasms to every one of Declan's, and he would read the guilt I felt over the imbalance on my face, then insist on giving me another. Being the center of his unrelenting focus was disorienting, and the fear that he would realize I wasn't worth the effort was hard to quash. Declan seemed to guess it and redouble his exertions without me saying any of that out loud. For the first time in my sexually active life, I was with someone who wasn't keeping score, whose main goal in bed seemed to be making sure I experienced every drop of pleasure possible without ever making me feel unsafe or robbing me of the opportunity to take the lead when I wanted it.

"You have me," he answered. "However you want me. I thought I'd made that plain?"

"Tell me again," I ordered, nipping at the lobe of his ear.

"You have me. And you aren't the only one who had a momentous day."

I stilled, pulling back far enough to look into his earnest eyes. "What?" The hope was hard to hold.

"I finally got word from UCD today. It took some doing, but I'm officially withdrawn."

I was unable to stop myself from grabbing my own face in gleeful disbelief, the very picture of Kevin McAllister after applying aftershave. "But are you still on track with UChicago? You didn't miss the fall quarter enrollment deadline?"

"My adviser gave me a sternly worded lecture on crossing an ocean every time I want to escape a woman who's wounded me, but yes"—he smiled—"I'm staying here."

I thought I'd known happiness before.

That was how we spent the night on Declan's kitchen floor, a few blankets serving as our bed, as we alternated between making love and drinking champagne. I lost count of how many times he made me come. It was long past the point where I thought I couldn't possibly have more orgasms in me, but I knew I would never forget the rapture of his reverent touch.

I was never able to walk into his kitchen again without smiling.

Another autumn came, as they always do. This one, in particular, was the first fall of my life without back-to-school shopping, sizing up my new teachers, and a new required reading list, but it did come with the same blank slate: I started a new job as a content writer for DePaul University. Three days a week, I took the Jackson Park Express to DePaul's downtown offices, where I wrote and copyedited marketing copy, the university newsletter, and web content for social media and the university website. I liked my coworkers enough to join their informal happy hour on Tuesdays and was hopeful I might end up actually making a few new friends. I wasn't sure about how I felt about content writing as a long-term career—it was so fresh and different that I was still getting my sea legs—but it provided me with a refreshing change of pace and gave me breathing room. This way, I could take my time and figure out what it was I really wanted to do while being able to make regular payments on my student loans and still have enough left over for rent. It wouldn't be forever, but I was grateful for it for right now.

The other two days a week, I worked from home —the apartment I shared with Declan.

Once we'd finally cut through all the bullshit that had kept us apart that winter and spring, we wanted as little distance between us as possible. We would have lived inside each other's skin if that was an achievable goal. If we were moving too fast, it still wasn't fast enough for either of us.

I packed up the beloved apartment I'd shared with George and Anika with a lot less angst than I'd been anticipating, knowing I'd be sharing my next home with Declan. We moved into a slightly larger one bedroom on Cornell than where Declan had been living on 57th in August. Our new place was closer to the bus for my commute and had enough space for two desks and two bookcases in the living room, though just barely. We had so little actual furniture between us that it was easy to consolidate based on whose alley finds and IKEA hand-medowns were least worn. After we wrestled everything up two flights of stairs ourselves (and even that wasn't enough to instigate a fight between us), I insisted we christen the kitchen the same way we'd celebrated my thesis defense even while the rest of the apartment was still strewn with boxes. It was ours, all ours, and that made it beautiful—even if the radiators screamed at inopportune times and our neighbors were fond of playing industrial music at a disconcerting volume.

It didn't take long for us to settle into a new routine. Declan was still years away from completing his PhD and spent plenty of time on campus, but more often than not, on the weekends, he studied at Viva while I read next to him—for pleasure and without guilt—because when we stayed home, very little work got done. In that small way, I got to keep a piece of my old life—but when it rained these days, I made sure we brought an umbrella for the walk.

I went back to calling my mother weekly, though our conversations were shorter and progressed haltingly as we tried to find new ways to talk to each other and non-academic ground to meet on. Mom put a herculean amount of effort into avoiding giving me advice or lectures on my future, which I appreciated more than I could say. She took a real interest in the tidbits I shared about Declan's dissertation but was kind enough not to ask about it, sensing it pressed a little bruise for me. There were still times I envied his sense of direction and my parents' tacit approval of it, but I tried to remind myself that wasn't the same thing as wanting to pursue a PhD of my own. I kept up with journaling in an attempt to untangle the thorniest knots in my head, trying to figure out which thoughts I'd put there myself and which I'd inherited, which ones still fit and which I'd grown out of. It looked like that would be a long process, but I didn't mind.

Declan had met my parents over a few Face-Times since graduation, but we'd already discussed him joining us in Framingham for Christmas, where I'd informed Geraldine that any topic that fell under the umbrella of higher education would be strictly off-limits. I told Declan I was afraid we would have to rely on a lot of games to fill the time with such a conversational vacuum—but he promised me he was a terrible poker player, so no one could resist cleaning him out. For the first time in a long time, a visit home sounded... nice.

When I'd gotten the news about the job at DePaul, we'd splurged on tickets to Dublin so I could meet Declan's parents and have a proper pint as soon as we'd dumped our boxes in our new apartment. I'd rarely traveled beyond the occasional school field trip, so crossing the ocean had been huge for me (and worth a little bit of credit card debt). I was able to work myself up into a pretty respectable panic on the eight-hour flight over whether his parents would like me, but Declan kissed my hand and said, "Darling. They'll take one look at you and threaten to clatter me if I ever let you go." He wasn't wrong, though it never came to actual blows. We spent two weeks bouncing up and down the coast between Dublin and Wicklow, alternating cozy family dinners with nights out in Temple Bar (and blessed hotel rooms, away from prying parental ears). It turned out that Guinness *does* taste better in Dublin. We even spent a weekend morning browsing Declan's favorite bookshop on the Liffey, and I cupped each new piece of his life that he shared with me in my hands, delicate and precious as water.

Four months had passed since my thesis defense and graduation—four months since the nights I couldn't sleep for missing Declan. Now, we made it a point to make our hot beverages (coffee for me, tea for him) together in the morning, starting our days by telling each other the stories of our dreams in the kitchen's gray morning light before heading our separate directions. Sometimes I couldn't wrap my mind around the seismic shift in my life, with Declan versus without him. We were creating the shape of our life together with all our new habits and traditions. I never wanted to take the miracle of that for granted.

It was early enough in October that it was still warm in Chicago, but there was the barest hint of a chill you could catch if you stood still and paid enough attention that said summer was barely hanging on. Charlie was flying in tonight for a weekend visit before rehearsals for her next show began, purportedly to celebrate my new job, but I knew her real motivation was sizing up Declan in person. I knew she was optimistic based on our phone calls, but I also knew she wouldn't put her eagle eye back in until she'd judged his rightness for me from a closer distance.

I was so confident that she would love him, love us, that I had been squealing my way around the apartment all week, scrubbing surfaces and telling Declan stories of our awkward and magical freshman year together—getting lost off campus after a party and getting yelled at by UChicago police, snuggling on one of our beds with a movie on a hot laptop until we fell asleep, the string of lovelorn one night stands Charlie left behind in the dorms.

"You're lucky Charlie had already moved away by the time you got to Chicago," I'd told him the night before. "If she were still here then, I would never have looked at you. I already had a best friend," I teased him.

"Of course not," he agreed peacefully, then hooked his arm around my waist and laid me flat on the couch, planting his hands on either side of my shoulders. His smirk told me he was confident there were some things he could do for me where Charlie would fall woefully short.

"Then again, you do have your own appeal," I amended, grabbing something very inappropriate.

"Thank Christ for that," he said, and then we didn't do much talking for a while.

Since then, we'd piled sheets and blankets next to the couch to welcome Charlie for the weekend— she wouldn't be sharing my bed with me anymore, which was bittersweet in its own way, but I knew she would understand. Now that Charlie had texted to say her plane had landed and I had less than an hour until my two favorite people met one another, I felt like I had downed a gallon of coffee with a 5-Hour Energy chaser. Declan laughed at my irrepressible excitement even as it complicated his efforts to knock out just a little more work before Charlie's arrival (since I'd informed him absolutely no work was allowed while she was in town).

"Sorry!" I yelped after interrupting him for the third time in as many minutes while watching the status of Charlie's Lyft ride inch closer and closer to our apartment on my phone's screen. "Sorry, sorry, sorry. I'll shut up now."

"The state of you." He chuckled, closing his laptop and pulling me onto his lap. "Don't be sorry. I love to see you excited. I can't wait to meet Charlie."

"You still have a few minutes to work! Possibly ten of them!" I said, gesturing between my phone and his closed laptop. "Go on, I'll be quiet."

"No, darling," he said, pulling me closer and resting his forehead against mine. "It looks like I'm done for now."

I grimaced, knowing he was probably right to give up the ghost of work while I was in such an agitated state. "Do you promise not to fall in love with her? Given the choice, I'd fall in love with Charlie instead of me," I said, leaning into his chest.

"Darling, I never had a choice when it came to you."

I smiled and landed a kiss on the side of his

mouth. "Good answer." I was lip-locked with him when the buzzer sounded, and I almost drew blood when I jumped off his lap, shouting, "She's here! She's here!"

A muffled "ow" escaped from Declan, but I only had time to shoot him a brief apologetic look before flinging open the apartment door and sprinting down the stairs to meet Charlie's car outside. She sprang from the back seat of a Kia Soul with a shriek, jumping into my arms with such force that I staggered on the sidewalk.

"You're here!" I shouted unnecessarily.

"I am not a hologram!" she affirmed.

When I could bring myself to put her down, I wrestled her carry-on from her grip and pulled her into our building, getting through all the usual small talk about her flight so we could save the good stuff for when the three of us were all together.

By the time we breathlessly spilled onto the third-floor landing, Declan already stood in our doorway to welcome her, grinning uncertainly.

"Good lord," Charlie said, taking in his height from the vantage of her five-foot-four frame. "You didn't mention that he was Andre the Giant."

"More like a really average basketball player," he

said. "At least height-wise. I have a terrible jump shot."

"Charlie, Declan," I said, making the official introduction. "Declan, the woman who just compared you to a beloved actor is Charlie, so make of that what you will."

"I'll take it as a compliment. Didn't Samuel Beckett used to drive him to school?" he asked.

"That's true," she said, smiling at the playwright reference. "You can keep him, Emma, but Jesus Christ, Declan, sit down. You're making me nervous."

Declan laughed and stepped aside, gesturing for us to come in. "So nice to finally meet you, Charlie. I'd tell you to make yourself at home, but I suspect that if you're with Emma, that goes without saying." Charlie nodded, accepting her queenly due.

We all crowded into the living room jammed with books and our IKEA couch. While I'd galloped up and down the stairs, Declan had pulled out a bottle of wine and three glass tumblers along with all the local delivery menus dropped in our mailbox so far. "For a welcome toast," he explained. "Emma told me that your first night in town, you two usually order in and catch up. If you want some alone time, I can make myself scarce."

I could see an approving glint in Charlie's eye as she took in the carefully collated menus and reasonably priced red blend on the coffee table. "I appreciate the offer, but I didn't come all this way just to sample Hyde Park's finest cuisine. I'm going to need some time with you to see if you live up to the hype. And I'm not going to kick you out of your apartment —at least not yet." This side of Charlie either made men fall in love with her or run away screaming. Her tone walked the delicate line between challenging and disarming, her smile adding a softer element to the knives just waiting to see if they were needed behind her eyes. Most of my boyfriends had been scared of Charlie, and for good reason, but Declan seemed oddly pleased by the protectiveness that radiated off her like Agent Orange, not discomfited at all. The three of us squished together on the couch, me happiest of all in the middle, sandwiched between both of my people.

Declan leaned forward and poured a glass of wine for each of us, then pivoted in his seat so his back was against the arm of the couch and he could see both of us without cricking his neck. "Cheers," he said, and the three of us clinked and drank. Declan held his glass in his left hand so he could play with my hair with his right, an easy smile on his lips. "I'm so pleased to finally get to know you properly, Charlie. Emma talks about you so much I should probably worry about her leaving me for you," he said.

I clocked the pleasure on Charlie's face—that there was nothing possessive or territorial she could detect in his tone, that he was being genuinely complimentary. He wanted her to know that he knew there was room in my heart for both of them. "Don't fret. Our love transcends the physical," she said, sipping her wine and throwing her legs over mine on the couch.

"Oh yes," I said, "it's very pure. You have nothing to fear." I pinched her big toe, and she kicked my arm, nearly spilling my wine.

"I'll be the judge of that. You two are terrifying," Declan said.

We both cackled with glee at the thought. I could feel the coiled tension that was always primed in Charlie loosening as she leaned forward and said, "I've heard the whole story from Emma's side, but I want to hear your version, Declan. How did you two end up here?"

Declan smiled, massaging my neck with one hand. "I ask myself that question all the time."

We were two bottles deep before we realized we needed to order dinner or we'd be too far gone for food to help. We were too busy and happy to notice our hunger; me with glowing over my two favorite people hitting it off, Declan with his earnest interest in Charlie's work on the stage, Charlie with Declan's stories about Ireland slaking her major travel lust. It was the kind of conversation that made me wish that much harder that we all lived in the same place, that we could have nights like this one as often as we wanted. I was boneless from wine and the as-then completely novel experience of my best friend liking my boyfriend, and vice versa, by the time our order from Pizza Capri arrived. After we'd decimated our pizza and tucked Charlie in on the couch, I knew her future visits would be nothing like they had been in my Adam era.

But then again, nothing was.

As Declan and I tumbled into bed that night, I cursorily apologized for Charlie's protectiveness. "Sorry that she gave you the third degree tonight. She can be a bit rough on my boyfriends."

"As she should be," he whispered into my neck as he pulled me into little spoon position. "She loves you. She wants to know that you're okay. I'm so glad you have someone in your life looking out for you like that. I'll answer all the questions she likes."

I knew that Charlie would love all his answers,

and that he welcomed the challenge of winning her over. I didn't think it would be a problem for him at this point. I pulled his top arm over my waist and settled in to sleep, satisfied as a cat in a sunbeam.

When we had to bid her goodbye at the end of the weekend, we were all downhearted at the thought of parting.

"So what do you think, Charlie? Do I pass the test?" Declan asked while we waited for Charlie's Lyft to arrive.

She pretended to consider that for about two seconds before breaking out her toothpaste commercial smile. "With flying colors. The provisional Charlie seal of approval has been upgraded." She stood on her tiptoes to give Declan a goodbye hug. "Take good care of my girl," she said. Declan nodded and released her, her heels dropping back to the pavement.

As her car pulled up and Declan loaded her suitcase into the trunk, Charlie clasped me in a fierce hug one more time. She whispered in my ear while clutching me in a death grip, "You really are the whole Emma with him. I even met new parts of her this weekend." I swallowed a lump in my throat and squeezed back as if pressure alone could communicate how much I loved her, how grateful I was for her love and protection. It couldn't possibly, but it didn't hurt to try.

There were tears in my eyes as she pulled away.

"Are you all right, darling?" Declan asked as we both waved until her car was out of sight.

I nodded, still watery. "I am," I said. "It's just hard to contain all this love."

"I see. Sometimes it has to come out your eyes."

I laughed. "Come here to me, you," I said. He stepped into my arms. We stayed like that for a long time.

ACKNOWLEDGMENTS

This book was inspired by a dream and a lot of weekends in Hyde Park visiting my best friend in college. All of the UChicago and Hyde Park settings (other than Viva Coffee) are real and worth visiting.

This book also wouldn't exist without the tenacious cheerleading and storytelling mindset of Jenna D'Angelo. Thank you for reminding me that the most interesting moments are the ones we get to experience together in real time. This particular dream would not have come true without you.

I also owe a debt of gratitude to the Boris to my Natasha since he shared a Den Pop with me at my first college party — Jeff Chaney, thank you for the beautiful cover art and Chicago touch.

Thank you as well to Jenny Sims, who taught me that I split my infinitives with absolutely alarming frequency.

But no acknowledgment section could be complete without Chris Walters. I wouldn't know what romance is without you.

ABOUT THE AUTHOR

Sabrina Burns is a reformed book snob. Romance was kind enough to provide her a light through the pandemic and all the darkness that followed, and she's never looked back. She writes emotionally grounded, steamy romance because life is too short not to swoon and be seen for who you really are. She lives in Chicago with her husband and the dog he envies.

Stay in the loop about new releases and join her newsletter at her website: sabrinaburns.com